DARK DESIRES AND THE OTHERS

OTHER WORKS BY LUISA VALENZUELA IN ENGLISH TRANSLATION

DARK DESIRES AND THE OTHERS

(NEW YORK NOTEBOOKS)

LUISA VALENZUELA

TRANSLATED BY SUSAN E. CLARK

Dalkey Archive Press
Champaign & London

Originally published in Spanish as *Los deseos oscuros y los otros* by El Grupo Editorial Norma, 2002

Library of Congress Cataloging-in-Publication Data

Valenzuela, Luisa, 1938-
[Deseos oscuros y los otros. English]
Dark desires and the others / Luisa Valenzuela ; translated by Susan E. Clark. -- 1st ed.
   p. cm.
"Originally published in Spanish as Los deseos oscuros y los otros by El Grupo Editorial Norma,
2002."
ISBN 978-1-56478-631-9 (pbk. : acid-free paper)
I. Clark, Susan E. II. Title.
PQ7798.32.A48D4713 2011
863--dc22
                        2011002834

Partially funded by the University of Illinois at Urbana-Champaign, as well as by grants from the
National Endowment for the Arts, a federal agency, and the Illinois Arts Council, a state agency

www.dalkeyarchive.com

Cover: design and composition by Danielle Dutton, illustration by Nicholas Motte
Printed on permanent/durable acid-free paper and bound in the United States of America

FOREWORD

Here I am, submerged in a sea of notebooks, some very worn, some half-written, others only a quarter. They've gone from here to there and back again, these notebooks, and when they were there, I didn't pay the slightest attention to them. Now, looking at them again, instead of simply immersing myself in the past, I feel as though I'm almost drowning. Not quite—it's more like swimming against the tide of the woman I was in my New York years. How I loved that city then! What constant, dominating stimulation!

Looking at these old diaries, I realize with dismay that I hardly talk about the city, I hardly talk about literature, and much less about all the work I was doing and what I achieved. All of that—those memorable meetings, long debates, presentations, and working alongside international human-rights organizations and more—was relegated to or engraved upon my memory and in various ad hoc publications. The *other*, the frustrations and the passions, the brief (or otherwise) love affairs, the fears and the attempts at appropriating love—all that *is* in the notebooks, in intense if sporadic bursts of writing, trying to let nothing escape.

Or was it just the opposite?

Only now do I ask myself that question. Writing as a way of putting everything that would disturb the flow of writing outside oneself.

Badly written notebooks, like the result of someone "getting rid of lice," as Cortázar put it, or like a dump for all your anger, like wastepaper basket for all the things you want to keep out of your mind so that you can devote yourself completely to the writing of literature—novels, stories, articles, and articles for periodicals (from the *New York Times*, *Village Voice*, or *Vogue*, to various literary magazines), and then lectures, classes, workshops . . . everything that allowed me to survive in the Anglo-Saxon world, contaminated as I was by the Protestant work ethic.

However, this is not an autobiography, nor are these my memoirs; they are simply movements of the heart and the body, tending toward the horizontal in more ways than one, and prone to various shocks.

Personal texts, never thought of as being written for anyone else's eyes, notes in the margin of what some would call life and which nonetheless I now feel to be themselves facts of the purest, rawest substance.

POSTSCRIPT

Thinking it over, looking from the outside in, I recognize that there is a dialogue here. A dialogue between the intention to write and then one-on-one relationships with other people. The impulse to put everything in writing is always an attempt to communicate, to reach the other, who, in the case of the published text, becomes multiple and multiplied. Bottles thrown into the sea, with or without an apparent message. Or, in the case of these scattered notes, meetings with the other, singular, as a way of writing with the body. The act of writing and the act of love, however unlike love it may seem, are one and the same. Equivalent inquiry, similar search. A shock for the other, a shock for oneself at the same time, and also much more—an attempt to rip away every slightest veil, to glimpse some secret in the mirror, in the dark, much as Saint Peter says that we see God. Movements of life in search of the elusive mystery, the eternal carrot: the heart of the word; that which is not what we call love—that would be too obvious—but includes and transmutes it.

As Alessandro Baricco says in the foreword to his novel *Silk*, when you don't have a name for things, that's when you tell stories. And sometimes, instead of telling them, you try to act them out—that is, live them like someone who's putting together a secret narrative that you can then jot down in fragments, arbitrarily.

POSTSCRIPT II

And, last but not least, my gratitude to Silvia Hopenhayn and Leonora Djament, who "invented" this book.

The story of my life doesn't exist. Does not exist. There's never any center to it. No path, no line. There are great spaces where you pretend there used to be someone, but it's not true, there was no one.

Marguerite Duras, *The Lover*

So she wrote more stories, and for each story she went out and had an "experience." And oh all kinds of things happened to her for she picked her men carefully for their literary value.

Spencer Holst, *The Language of Cats*

DARK DESIRES AND THE OTHERS

October 2, 1978
On the Eve of the Trip

You'll think that I died, and something like that is indeed happening or has happened. You can't tell anymore what's alive and what's dead, or rather, who's going around these worlds, seemingly dying. Remembering is like being left hanging from something that you don't have anymore—if you ever really had it—one reason to be more or less agglutinate, magnetic. Valid.

Remembering here and now, in my house in Buenos Aires, as if I were at the top of a mountain, and even further, as if I were lying at the bottom of the sea, which is where these things tend to happen. Sometimes yes and sometimes no. Sometimes the memories flow when it gets dark; they appear and they fade, they amaze us at the turn of a page and perhaps we should hurry to retain them. Perhaps we should offer more to memory, that form of madness.

I found a piece of paper. I found a writing pad—and I write and I write and I write. I'll write until the ink runs out and there's nothing left of what I care about to jot down.

Here there is order, calm. I don't want to leave this house anymore. I don't want to be distracted. I prefer to keep seeing objects that I'm fond of, encouraging the winds of inspiration, getting up early and sometimes running through the park to buy something to eat or more ink. Refill the cartridges. Cartridges of ink to write a bit, fire more shots, all made of words. And now—now that the phone isn't working—how I long to stay here shut in between these caressing walls! I feel so good facing myself, facing mountains that look like water, but which are really wool, mountains woven stitch by stitch, only suggested. A small tapestry that will accompany me on my trip, though I no longer want to travel.

I'll go all the same.

The house is beautiful, I like each and every thing, and the cats are playing in the middle of the room and tralala tralala. I keep on in my singsong and can't get away from it. And again my doubts: "To go out or not to go out? To bathe or not to bathe?"

How I need the little securities of life, or should I say, how I'd like to have the larger ones! I would like not to have to take the plane or the boat, not to climb once more into that enormous floating belly, to float in that endless amniotic fluid, the ocean—and go sailing peacefully toward other latitudes, writing my novels. I have to learn how to write during this trip, an errant writer so to speak—a roving writer.

Getting Ready to Jump

Further along the dates will have to be erased, but at the end of '78, the person I was then was getting ready to jump, knowing her absence will be a long one. She's been invited to be Writer in Residence at Columbia University for a semester, and that will be—she intuits already—the longest semester of her life. She breathes in huge gulps of her city's air, the verb a lie at the time, because the air had become unbreathable. With vandal-like delight she is disemboweling her library. Some books will have to disappear—the word alone produces goose bumps—others are simply dismantled in order to preserve this story or that essay or those three chapters that she knows she'll need for her course, or that she wants to keep with her in spite of the weight limit on planes. Get rid of everything to be able to leave as lightly as possible. She knows that if she stays in her own country, she won't write anymore. She can't show her latest work to anyone. She's afraid of putting those readers in danger. She also has notebooks and notebooks—disheveled, awkward diaries with no continuity at all. From those she likewise vandalizes—or, in this case, rescues—some fragments that will later form the microstories of a volume titled precisely *Libro que no muerde* (Book that Doesn't Bite). And it didn't, really, unless we say that irony has a bite. Those were certainly times that lent themselves to furious biting. She did what she could with regard to the situation; she got involved and she wrote and later she wrote partly about her involvement. These pages however, only took in the shrapnel— shrapnel that was noted down in new and multiple foreign notebooks. So that all that's left is to write the good-bye bite:

Her loved one of the time, ex-loved one now because of his abandoning her when everything seemed to promise the opposite, reappears after almost a year of absence in order to declare his passion and his anguish and to confess his error. The woman I was then has one foot already in the stirrup and treats him with disdain, and when he desperately swears that he will never stop searching for her, and asks, using these exact words, "Now what do I do?" she answers, "Become a man," and turns right around.

So that's where, in New York, and without realizing it, her notes about herself, about her efforts to become a woman, begin.

The Starring/Dying Role

The moment has come to say it, to become consistent. This is who I am and this is my truth, however heavily it weighs on me.
After so much talking through other mouths, creating characters,
HERE I AM
In body and fantasies,
  In desires
Spectator that I am
  (and extraneous)
Protagonist sometimes
  Agonist others
  Heavy prot/uberance
    milking words,
    that leakage.

The best way to be the protagonist of the story without being the protagonist is to be the author of the story.

Having recently arrived in New York, an analyst whom I saw sporadically cursed me with the following:

"You don't look for men, you don't look for lovers—you look for characters for your novels."

I stopped seeing the analyst after that session, because I didn't think he could understand me, could understand that, for me, life and literature, love and literature, are the same. Now, though, I worry about it, because I see myself in Spencer Holst's character, the one from his "True Confessions Story." It's true that I only quoted half of the paragraph, the part that fit best. The rest goes like this:

". . . for she picked her men carefully for their literary value, seeking always someone sinister for her unhappy romances, and after each she would simply write what happened, the simple truth in a sorry style."

Okay. I'm not *that* bad. I'm hardly so unhappy, nor my style so sorry.

I moved to New York in 1979 after having lived the most leaden years of lead in Buenos Aires, acting rashly and then writing about it. I traveled intent upon staying away a long time, having been invited to be Writer in Residence at Columbia University, the alma mater of my maternal grandfather no less. A great honor that only the Dons of Latin American literature had merited . . . and yet, what do I write about in my journals during my almost twelve years in New York? Not about my literary successes and other dazzling exploits, no—I write and I write and I write about my confrontations, tribulations, and joys with the male of the featherless biped species to which I belong, and which I am always exploring, simply because I'm a writer and because I have a certain skill with words.

7

The Male of the Species

The male of the species also has his little heart. It surprises you every time you rediscover this, without really wanting to, and then all at once you start putting two and two together and all the available evidence comes together to demonstrate that, yes sir, the male of the species is also a human being, although he generally tries to hide this fact and very often succeeds.

Not that I hadn't suspected this all along, but it had only been a flash of something, something present but not really well defined enough to make it feel real. Through repeated contact—sometimes rather intimate and highly pleasant forms of contact—I've learned many things, but it's hard to say if what I've seen are true feelings. Tenderness, yes, there's been a lot of tenderness, because at bottom, that's what I choose—but after that? Tenderness can easily turn into something clingy.

The second turn of the screw might turn out to be something even more difficult to confess: the recognition that I am a lovable person, in other words deserving of love from the other. If the male of the species is capable of giving love, the female of the species should be capable of receiving it. It sounds simple, but that's where the trap is; in fact, it's horribly complicated.

I think I write, among so many other motives, to reach some kind of acceptance, some kind of profound recognition. Not of exterior recognition, the applause that's also implicit in that word (a career, if you can call it that, stretched throughout a life)—no. A proprietary, nontransferable recognition: know thyself and all that.

And I say that to write is a fulltime curse, because the long periods of drought hurt more than all the pains of writing put together. Because the pains (and horrors) of writing are usually infected with an exultant joy.

The marches and countermarches, the eternal struggle against the weariness of writing. And that's how, all of a sudden, an idea emerges: try to see the face of the internal enemy, the one rising up against me and who opposes even the simplest desires, especially the desire to write, which should run free of any obstacle, like a beneficent river (sometimes raging, sometimes out of control, bursting its dams, but always a river, always something that flows, even though at times dryness takes hold and it turns into a tenuous trickle incapable of quenching my thirst or of irrigating anything at all, seeping right into the earth). An underground river. And the internal enemy putting her foot onto its point of egress, preventing it from bursting forth.

Let's see, internal enemy, you there, show your face! I'm mature enough now to know you, to deal with and even love you.

That's what it's all about—to feel affection for the internal enemy. If you do—if I'm able to achieve that—these texts will be essentially about the apprenticeship of love. It's a chronicle, in other words, which can at the same time be a step forward in my apprenticeship (and, as always, two steps forward, one step back . . . but I don't want to get ahead of myself, admitting to the inevitable backsliding).

Later the other stuff will arrive, the actual practice of love. Later or simultaneously, which would be ideal. Because enough of separations and splits, to want to say *I want you to* . . . like when we used to play tag and the world would stop, or to pretend to stop in order to think and regroup and reestablish order, and then start moving again. Enough of so many cuts and breaks, enough of focusing on pieces of myself. This will be an attempt at integration; the internal and external enemies and the inter-game that connects them.

"Tag, You're It"

I say, "touch me and I'm it," and then I won't play anymore. And I don't say that because of the famous child's game, but purely to express my desire. I want him to touch me, to leave a mark on me, a mark of love, just one little stain, at the very least.

If we have to play as though it's just a joke, without really getting into the real game, at least let its memory stay with us. Touch me, leave your mark on me, that's all I ask of you; and then I won't play, I won't play anymore.

Inter-game. Game. Whatever I do, I can't get rid of the word *game* so easily. I would like to throw it away as though it were a peel. Peel upon peel upon peel, perhaps, in the best onion style—in other words, establishing my self.

Advice: treat literature with the same disrespectful veneration as fans treat soccer. Play with words.

Playing with Males

My vocation since childhood: that beautiful little girl over there in the park, the one with the long curls, and with such a serious look—hands behind her back—that's me.

I stand guard.

A few steps away, my expression almost as tightly clasped as my hands, I watch over the bench that I've spread my toys on. Bait made up of little trains, various little cars—and all the boys in the square in front of my bench stretching out their tentative hands.

"They're mine," I'll tell them when they finally touch the little cars.

And my invitation will fall almost like an ultimatum:

"Do you want to play with me?"

The scene with the little cars in the Plaza San Martín is stamped on our family narrative, just like my odyssey to sit on top of the big ant pile. The *tacurú*. A personal anecdote, which in all generosity I ended up giving to the Sorcerer, the most repugnant of my protagonists.

In Corrientes, at the hacienda of some rich relatives we visited every year, one fine day at nap time I escaped from bed and went out into the fields, something I'd never done, I who usually chose to escape to the kitchen to hear the workers playing the accordion. And out in the fields, under the burning siesta-time sun, I sat on an anthill and the ants miraculously didn't bite me. I destroyed their ant-castle and they covered my big body with their tiny greedy bodies. When my family found me, I was staring, enthralled, at my arms, and saying, "Beautiful creatures!"

Beautiful they are, as we shall see. The majority of creatures are beautiful, in fact. Especially the males of that species of featherless biped, the human being.

Thanks to the ants and to the "bite" I did eventually receive—delivered by an infernal parasite that got under the nail of my big toe during that same vacation—my father decided that Corrientes was unhealthy for girls and we never returned. My father decided few things in our house, but as a doctor, he always had his say about matters of health.

So that adventure ended along with the very vague memory of accordions at nap time.

The Corrientes adventure ended and the Punta del Este one began (Petitina needs the sea air to cure her ears). That's when the shelled animals began.

Latin Americanisms

The Eastern Republic of Uruguay, Punta del Este beach.
At three years old, I push open the swinging door in the hotel that separates the dining room from the kitchen and I demand:
I want bugs,
    referring to that delicacy—not exclusively—which are mussels.
Prophetic words, those.
A little more to the east, a little higher and a little lower (especially lower), I kept on demanding "bugs" (as the Chileans call them), and that's how I've roamed and been permitted to roam the continent—not always by the oral route, and at times with delight.

I would demand other foods too.
And also words—those nourishing sluts.

A Dream

Last night, having finished writing about childhood very, very late (a thousand o'clock) would you believe that in the middle of some rather confusing dreams, a very affectionate child appears, with something animal-like about her, who then suddenly becomes uncomfortable, poor little thing, so I take her to the bathroom and she pees, telling me how important it is to be sitting in the right place, and then she makes caca and we're both very happy. And I tell her she's done very, very well, but that she should let me know when she has to go to the bathroom, that I can't guess these things.

Take *that*, I say now in sleeplessness. How careful we have to be with the little girl we once were, and what wise uses we have to make of her poop . . .

So many memories and dreams I'd like to jot down so that they don't escape us; "moments of being," as Virginia Woolf wanted? Sometimes I miss journalism: putting yourself suddenly into unsuspected and surprising worlds.

A desire to write EVERYTHING

And the other side of the coin:

All this because the other day Federico Allodi came by and began (*une façon de dire*) to persuade me to write my autobiography . . . something that Elena Urrutía in Mexico had wanted a few months back, and I asked myself: What use would autobiography be if what I'm looking for when I write is to put myself in someone else's skin? My own skin is uncomfortable precisely because it's so familiar.

They both forget that I'm a novelist. My desire forms itself around tenderness and callousness when they arrive—mixing together but not interfering with each other. Softness to the touch—the hand that writes it, the pleasure of the hand—and a lot of callousness too—interior—are necessary to feed stories.
Because

> Where I place my eye, I want to place the bullet
> Where I place my fascination, I place the pen
> Where I place my finger, there is the wound.
> As if laying an egg, I place a story
> I don't place words: I take them.
> And I often put my foot in my mouth.

And that's how, from the other side of the story, one *narrates* a story. If I narrated as I live, if the voice were the same, if the perfect autobiography existed, the story would have only one side, or maybe it wouldn't be real—as far as a story goes—or we wouldn't have really lived it (Möbius strip of the necessary options).

If once and for all I could get the hang of the picaresque style, I'd have some nice stories to tell. And they'd be my very own private property, not thefts, even if only thefts of the imagination.

I've been writing this diary for twenty years. No. For more than forty: it's a diary that's been writing itself since my birth. It must be because of the recurring theme, writing with the body, that it keeps such a close relationship with the most profound essence of what writing is, the *raison d'être* of the writing almost as much as or more than the *raison d'être* of the writer. Because writing with the body is an attempt to decipher symbols that are sometimes disguised as specific events. It's an attempt to unveil the mysteries while going about one's life indifferently. Or, even better, it's a way of tying little knots to make the finest of rugs, the least ostentatious, the one that you appreciate all the more looking at it from underneath.

I am the one who could never speak the word love
because she always got lost on the side roads. Because she felt the attraction of danger. Because fear called her by name. (Her own name, not fear's name. Fear doesn't have a name; it's just the steady beat underneath a smile.)

My own word games called out to me, and what resulted were juggling acts—searching for what can't be said.

They gallop quite fast. Faster than I can tolerate, and faster than I can perceive at first glance. And they lead to my headaches and various other weaknesses. Perhaps what I'm looking for after all is the unifying thread, something that should unify—surely—all the aspects of this plot, the different textures. The different weavings. Although perhaps the men who approach me turn out to be the weavings, after all, and I the weaver, as befits a woman. One more parka. Textiles: text.

I am Crying

I come from a long matrilineal line and I respect it and cry for it because I am its missing link. I am the generational break made flesh not only because I realize all of this, but rather because in some way I am compensated by the fact of realizing that I realize, etc., and I write in an infinite number of notebooks, letters, papers, and other writable surfaces, all to say the same thing. And that same thing today is this: I adored my mother, and this was a mistake. I adored her like crazy. Today I think that the only creature worth my admiration is my daughter, because she doesn't let on that she knows—but she knows.

I cry, I cry. This circle of love has trapped me and I can't ask anything of it. What to ask of a mother who takes everything and leaves us naked? What to ask of a daughter to whom we'd like to give everything and can't? And I, crying—in what corner of myself am I?

When the tears stop flowing, discovery: that centripetal and admirable mother is mine, that daughter whom today I consider wise is also mine. Therefore: leave what's mine aside and go in search of the other, the complete otherness.

That's why I told Laurie no, no, because of not being totally other, for being in happy possession of very maternal breasts. No, no to breasts. I want a hairy chest to contentedly cry on (remember, Jorge). To cry nonstop, to be able to stop crying. With pleasure.

The story of crying. Like threads or rather like crossroads when I know that invariably—and that's why I cry—I've started to cross over to the other side. In other words, crying as though in farewell, but I'm not the one leaving, not in the process of leaving. (It's so easy to leave, to distance myself, leaving behind a promise.) I stay in the same place, but I'll never be the same.

Then there's the story about rice pudding and the door that opens for us to go outside and play. We open it with some, and others we let play by themselves. And, what's worse, sometimes we play all alone, even in front of them.

Whoever plays at the edge of the abyss, plays, and I was even able to play at erasing the abyss. The abyss is still there, luckily, and whoever plays at erasing the abyss, always plays dangerously at the edge of the abyss.

Playing with your hands, things change. Whoever likes to play with himself can sometimes forget the abyss, but never the emptiness.

Jack off, but please, don't make a mess!

Writing, writing in an infinite number of notebooks, many times little allusive stories emerge.

My Golem

With that expression on his face, and that frown, I think he isn't going to be able to take my hand; nonetheless, he does, and he has such long, soft hands. Hands like those I've dreamed of, not like the other one's chubby digits.

With that air of being elsewhere, that skinniness, I don't think he'll be able to talk to me of love, and nonetheless he says that he wants to share everything with me. He tells me that I stir so many things inside him that he wants to be with me all day, every day, always. The other man, on the other hand, is distancing himself from me. He doesn't reject me, but fears me—or so I think. The other man is a little ridiculous and I love him.

This one takes me by the hand through secret streets of the city like in my dreams. He discovers new squares for me and unexpected doors. The other man always takes his car; once in a while he'll open the sunroof, but he never looks at the sky.

This one shows me the moon, he gives me a flower, and he talks about spending whole days caressing one another. With the other man, we've also caressed each other a lot; it was the purest thing we had.

This one talks to me about traveling with him to those places I prefer. The other man gets scared as soon as the remotest possibility of leaving the city center comes up.

Neither one of them takes the slightest step toward a true encounter. Who gives? Who will be willing to give of himself until everything explodes?

One offers with words, the other takes away the happiness we were able to achieve—sometimes very intense—with words. And me? Where am I in all this, and why do I dilute myself?

The problem is to love or not to love. It's not being confused. It's knowing how to surrender without leaving the pieces behind. The problem is avoiding anthropography.

All because there have been, there are, and there will be men who awaken multiple kinds of imagination in me. And there is a city, New York, which for me has the soul of a loved one.

Today however I feel the absolute need to tell stories of actual physical love. Today I would like to tell my love stories with complete candor, just as they happened, as chronologically as possible. I have journals, various annotations, outlines of stories and novels, some other literary attempts, even dreams. Now I think I should give up any pretense and write it all down, just like that, like telling it to a girlfriend. I don't know about telling it to a male friend; they're usually the ones to talk, and they don't listen. I do listen and listen and sometimes I urge them on, perhaps simply because I'd like to make what they tell me into my story—because I feel like belonging to or integrating myself into the masculine world. That's why I have this imperious need, which began so long ago, almost from the beginning, to outline my Chronicle of the Conquest (conquests?). It could be considered as mere ornamentation, gossipography, if you didn't take into account the fact that inside all of it is the search. The problem is the tangled mess of stories, the temptation to embroider—not to disguise, hide, or invent, but rather, thanks to the dark side of language, to highlight the situations in all their subtle half-tones. Chronological order will help me. The tedium of narrating what's already known could turn out to be my worst enemy, and please! no epic or bombastic tendencies! Or the poor-me syndrome.

So I'll start at the beginning.

Thousands of notebooks, hundreds of thousands of spiral notebooks that not only have lost pages with time, but have gotten all crumpled. Little spiral snakes making up one big notebook snake. With teeth and a few bites—and vice versa.

Perhaps it would be best to take note now before it's too late: I don't claim to be using all this spiraled material now. I'm imitating squirrels, hoarding for those long senile winter nights when I'll no longer have the skill for other things—only to shuffle memories like someone gathering little figurines. And what if I were doing this because senility has already arrived prematurely? And what if, as an old lady, I no longer give a damn about these things, and only want to enjoy myself?

And then there's the option of donating it all to the Boston Library,
although this material is mostly for me—to be able to see clearly.
That's why it's better to do it now and not leave it for when seeing
clearly no longer has any importance and isn't worth a damn.

This wandering through the rough and pathless territories of the
soul and my passion for masks: one and the same thing. Masks
hide the face, only seemingly leaving the person intact and un-
touched behind them—because the mask transforms you. And
not only that: the mask tends to be the mediator between the
world we know and the spirit world.

I hang the wisely chosen masks on the wall, and it's as if I've pen-
etrated them to lose myself in other worlds. Or to travel through this
world that, seen through perforated eye-holes, is made more human.

Carefully choosing the outfit for a certain occasion is like putting
on a mask: you assume another identity.

What most often escapes you of all the things that happen—that
pass through your own mind in bursts? Things you think should
be written down but finally remain lost (or almost) forever in a
corner of your memory and never again emerge.

I went about reliving the sudden pain of certain loves that come
back to me in waves. Remembering San Remo, feeling that some
streets of the Village are just like those in San Remo, or better yet,
that this spring is also the spring in San Remo two years ago. Not
a very encouraging anniversary this, but in homage to that anniversary and everything that it meant . . . it would be interesting to

be able to write the story of that meeting, that enlightenment . . . incorporate it into something, the novel I'm writing, even though the novel may rob it of any virtue, devour or assimilate it.

Assimilation is good—no more fragments, enough already of things in tatters, destroyed. I isolate facts to give them more form, as though the facts were mortar, a moldable material and pliant between my fingers. If the facts are indeed pliant and moldable, it's only because of life's continuity, because of the umbilical cord that ties us to other facts, to thousands of facts that give this fact its most secret form.

Everything that I have to let go of to write this story! Everything that needs to be purged!

In the end, as in a translation, beyond what is mere anecdote, all that remains is what you touch without wanting to, and this is definitely the most valuable material.

It's like putting a tapestry together, knitting with different colored yarns; plots, schemes, changes in texture, thickenings, hollows.

Michel

I love Michel now, with his Eastern approach to time and nature. "What do you do in real life?" I asked him when I met him at an inauguration.

"I observe nature."

"As in an ecologist?"

"No, as in someone in love," he answered, and I couldn't help but love him.

Michel. Big blue eyes that I discovered at the back of a huge crowd at an art opening and which rowed toward me, helped somewhat by my friend Rosario who tends to know so many things. I was practicing what's known as Cool Seduction, and Rosario was laughing at me. However, this technique did give me some beautiful pleasures; a technique almost, almost the Vietcong type, consisting of a delivering a light blow—perhaps the fillip of a look—after which one retires to a corner to await the results.

In this case, the results didn't take long. The blue eyes from over there at the back of the room rowed toward my zone of influence, and in a flash of true inspiration, Rosario introduced us, without knowing who this other person was, but knowing me very well.

When you see a pair of eyes that attracts you, it's an iron law, a law of fire or hot, magnetizing iron, that their owner is also attracted to yours. When their eyes attract you, when you fly to their call without thinking.

And that's how I had those days of profound happiness and affection with Michel, while both of us cried "Miracle, miracle!" and caressed each other.

I've become soft for him. Someone else might touch me and I would like it—we would like it, why deny it? He's been looking at me—I know he wants to go back, but I've become soft for him, for his soft touch, and also by imitation, out of sympathy. I lather myself in creams as I think of him. I think of him even when I'm not lathering myself in cream, and I still become sweet and soft. He goes away and it doesn't matter—I know he'll come back and so it doesn't matter that he goes away leaving me a space in which to think about him. General rehearsal of love with lights and costumes—in other words, undressed.

The anecdotes about all the women who clambered over themselves to get to Michel at that party, I'll leave perhaps for a novel. I've never ever seen women trying so perfidiously and so often to steal another woman's man. It's true that Michel is some years younger than I—and they. But what poor wretches, no? since this man is all mine at the moment. Even I realized that, and I've doubted all my life—I didn't doubt it that night when Michel told me he was in love with me, and all the women threw themselves on him about to eat him alive, good god! I was sure he was mine, mine that night and the next morning and after the flood because he'll go to Canada on his way back to France, and then not mine, or anyone else's, at least not on this damn island of Manhattan.

Where exactly is the delight with Michel? It's in the caress, those long, really long caresses when one usually rolls over and curls up, but not with Michel, no.

With him, we spent so much time passing our hands over each other's bodies, recognizing each other.

"Do you feel what I feel?" he asks me. And of course I do, because the electrical current that's traveling through my body (what else can a current do?) doesn't stop at me—it completes its circle through his body and then it comes back to envelop me again. A Möbius strip of purring delight.

What a drag that full moon of March 15th that tore us apart from each other! The moon woke me around two in the morning, laughing in my face. It seems she let Michel sleep, but he knew that the next day we'd be together again. Without telling me he'd postponed his trip one more time in order to cry out for more, applauding the miracle of having met and recognized each other.

Why do I look for him in the corners where I know very well that I won't find him? He told me where he was going to be and I even suspect that he may be waiting for me. Waiting, yes. He always waits, that's his most sublime attribute, the step he climbs in order to be able to touch things completely with his hands. Touch with his five senses and one more, if need be: the bonus of those who are leaving, those who are never complacent.

How did that saying go that fell into my hands just when I was lamenting Michel's departure? If you love something, you must set it free. If it comes back, receive it with open arms. If it doesn't come back that means it wasn't meant to be.

Then I received his card, full of sweetness, and I must be going all soft and sentimental because I'm mentioning the letter instead of talking about his skin or his cock.

I'll leave a space to do so, to fill it with the other side of the matter, that Cyclops. That tender, slightly melancholic being who in that precise—beautiful—moment would get so, so rigid with its balls hanging almost at half mast, the skin so stretched, so tense. And become so very active. I would like to describe it all but I don't dare. Or, more precisely, in that moment, I can't dive in and take off, sliding into the secretions, oh those thick warm secretions, pure delight.

I let Michel leave (getting angry, it's true, stamping my feet a bit; he didn't come back and now I miss him). I think that if I could choose now, I would choose him. Forever—for his absolute lack of complexities and moodiness. Why did I doubt him then? Why did I think that he was a bit simple, or that his arms were a bit short and that that this was a symptom of some deficiency? I can never accept that someone—whole, normal, perfect in all that human perfection means—loves me.

That's why I'm sketching myself now, trying to recuperate the best of my forms: to be able to accept myself, me—and that way, be able to recognize, accept, and instigate the acceptance of the other.

(The same story as always, but it has to be incorporated in all its depth in order to understand it with your guts and not just with your head.)

I bought myself a flowering plant that awakened an enormous amount of tenderness and quite a bit of pity in me. Pity because the flowers are going to die, since I don't know how to take care of them and in this studio apartment in the Village, they'll get so little light.

What to do then with this overflowing tenderness? I don't want to lose it. I want to share it.

Thinking about love as if it were a Navajo sand painting or a Tibetan mandala or one of those Australian aborigine drawings made with flower petals. Something not made to last. With complete devotion you compose it during a whole day and a whole night, but before dawn, it has to be destroyed in order for its true powers to be freed.

Does everything have value? Is nothing worth throwing out? And the weaving, weaving of the web in the clearness of the day. For now, writing is something I can do only during the day. Building, piling one memory brick on top of the other, and the twilight becomes impenetrable, not to mention the night with all that it encloses and the impossibility for now of perforating it with the written word. But night's letters are really the ones that nourish memories. During the day, all that happens is the simple unloading of the dead weight and then off to something else that—as I remarked somewhere—always turns out to be the same thing. Always a chain of searches (the human being, that searching animal), it's just that for the moment the chain is limited to what's called love and replicates in its path the heart line on the palm of one's hand plowing through the head line and below the little mounds of each finger. And when the heart line starts forming a chain, well, well, palmistry tells us how to read such complications.

Michel left to go resume his solitary meanderings, this time on a river in Canada, and he had to hurry up, before the thaw began. Hurry up, yes, before the thawing of our passion drowns us like rats. No. Like lemurs, because rats usually know how to swim and we felt defenseless.

The trees that were his are mine now. The full moon from the time you descended alone, sliding down the snowy peak, you left to me too, and now it's mine. You left me the snow as well, and it's not cold—it keeps my soul warm. Your long trek through Nepal I've kept in a little box. I have your fig trees on Easter Island and the flight of the huge flocks of pink flamingos that so dazzled you. Like a grasping of your interior time, the sound of your words, the letter in which you told me about love: I have all of it, I just miss you, and what does it matter.

I've already forgotten about the phallus. Romantic that I am, I already forgot about the phallus or at least that's what I think. I think two erroneous things, as usual: the romanticism that a forgotten phallus can imply, and the fact of thinking that I forgot the phallus. If that were feasible (phallopheasible), I wouldn't be writing these sorry pages. I would devote myself to embroidery, or something else that keeps the mind away from bad thoughts or actually rather encourages them by letting the mind take pleasure in those bad thoughts, one by one, without anyone noticing.

The morbidity of the seeming purity of domestic chores. The so-called purity. It reminds me of the stories my friend Dedé told, virgin at twenty-four and always asking the most indecent questions about sex with such subtle innocence. And when she finally decided to tear her Achilles' heel, or, rather, a somewhat more sensitive piece of flesh, the hero of the day gave her a certain oral attention, and she asked (always asking, she was) how it was done.

"Like eating an ice cream cone," the explicit one replied.

"I eat my ice cream with a spoon," she clarified, so as to avoid confusion.

The Binnacle Notebook

And where is hate in all this? I don't think there is true, solid hate. Only a bunch of arguments and a few grudges. Maybe what I'm looking for here and in so many other notebooks isn't the justification of love—*if* there was love and then with whom and when—but rather that of hate. To finally express hatred and not a comfortable acceptance of the circumstances.

Today I think I'll shut myself up in this notebook, in this little shell, and just look and look and look at everything that's in here to be written down. To write things from there—categorize them—even if only to get them off my back and be able to leave on paper the burdens that we all carry, to be able to flutter around then at will.

Another time—like the one in *illo tempore*—in my ex-love Buenos Aires, when I made note of the names of certain guys that were all weighing my soul down, and then burned the little piece of paper and threw the ashes into the Palermo Lake to announce my internal freedom, so precious.

And today: like the lists of lovers that I made and remade several times (each time more extensive, luckily) and that must be around here because I never decided to destroy them; I got up to the seventies, and number seventy, as I promised to Nenuca, was important—although not, as I would have liked, long-lasting. But who knows? He appears to be returning, but I fear that it will be too late, as far as I'm concerned. That's why I became so indignant when he went away, because I knew inside that I would sooner or later cut the cord.

Once again I will try to write, as I have in other circumstances, my much mentioned Ode to the Phallus (the inconstant). I've already tried it on more than one occasion, my failures obvious, but now I try my hand again, writing in two notebooks which have multiplied and are now three.

New York, New York, what a marvel, and this now rainy spring, but the other day so perfect, painful in its perishability—with the apple and cherry blossoms twinkling like stars in the sunny air. The beautiful and the ephemeral and the feeling that everything dilutes in our hands. Now fortunately the rain has put everything in its place, put an end to beauty's very perishable perfection, bringing along all kinds of inconveniences, and that way we feel safer, at least I feel at home.

People and things that are too beautiful make us afraid. And situations too, because of that immanent sensation that they won't last longer than a sigh. And why would we want them to? As if we were that constant . . .

Be careful of waking the sleeping phallus!

I have a few unconnected stories that I'll have to write down before they escape me—I have some good characters and situations.

I don't have . . . I don't have . . .

What don't I have?

Maybe the coherence, the connecting thread that I'm looking for in four notebooks.

I have the devil on my heels. Good title:

The Devil on My Heels

And now here comes Carmen telling me that Ekeko is the devil, but I already know that, more or less. From the days of Christian and Exu of the folded cock that I'll tell about somewhere else, gifts I make just to my stories. My characters for the moment are becoming mythical.

Someone with a little mouth is crying out, but the cry doesn't amount to much, it's not a sonorous sound, and that someone is a little man named Ekeko, full of all sorts of presents, who has his mouth open forever, and it's a little mouth because he's a little doll and the only thing he asks of us is that we put a cigarette in his open mouth on Fridays at any time of the day or night. He asks that we remember him once a week and the rest of the time maybe he'll remember us and will give us what we want—that's what he's good for, open-mouthed and full of the offerings that we've given him, ready to be obliging.

What kind of motor is it, gratitude, that it gives us life? And what kind of fuel does it use?

I live wrestling with what can't be fought; the things that are worth battling tend to terrify me—they drive me away.

To be alive and kicking, making my way through exotic lands seems to me a gift of the gods. To be alive and fucking, well, that's even more interesting.

The stages are getting a bit rushed. At the end of my stay in Barcelona was the stage of wanting to be a hunter and going out with my hunting gear over my shoulder, in search of some tasty prey. Here in New York, it was already too late for feeling playful and knowing—perhaps—how to play my cards right. And now this third and I hope final stage: like Zen archery, it's not a sport but rather an almost religious ritual. To become one with the target, to forget oneself and forget the target and try to become one with the cosmos.

Become an unmovable center.

In reality the true target should not be a person at all: the target is love. And because inevitably the personal and the possessive enter into the game, I tend to miss love entirely, and only managing to get in a few shots at the other person and then some at myself. Watch out with those arrows! I warn myself. I wasn't born under the sign of Sagittarius for nothing.

Be the unmovable center. Be the opening where sap flows freely, the interstice where truths can sneak in, be the loving hinge, like the print by that sublime Mexican painter named Vlady.

The decade of the '70s was one of searching. Now the one of non-searching begins, the one of letting oneself go, in order to find oneself, as the Tao says.

The era beginning now is one not of patience, but rather of not being impatient, which is different.

Rereading now Borges and Cortázar for the hundredth time for work-related reasons, I tell myself that there are so many things I don't know, that I once knew and have forgotten, so many loose threads that I can't tie together, and I try to console myself. Maybe knowing is a refuge, a safe haven, and this not-knowing is an attempt to keep navigating through unsafe waters, yes, and today, in a certain way, I am able to resign myself.

In Mexico, Alba said:

"I'm no longer anybody else's better half, and I'm not looking to be. *I* am my own better half, and whoever wants me like that can have me. Exactly as I am."

Crime Scene Unit

I am what others have left of me, or what others have drawn me as, with their hands
(Be inside the caress/existing because of being touched)
Being freed from numbness without molding myself
By pure purring

Here will be—or would like to be—the telephone directory, ladies and gentlemen, a long list of names and of men (many masked), in desperate need, impossible to fulfill, of writing it all down.
To be able to understand?
To know?
To forget?

What?

And that coincidence of having written in this same notebook the sentence *Crime Scene Unit.* Nothing to do with anything and yet so much. I was in El Paso when I read it on a police car going by and it caught my attention and I noted it down at the beginning of my notebook where further on I would make notes about my own—very different—character. Which would end up being, why not, a sort of investigation instead of a crime. The crime of love? (The place I was thinking of just a few minutes ago).

But not anymore. Luckily. Finally stop letting myself be shaped— stop being torn up—by others. By *the other*, each one at his own time. After so many years of struggle and revolving around that unhappiness and looking for it, I think I've finally reached the goal. That is to say, of accepting myself.

Man as Horse

I met him in a park when he was still trotting around peacefully. I ran into him turning a corner in my life, those corners we all have and that we tend to frequent alone so that nobody suspects. Corners where we manage to put our feet into other people's corners, corners where we discover ourselves little by little.

He was grazing and I didn't really know what to expect from him with his hairy muzzle. He was there and he wasn't there: gentle eyes, eyes that seemed to be looking just for me, one could have said. Anyway, so I went out to meet him, and we loved each other a lot in the beginning. He still had some human molecules in spite of being in the middle of a complete mutation and I should have foreseen what would happen later: those missteps, just before a leap.

These things happen when one falls in love in a park. Can you really know, when you're in a park, whether you're dealing with people, horses, ruminants, beasts of prey, or insects?

What led me to make a mistake was without a doubt his ca-resses—since when does a horse touch you? And with a gentle hand, not a hard hoof with a shoe and everything.

But it's not the same anymore, it's not pure gentleness anymore, it's the bit and the bridle now. And inverting roles, I have to ride him now, nothing metaphorical about it and not at all pleasant. I have to tie myself on well not to fall off all the time, and at the same time to get used to falling off all the time.

Of course it would happen to me: meeting guys who are turn-ing themselves little by little into stubborn horses. I should have gotten myself one of those that go around and around in a circle, a humble stick horse. As if I liked merry-go-rounds.

Today Pedro C. defended seduction, something that makes my hair stand on end because it reminds me of my mother. But I un-derstand, in his case: if you took it away from him, there would only be a huge vacuum in its place.

Today Randy said that all conversation, all communication is for her a struggle for power.

What do I care about all this now? Today I was sniffing myself—all of me carries a very tenuous odor of sex.

Life has slowed down for a few days. I want to get the most out of things in these last days of sun. Only there isn't any sun. It's got-ten cloudy—I'm referring to the meteorological condition only. Still, it's nice to be looking outside and seeing and discovering that some ray of sun is about to peep through.

What few seasonal changes a human being sees, after all, in a life-time. One winter a year, one spring. In the end, there aren't that many to add up.

And what do people do in those countries where the weather is the same all year? What do people do with the same, foreseeable, life? I complain about the changes and the moves, about insecurity. And the opposite? To know you'll be in the same house all your life, next to the same man, seeing the possibilities moving farther away, knowing they'll never be reached . . . it would be unbearable.

A crisis of inspiration. On to something else, no? I'm lacking that initial kick that I started these notes with.

Masks. Seduction and the male language.

Seduced and abandoned?
Is that why I reject seduction?

Oh dear. Always my relationship with a man. And writing. A man and writing. Now I see, and it doesn't make me at all happy, not just realizing it but realizing it *now*. Only now, after so much time. And it's what I've been writing for a thousand years, or let's say twenty-four. And now I wonder why I threw away those three or four chapters of my really bad novel about myself at eighteen with Rodrigo as protagonist. Good proof of this mediation of literature in my love life, and also of my tenacity in that respect. Let's call it loyalty.

I wanted to write about Rodrigo at eighteen, his relationship with the big old house in the Tigre district and with his mother—house and mother, both mixed up, both just as decrepit and omnipresent (the house even more decrepit than the mother), and his little bed, almost a cot thrown in a corner and abandoned. In the novel I slept with him, something I only managed to do in life many years later. But in some way, Rodrigo was my lover at that time and the mutual fascination was enormous across those twenty years that separated us. The novel of course was high melodrama. Unbearable. Later (or more or less at the same time), I met Enrique, another very attractive fortyish fellow, and with him also as protagonist I wrote a really long "heartrending" story. And I went to bed with him too, years later. Nothing like repressed juvenile sexual anxieties to produce bad literature. At least in my case.

And I wrote so much about so many others. I only could produce good work about those I'd really digested, for better or worse.

Hic et Nunc

It sounds good, but what does it mean? So many, many things sound good but what do they mean, we ask ourselves with the complete and worrisome conviction that we will never know. Here and now we will never know.

What galloping insanity for this woman—who proposes to write about all of them—to try to describe good men as they act in private; maybe for the benefit of those who will follow in future and comply with these directions? As if she and they didn't know that each act of love is different, that each answer in each person is absolutely personal and nontransferable. If it wasn't that way, there wouldn't be any otherwise inexplicable couplings. If it wasn't that way, I ask when, in what heavenly fart she who writes this would have developed that crazy crush on the one her closest friends so affectionately nicknamed the Lousy Brute. With orgasms that made his already bristly hair stand on end.

36

Just wanting to enter the lives of the others, put myself in their houses, make them prepare my breakfast, but with the growing suspicion that I'm never going to let them invade my own little house-soul.

Even poor Ch, the love of my life, who when he had to leave for work at dawn, I made coffee with milk and salt, an unsuccessful gesture, easily translated: Don't get any ideas, you—this isn't my job because I'm by no means a submissive housewife. I'm the black widow, the praying mantis. More or less, let's say (the salt of life).

And what do I do now with this enormous cobweb where the hides of so many, many males are hanging while the males them-selves have gone away?

Now I tidily unravel the web, make a ball, and tidily store the dried skins in the pages of this journal.

Later I tell others that they have to surrender their flesh and blood, tear themselves apart if they want to write, but here I am escaping once again, trying to get away through the tangent, to renounce everything and wondering why tell about all these stupidities? like a leitmotif of impotence.

And here I am and this is me with my nerves exposed.

Make of me what you will, since at the end of the day you won't be able to make much—total surrender renders us invulnerable. That's what I believe. Today. Tomorrow will be another day.

(Nobody can beat me up because I'm nowhere.) I'm not here for the others.

I'm here for me and I'm tearing myself to pieces and tomorrow maybe I'll gallop underground and leave little bits of myself at each stop.

I—the others.

What a soup of such bad inclinations, such uniting of undefinitions. This is going to be (going to exist) in order for me to find my form and to give a limit to myself.

He (which he? which of the so many mixed-up *hes* that make up my album?) knows it, perhaps. Maybe they all know and so they distance themselves from me in disgust, as though they've touched a frog without wanting to, something slimy that they don't understand and that doesn't have any form at all. That's me. Like a slimy something that doesn't have any form at all is how I feel now, because I don't have any form, not at all. Not even when they sketch me out with caresses or try to take my hand.

It seems I'll have to live through (if time is on my side) a sizeable number of emotions. Or I would, rather, if it weren't for the fact that I'm starting to run out of emotions. But no. I'm just saying that to calm myself down, to make myself believe that the anguish has been left behind—the anxieties. In reality, and perhaps luckily, there will always be men (more or less frightened themselves) who will cross my path. Sometimes like chickens crossing in front of my car, and I look in the rearview mirror to see if one of them has been thrown to the side of the road. It doesn't bother me (at least that's what I think), but I like to collect their feathers, and sometimes I adorn my hat or tickle myself with these, or clean my teeth with the shaft, or even use it write such heartfelt lines as these. Some feathers are colorful, and some aren't even worth sticking in a feather duster. There are drops of love that still bleed from some shafts and sucking on them can be sweet or can be bitter and I suck on them as I'm doing now to retain their essence.

I was finally able to restrain myself somewhat. I sit down in front of my desk, I write, and I see some folders lined up. I see books (Anaïs Nin, Virginia Woolf—she trying to be so tidy, and I muddling everything up).

To shake others up. Take them by the shoulders and shake them vigorously until they see straight at last. And me? Always shaken up: the human cocktail shaker (I already said it, or will say it further on).

I see a mask, one made of pasteboard. It interests me because it hides me. A little box that has such a serious writer drawn on it. I see a souvenir from Mexico, a photo of my daughter. I look and I look and above all I listen to the singsong of my sentences, damn it . . . I also listen to others and I know that there are more stimulating things calling me, like hunger.

It's one of my themes, hunger. That's why I'm staying awake. Not for me, for others.

And there are so many.

To become aware, what for? Why aware? Free, free, free, I tell those who have the gall to approach me, and then I'm tied up just like any woman (like a *roulade de boeuf*, as the guy I nicknamed "Duck" used to accuse me of). Why bind myself to the constraints of a novel? Why bother writing this stuff, I repeat to myself, let's be serious, let's do a novel instead.

Serious, a novel? Who says?

What mobilizes and what immobilizes, is it the same thing? The other side of the same thing, just separated by fear?

I remember fear.

What bad luck, no? to act as an opener of eyes, to put my fingers in the wound and other such nonsense. She makes others feel tied to conventions and then they end up fleeing from her for just that reason. Or is it something else? Is it simply that she, without meaning to, frightens them away?

But also to shock them into being serious, for a change. The Sublime Poet says: You don't venerate me.

And I answer him: If what you're upset about is my not having given you a venereal disease, just wait, my boy, keep trying, wait and see, you never know.

I have an already finished book, I have six published books. I *am* an already-written book—is that where this panic comes from? I go underground crisscrossing dark desires. But no, I'm afraid not, that's not it at all: desire is generally clear, not dark—what ends up being dark is rejection. And worse than the fear of being rejected by the other is the tremor that shakes us when we perceive—too late—that the rejection was our own: I was the one who broke the toy. To see what was inside. And what usually happens—it's well known that there's no such thing as a perfect vacuum—inside we only find a heap of smelly guts that we, with great enthusiasm, will—if we can—make into a heart. From guts to heart. But it will be too late.

New York Wedding

He's so blond and light-skinned, so transparent (if only in appearance) that he looks like an angel. Who knows what I look like, I will note here only my exterior darkness. And here we are, the three of us—there's always a third person, discordant, always a witness—sitting in front of a table in an elegant restaurant, the kind with candles everywhere, and we're planning our wedding. The third, discordant person insists that she'll marry me; he, however, does not, if it's a question of a marriage of love: but no, this is about a marriage of convenience. For both of us. I have to get my US citizenship, and he has to make his mother happy, a mother *comme il faut*. And is your mother going to accept your marrying an older woman?

"She'll love it that I'm marrying a Latin American writer. It'll seem exotic to her."

"Then let's do it," I tell him. "My only stipulation is that we spend the night of the wedding together."

I love seeing him bat his long blond eyelashes, sadly shaking his head.

The third, discordant person who is an important lawyer for an art foundation raises her likewise golden head and laughs. "Since I can't marry the bride," she says, "at least let me walk you down the aisle. I have a great tuxedo."

There are no guides! In a story like this one, there isn't just a single line to follow and finally be overtaken by the vertigo of wide-open spaces. The pieces of the puzzle are all there. Or almost all of them, although they have to be arranged as the story advances. What's not there is the final model. Not at all, nowhere. Just the opposite, in fact; on the other hand, the other one, the story about the Ambassador and Bella that I say I'm writing, that one is all there, all of it so elaborated, step by step, that I don't even feel like writing it anymore, filling it in. I prefer to dive into these unknown waters—if waters they are; I don't even know if they're liquid, or if there are marshes or quicksand ahead.

Therein lies the danger: that which seems solid may be liquid, or an avid conjunction of both states that ends up swallowing everything. A molecular problem—lack of cohesion. There's a form of friction keeping things from cohering and making everything move beneath the feet of anyone who, believing that they're walking on solid ground, begins to sink. Like the isolating friction of the sexual act: on two separate occasions, not so far apart, I told two very different guys:

Watch out, you asked for it. This is a quagmire, this is quicksand. I advise against entering. Neither of them paid much attention. They both dove in or at least put their toe in and the one who ended up sinking was me, as always, sinking into myself.

Let's talk about destruction, my only possible connection, the only thing that keeps me united (cohesive would be the word: the friction of molecules in their infinite possibilities of mutual rejection).

Later I'll use the old, stupid cliché as if it was a glorious truth itself, saying: One renounces love for fear of rejection. And meanwhile, what do I do? I claim to love and reject at the same time and finally I achieve what I wanted, to be rejected myself, and then I feel proud, confirmed in my doubts.

Deforming mirrors for others, when will they recognize their faces in these pages?

The longing to awaken the other's desire, and then to frustrate it, the only way to keep desire alive, because there is no doubt that desire, when satiated, dies. Perhaps I want to do something like that to the others (*the* Other), and then the other ends up doing it to me, out of pure revenge, because of my constant provocations. It's a game of mirrors facing off—bloody mirrors—the eternal *mise en abîme*. The immediate response of someone passing from defense to attack.

Memory tends to be on the side of those who don't always have a good memory. That's why I—as forgetful as I am—remember the men who in one way or another have been connected—plugged-in—to my life. And so the mirror—they are the ones who show me the other half of myself, my equidistant image, opposite and inverted (thank you "Jack" Lacan). That's why they are never women, although that particular fantasy never stops titillating its way through my most unconfessable zones. But it's only a fantasy, appreciated as such, because with a woman everything would be like staying on this side of the mirror, without every trying to cross through the image. Anyway, what people call an inversion—as in the old statement, "she is an invert"—turns out to be just the opposite: staying fearfully on this side.

When will I write about the encounters always about to take place in museums, in the reflections of shop windows, in the looks that from different angles converge into one single painting?

To sink oneself in the other, to look for salvation in the eyes of the other. The lifesaver. And then what? Drag him to the shipwreck or drift away, floating through the crosscurrents?

I'm going to go down a one-way street and I do hope that's what it is, because I'm sick of the coming and going, the starting and leaving, the things that are never decided.

Of living and then drifting, of an ode to shipwrecks. (Rather bleak, but I'm still here.) Of eating oneself up. Of cannibalism. How much free rein does tension need? More than can be calculated at first sight. That's where the glory of destruction and desire must reside. The ferocious temptation of rejection.

The one who has had many men, I am the singed one, the one who knows how to be reborn from the ashes—and with a pontifical dignity to boot. Inhaling to take up space, breathing deeply.

Space is what it's all about, no doubt there, it's about space, the space that belongs to me and that they all want to occupy for me. And I struggle to keep it, and every time I say *Here I am* in a little while I find out it's true, there I AM, but I'm alone. Nobody nearby. Not even a Cheshire cat smile. Nothing. Because of the simple fear of contamination from those who see themselves as protected by their masks.

I've learned, not without some pain, to tear the mask from others, but my own mask has become my flesh.

Sooner or later, I will also learn the merciless lesson of cutting ties. But for now it's impossible to cut—only tell about the ways I am tied. And tell the story backwards, counting with my fingers.

Later, one manifested himself. I can't say he appeared—we were rather close friends until we became, oh what a surprise for me because I thought he was so different!—morethanfriends. That's when I started calling him

Pale Fire

Like gods, like days,
Like the corners where I sometimes find him again,

44

Silent and composed (remorseful)
Sometimes groaning,
Sometimes trying to show me his claws.
Sometimes for, sometimes against.
Awake, yes, and sometimes desperate.
He never blinks,
Observing me at all moments and sometimes criticizing me
(not for lack of trying to criticize me *all the time* instead)
Never understanding me, denying me the space to be in myself.

I call him Cat because he loves to be spoiled and hardly ever returns my caresses. Like a cat waiting for a friendly hand (and we're
not talking only about hands!)
    "It's beautiful, no? Everyone likes to stroke a cat."
    "It depends," I answered, determined. "There are people who
are allergic to cats and there are feral cats who live in sewers who
scratch when you least expect it, like someone I know who takes
away his hand just when I'd like to hold it."

To whom should I direct my cry, my shout for help?
Where to open my hand so that he takes it? Whom to invoke—
implore—in these circumstances?
Such distress. Such sleeplessness and upset.
My hand is good; my hand doesn't drag or push, or lead to anything.
My hand is good—it's only its heat that is conducive to other things,
My hand is good.

You give the peace of knowing you're solid, but that solidity kills me,
dislocates me. I need you to be strong and tender at the same time, and
not to be afraid (afraid of surrendering, the same fear we all have).

Because, oh Puss in Boots, you're not five years old any more—no need to think that when someone takes your hand, they're going to drag you off to someplace you don't want to go. When someone takes your hand now, it's only to share a bit of human warmth.

That's what I say, what I instruct, what I try to inculcate, but later I know it isn't true. I give my hand and I take it away. I too succumb to fear, although I like to proclaim the opposite.

(On one hand I'm the one who for a long time has been trying to write a long novel about the Ambassador and Bella without getting anywhere at all, and on the other hand I'm the one who lets the novel get woven on top of her, and the fictitious narrative gets mixed with that other spurious element—what's it called? Reality.)

Here I am, or at least that undefinition so addicted to the wound that makes up my self. I bleed, and not only monthly; I cut myself and I gnaw away at myself, but I don't know how to surrender. With fury. Yes, that's for sure: with fury. Fury that sometimes abandons me and leaves sadness in its wake. Fury that I hope will last and keep me going. Fury against all those who try to touch me and do so only with their fingertips, and then sometimes pull away, afraid. Something burns them, something surrounding me, something merciless that comes out of me even if I don't intend it to.

At least, this is what I claim on my most Valkyrian days. On the other days, I just mope around, succumbing to the temptation to feel wretchedly sorry for myself.

With the Cat, I ended up re-nicknaming him "Pale Fire" without his knowing. I have my reasons. Although some day I'll remember that single night (out of all the many nights we spent together) when he took me in his arms with a crazy enthusiasm, hugging me, kissing me, fucking me with fury and desire, roving up and down my overflowing anatomy.

"It's fantastic, I felt like my whole body was a phallus, my whole body tense and excited like my cock," he was able to say afterward in an uncharacteristic outburst.

And didn't I say, as soon as I had turned around, out of pure condescension and acceptance, "Of course, like a cock, because you finally acted like a man . . ."

After all, though, acting like a man isn't everything. What's needed is a prudent combination of this with tenderness.

Our desires are listened to, but only halfheartedly. Do we have our own private god, made especially in our own image and likeness? Because, as for mine, he listens, I can't say otherwise, but the poor guy is just like me, and only has one ear.

This is the end of a story that had its bright moments, but they were only mirrors—my good will reflected in the other's desire, happening light years away, somewhere else.

Are these what adult friendships are like? Getting together for a time, knowing that nothing remains? Or very little, anyway.

House of Cards

She has the soul of a watchmaker and thinks she can take apart the mechanism. He has the soul—if indeed he has one at all—of a lark hunter. What he's building with hundreds of little pieces of polished wood and tin are giant sparkling traps with mirrors, promises that will never be kept—just the opposite. That's why they shine so much.

At times she tries to understand the trap but some pieces are always missing. He's been careful to take them away in good time and put them in his pocket, waiting for a better moment, and when she stretches out her hand to examine a piece or play with the mirrors, he kicks the mechanism and takes it apart before she can really indulge her enthusiasm. Sometimes a tiny bit of metal falls on top of her, wounding her.

He loves to kick mechanisms, he doesn't hide it, she knows that and still comes back over and over again and lets herself get caught by the mirrors.

There are times when she moves away, indifferent, and then he hurriedly builds castles with only the shiniest cards. And she, who has a weakness for shiny houses, doesn't stop to think and believes they're playing again. She accepts, and rebuilds a fallen tower, or takes down one of her own drawbridges. Until once again he decides to show her that it's not her castle, nor her game—it's just one more of his traps for larks, a synthesis of misery.

I've been kissing so many toads to see if they turn into princes, I'm going to end up liking toads.

A Letter

My Enormously Adored Alicia,

After a good many months, I'm returning to my computer to write you this letter, which as usual is going to be chaotic and, to top it off, full of complaints. These because I can't be talking to you in person, damn it, I miss you so much. Instead I have to type really fast to try to put my ideas in order and tell you something more or less coherent. I'm a mess, dear sister, which I'm sure won't surprise you, although I should know how to control myself at this stage of the game. I'm not going around looking for trouble, no, sometimes it just comes on its own, falling from the sky.

So let's back up and try to be meticulous. In December, I came back from a vacation in Mexico finally feeling like a grown up—in control, or almost, of the situation, and eager to do things. I did them, and I wrote rather well, and finally had to go back to feeling resentful a week ahead of time, that is, on January 28th, because of the new courses I was to teach at Columbia University. They hadn't started yet, you see my dear, but I still arrived with my tongue hanging out, to prepare for them and with the hope of seeing my Latin American, whom I call "Pale Fire" now. Even though he had kind of acted like a pig in my absence—no communication, not even a card or a letter or any kind of call, nothing—I attributed it all to his usual smallness of spirit and his inability to show any emotion, and I told myself, you have to accept people for what they are, and he'll be different when we're face to face, etc., etc. (etc. referring to other parts of our anatomical intersections). And can you believe it?! This shifty character went out of his way to put off seeing me! I arrived on Tuesday, and on Friday, I woke up in a towering rage and threw the phone across the room and stamped on it until I felt calm again. Then, a few hours later, it rang and, what a surprise, it was Duck, yes ma'am, the one in the beautiful and tearful European story, the story of my desires two years ago in San Remo and vicinity. "I'm here on vacation, alone. I didn't come for work or anything like it, simply to see you,

49

just for that, no more no less, like I promised just before you left. I read in some prestigious newspaper that you still lived in New York, next to an ancient cemetery, and so I did some research and found out that you were coming back from Mexico this week, and here I am."

I received him. I found him a bit soft and spongy, I must admit, rather ugly but as tender as always (yum, yum). And I sure needed some tenderness after that dry Latin American brother, better known today as PF, Pale Fire. So we renewed contact, saying Sorry, and everything would really have been great if:

a) Duck wasn't a shit. He's never going to change his life, leave his wife—whom he swears up and down he hasn't slept or even communicated with in eight months—and chuck his emetic, quasi-government job; and

b) I wasn't so neurotic and didn't see a betrayal, a lie, a con, stinginess in everything.

Not that there haven't been interesting examples of all this and more, it's just that, I don't know, I think that on the whole his gesture of coming to see me should weigh more, and likewise his undeniable fixation on me—which more candid or perhaps more sensible beings might call love—and likewise the manifestations (all of them verbal, that's for sure, because as soon as it's about giving me some item of clothing, or something written down on paper, or whatever symbolic gift it might be, something that would last longer than a few spoken words that, as we well know, are carried away in the wind, it's another matter) of his absolute certainty that I am the *only* woman in the world that could make him happy.

Nevertheless, there's still the hunch that I can't trust him since his old cowardice or let's call it his cowering during the days I really thought I loved him. Or the fear that he's half-crazy (as if I were completely sane . . .) A guy full of fetishes and fears. Just imagine, he keeps having these what I call "ghost heart attacks," something like the terror of a real heart attack or of dying, which leave him stunned when he least expects it. He spent hours talking about having a heart attack, and so of course it had to happen. We separated one afternoon—he went shopping and I to run some errands. We were supposed to meet at six o'clock at the Center for Interamerican Relations. 6:30 and no sign of him. Well, he's disappeared again, I told myself. Fuck him, he did this to me two days earlier during some kind of panic attack about what all this would mean to him, but twice? forget it, no sirree. So my decision was, even if I saw him, not to acknowledge him. Anyway, he called the Center around 7:30, oh God, I'm just leaving the hospital, I fainted, come to the hotel quick. I'll be there within the hour, I still have some things to do, the merciless one answered . . . and all to find him recuperating from his damn attack, still panting but with his sense of humor intact, luckily, since that's the best part of him, excluding some private aptitudes. To sum up: he went shopping (and I seriously suspect that he was thinking of buying me something and that's what did it: guilt is eating him up inside—I wish it would on the outside too, then he would be skinny). He started to feel bad, worse and worse, until he lost consciousness. *Brring, brring* a call to one of his friends at the Consulate, a visit to the doctor on call. Doctor, doctor (with the Consul as interpreter), am I going to die? No sir. Electrocardiogram. Doctor, doctor, do you think I should return to Buenos Aires? (How about that!) No sir. Doctor, doctor (by way of the Consul), it's been years since I've been sexually active, and now I think I'm overdoing it, do you think that could be the cause, should I abstain?

"Listen, sir, did you faint in bed or in Bloomingdale's? What almost gave you a heart attack wasn't sex, it was the prices!" the doctor, a pragmatic gringo, clarified sensibly.

Which took away the worry about his health, but left his guilt intact. The next time we see each other, you and I, we're going to make a pilgrimage to the sanctuary of Notre Dame de la Bonne Culpabilité. There has to be something like that in that devout country called France. Sister, we are surrounded by idiots who feel guilty . . . good thing I don't. I feel ferocious and despotic, but never guilty.

Unfortunately for me, just now I'm getting tired of putting the Ugly Little Duckling down in this letter. It turns out that I went to fill my stomach, interrupting my train of thought, with some good pork ribs, and as everyone knows, once your belly's full, your heart is content. Content? How ridiculous! But at least my sacred fury is appeased for the moment.

At this point in the letter, knowing you like I do, and knowing me like you do, you'll notice that all of this is being used as literary material, just with your name at the top—a sort of novel spurred on by anger. A return to the epistolary novel, or at least to the cathartic one. That's what I hope at least.

Bad rice, bad rice, the guy yells every time he's finished fucking like a god. To appease them, he explains. You have to complain about something so that the gods don't take away our excessive happiness.

Jesus, that bit about being conscious of gathering literary material while eating pork ribs (they were delicious) succeeded in killing my impulse to write with total abandon. I hope it comes back. At this moment, Vicky (who's here as a tourist) and Marta have arrived. Reality. But since they're coming from the Chinese New Year celebrations (the year 4678 to be exact), their arrival sort of coincides with the bad rice idea, and besides, they're full of good omens in the form of colored bits of paper. A good color, red. The only thing Duck—such a cold-blooded animal, though he did have his hot moments—ever gave me is a very beautiful red hat that he decided to buy, just like that, spontaneously, what a miracle, just passing by Bloomingdale's, maybe to exorcise his fainting spell from a few days earlier.

Bad rice, bad rice, but good pork ribs, I'll tell you. Then I told the aforementioned what's this about assuming that Orientals also feel guilty for being happy? I'm afraid it's purely a Judeo-Christian sort of guilt, like so much else.

Not only did he buy me the red hat as a mini-proof of his love. I won't believe his lies (I accused him of lying so many times) this time. He also gave me a (red) cloth rose tied to the hat of a certain a certain ceramic statue that is almost all tongue. I told him when I saw this little doll in the shop window: look, it looks like you, since you stick out your tongue so much to be funny. Yes, yes, he recognized himself and ran in to buy it for me, not because he likes sticking out his tongue to be funny, but rather because it reminded him of other, less infantile activities. So now I have a mini-altar: the guy with the tongue, insolent, and underneath, hanging on a nail, the paper where Duck wrote: I'll never be cured of you. And the little heart from Limoges that he gave me on the other trip, the real one. But that's another story, there are a lot more stories with the same protagonist.

And now my fury has dissolved. Maybe I should have written to you earlier, so that I wouldn't dump all my anger on one person. But no. Maybe my fury will be positive, energizing, after it it travels 10,000 kilometers, arriving on an expansive wave of bomb-fury.

I live struggling unto death with everything that's about to leave my side, leave New York, and I wonder why I chose to stay in a city like this, adrift, where people are always passing through and falling in love with me (more or less) and where they only ever succeed in awakening my galloping rage. That's what I get for not playing with the home team, you'll tell me, and you're right. It's just that the home team either doesn't pass me the ball, or I don't see it, or it gets away from me, or it doesn't interest me, or—something about those human disconnections; what I really want is to play, you understand, run from one side of the field to the other, make decisions, do my kicks, my dribbling, not stay at the back of the field with my legs wide open, turned into an arch.

Soccer metaphors, you see, I owe to our country, or rather, to our government, which managed to put soccer in our *mate* and made us suck on sweaty T-shirts through the straw. The histamine of the great sporting feats.

Forgive my handwriting, forgive my putting away the computer, because at this stage of the game I prefer to draw you little words. I went out braving the storm, as they say here, to buy some note-books (one is Chinese, with red and black covers, such literary—and liberating—colors) and I came back to my private lodging (this is an Occupied House) and finally realized that it's not worth putting all of this on paper, that is on durable paper, because the story is already over and done. Over and done with, and I have no right to dig it up again just to try to understand.

So I'll reopen your happy missive, which so warmed my heart the other day, and try to respond to it directly. I loved the part about your Jean-Pierre. I hope, you chubby lovesick woman, that you don't go messing it all up like I do. Or that you don't go

54

idealizing it too much and expect miracles from him, like you usually do, which is just another, more subtle way of screwing things up.

After all this, I'm giving up on the idea of the web-footed novel. It's not worth it.

And now what do I do with all the pretty notebooks I bought?

I'm always thinking that my love life is so important and then I realize, ha ha, it's just the same old shit. So once again I'm without a literary subject, or I'll have to go back to the story of the Ambassador and Bella, which is blocked for some reason I don't understand. And I even have the novel's whole plot worked out, all ready, on a silver platter—and I worked hard on it. I'm afraid the truth is that I can't touch any subjects that are close to me, because at bottom they make me feel very alone. Everything seems so strong, so radiant, but underneath—that terrifying solitude. And nobody, my friend, nobody is capable of accompanying me in the struggle to come out ahead and not let myself be crushed. And Duck, who says he admires me so much, hasn't even been capable of methodically reading what I write—only a page here and there, he who's such a compulsive reader. I'm afraid that he can't even tolerate any of my humble triumphs.

Here goes a note in the margin: Duck came by with the firm intention of convincing me to return to the fold, that is, our native country. And on the second day of his presence in this one, I had to participate in a conference on censorship—a subject we're working hard on—and he accompanied me and in spite of his slight knowledge of English, he caught enough to understand that he shouldn't insist that I return, but rather dissuade me, because it could be unhealthy for me to go back. Though I barely spoke to him about my work in the Fund for Free Expression, etc., etc., and I can tell he hasn't read my story "Other Weapons," which of course will never appear in Argentina, but has in Mexico and here.

That having been said, I won't go on with the topic. All the other work, the denunciations, the struggle, is going on elsewhere. Here, only the sentimental passions. But the others also beat strongly: I have to write, I have to write, I set myself a goal for this year and now I hope to put the gentleman problem in parentheses and devote myself entirely to literature. But it does get in the way, damn it, since I sure do like those rolls in the hay! I wonder why I complicate life so much in that respect. To the point of being afraid now of those encounters and not wanting to become involved again. Everything always begins so gently, as if it's nothing more than a happy-go-lucky interlude, and then, little by little, with each swaying movement, with each shake of the ass, it gets more complicated, to the point where I feel anxious about a call or reply that doesn't come, and in a little while, I become absolutely furious, and won't let anything lasting be built. Not that much could be built, don't think I have many illusions on that score. It's true that for example the man who occupies me at the moment is not by any means the be-all and end-all, but from what he says, he came into my life with the profound intention of changing himself. Changing in word only, it seems to me, though I must admit that, in general—in these cases—I become rigid and not very patient. Everything has to happen right away. I demand a forced change, a real transformation. Whatever happened to my being a miracle worker? That's how this started, with his most absolute transformation, over there in Europe, but it didn't last. A masculine Cinderella, Duck, who later got back the grayish color of someone who spends his days inside, working, now coming here to meet up with me again in full regalia. How to give him back the skin he had when we frolicked through Europe, in a happiness that seemed eternal, perhaps because it had a limit? We'll win, I told him as I accompanied him to the airport in Barcelona, and he held me close and answered, "If it's necessary to win, I'm sure we'll win. But I don't know. I don't know. I'm still very confused."

He's still confused. Two years later, after thousands of fainting spells and multiple ailments, for both of us—and, I'm afraid, some unconscious intentions, or desires, at least on his part, to die. That's what he told me when he went to see me off at the airport in Buenos Aires when I first came here, that he felt like killing himself. And now what do I do? he asked me, as if wrapping everything up. Be a man, I told him, feeling like a queen. A queen of shit.

And now he comes looking for me, as if I'm his panacea, as if the panacea wasn't only in his little heart.

I've had enough, why write about all this.

Ciao, I'm going to sleep.

Duck

I would like to tell our love story, but all that comes out are the fights. I'm in the taxi—once again I'm in that taxi—and I see Duck calmly crossing Park Avenue at Thirty-second Street. What's he doing here, I wonder (I wondered then) when he should be waiting for me at Sixty-eighth?) I get furious again, and this blind fury makes me tell the cabdriver, Run that man over! Run that man over. Luckily, I didn't say it loud enough then, and I'm certainly not saying it now that I'm alone again—how boring; that's why I'm writing, I write and I don't say Run that man over aloud, because, really, what good would it do, although the anger is still here, as well as the urge to step all over him. The pedestrian in question wasn't even remotely who I thought he was—the one who was supposed to be waiting for me fortysome streets ahead. And I tell myself, in order to take up the love story again, the feeling of love, and not lose myself in the magma of rage, I tell myself that time doesn't exist, actually everything is a vast plane that we circulate through with blinders on, half blind, and that December is also now and it is especially and always that splendid May of two years ago and it is now forever because the door of love opened and let me see something on the other side, see and touch and taste, luckily, and now is then because even if we say that the door closed, the feeling will remain inside me, has formed a part of me since that moment.

So I told him and told him again and will keep on telling myself for eternity: Run that man over. Yes, to the New York cabdriver who luckily didn't hear me, and even if he did hear me, in this city where he must receive far worse, far angrier demands or protests on a regular basis, it would be no big deal, no?

This man was naturally not my man although he was wearing an almost identical raincoat and was the same height, and had the same way of walking and for me was the man who was supposed to be waiting for me at the Center for Interamerican Relations on Sixty-eighth Street (one block nearer the corner that would have been the right one) and was supposedly not there and so I had to ask myself, why assume he isn't there when everything indicates the opposite? He had come so far to find me, he was completely enthralled, totally miserable without me, he loved me, he couldn't live without me, etc., and more of the same kinds of confession of vulnerability that make men ruthless.

His turn had come.

My clairvoyant desire to run over him was just beginning—I wanted to run over his defection, his surrender. His fears, which can't be combated by anyone caught up in them.

His ghost crossed Park at Thirty-second, where it's still called Park Avenue South and nothing is the same. In any case, he wasn't waiting for me in the luxurious rooms of our meeting place, and I knew it, I told myself, I believed it, and I still believe it, I told myself so many times: this is good-bye; and it was actually a kind of relief.

It was only the beginning of multiple good-byes, as usually happens, another return to that which is forever saying good-bye.

I want to be loving him forever in the dazzling moments of transformation.

The time of writing. Run that man over, driver!

There are things I know and I forget and when I think I have new ideas I find them imprinted in the writing I did before. What is it now that I want to forget so deeply that I can't even write?

Then:

- I told Pale Fire shortly before going to Mexico:

What you're lacking is tenderness, and I think it's the only thing that matters to me in a man. I'll give up anything but tenderness.

You can't say that I've had much luck in this, but what can we do about it—that's how things are.

After spending a few days in a forgiving mood, I wake up furious, pick up the phone, and scream insults at the man not yet called Pale Fire. It's been four days since I got back from Mexico and you haven't called, I told him, go to hell, I told him, who do you think I am? And so forth and so on.

"I know. We have to talk. I've got a ton of work and I have the flu. Maybe today I'll go to Rosario's house."

"The hell you will. I don't want to see you in public. Don't fuck up my night. If we have to talk, talk now."

"No—I just got out of the shower. I'll catch cold. I'll call you on Sunday."

"Go to hell!"

And why all this? So that Duck could be free to advance with his fleshy webbed feet and destroy all the seedlings? (But we hadn't planted anything, honey, let's not deceive ourselves).

Duck did call that same afternoon, completely unexpectedly, and I went with him to Rosario's house and I felt the gods must have heard my wishes. Because . . . in Mexico, each time I went in to some ancient chapel or church, I wanted to make a wish, like in the good old days. But I restrained myself. I had wished so much for Duck, and look what happened—I'd lost him forever.

But I hadn't!

That, I have to admit, made me feel that life had compensated me.

Poor Pale Fire, every time he breaks up with me, someone else shows up. He deserves it for being such a sad sack.

Sad, no, let's be honest: the happiest part of him is his sack, his balls—tight, terse, tasty. And in his rare confessions, one time the story of his cyst came up, a cyst he thought was a third testicle; he was scared to death for days, considering suicide (he was seventeen), until he finally decided to tell his father, and it was a sebaceous cist and they operated and adios baby. He was free of his guilt, his burden, but I felt muzzled. Because at the time he was telling me The Dramatic Episode of the Third Ball,

I, along with a friend, was inventing the *tripolotos*, a race who sometimes rivaled the cyclops, and who prospered particularly among the military castes. But we never could write our illustrious masterpiece, perhaps because of my obligation to keep such matters as were revealed to me while practicing my profession confidential. What profession, you may ask? That of Complacent Ear: sole receiver of certain confessions of the Cat, today Pale Fire—and a profession that I will soon have to renounce in order to write a novel.

Next Sunday with Pale Fire. He with the flu—that at least was true—stuck in bed.
PF: It's like a bank. You invest what you think you can or should or want to invest.
Me: Not really, because what you don't invest counts against you. What you take out, what you deny. Think about it: affection doesn't run out. The more you give, the more you have.
PF: True.
Me: What's awful is the vulnerability; the more you give, the more chances you have of being rejected. And that's what's unbearable. (Look who's talking, I say now, muted.)

I sound so wise. Sometimes. And then I go put my foot in it wherever possible. And then some.
The centipede of self-destruction. That's how I should sign this.
Quién soy yo, who am I.
In front of the mirror.

Put together a jigsaw puzzle, rebuilding the heart. Should I dedicate myself to breaking hearts in order to keep my head unscathed?

PF: Maria Luisa looks marvelous, triumphant, now that she's separated from her husband. She looks ten years younger. So many women would do such interesting and beautiful things with their lives if they didn't have a man at their side demanding submission from them . . .

Does he want me to change, then? I wonder what he's been trying to get across with this strange little speech. And I also wonder why I want to know what he's been trying to get across with this strange little speech. (Why try to penetrate, why try to find out if the result is the same? . . . just a vivisectionist's mania to put people under a microscope and observe them in vitro. It comes to me from a long while back, from the long ago times with Rodrigo. And now the mania is reversing itself: to see myself, to know why, as if it were easy and worth the trouble . . .)

I think I remember: in my very good-looking years, I wanted to break men's hearts to see what was inside. To eat the egg, you have to break the shell, I would tell myself—as I swam over the obviousness of this metaphor.

(a reality for each taste and every color, an attempt where everything is transformed and a woman breaks into a thousand pieces and she is all of the pieces, every bit of her, and all the bits the same and yet different.)

Today I feel French and will announce my wise discovery of a few days ago. Relating to Duck, naturally:
Some have *savoir faire* and others . . . *savoir défaire.*

I told him, but he didn't react: his ignorance of other languages is enormous. Strange for a guy who knows his own so well.

"You're so intelligent. I like you a lot," Tom says to me.

"You've got a fantastic sense of humor. I like you a lot," Duck says to me.

"I can really confide in you. I like you," Pale Fire says to me.

After all this "liking," is it possible to find one man who really appreciates me?

Rereading old notebooks, all those notes from the times when I thought I wasn't writing anything. And this one, dated in Mexico:

Love? I never come when you call. You always call me from the most inhospitable cities. You don't do it on purpose, but will you come look for me some day?

And a year later, recently back from Mexico—fulfilling the eternal return saga (the cycle)—I find that love has indeed, in some way or another, even though it isn't whole, come looking for me. And what do I do? I cradle it for a while, and then I throw it out on its bare feet.

Bravo, bravo, I applaud myself. This gives me more material, so I can complain. Or at least material to write this long lament.

It does have its comic elements, I have to admit. And its many and enormous coincidences, turns of the screw, recoveries and *reprises* (retellings).

Res non verba, that should be our motto, and Duck couldn't produce a single *res*, a single testimony.

"I came ten thousand kilometers to find you. Doesn't that seem like a lot? As soon as I knew you were still living in New York, I made inquiries to be certain, and here you have me. I came to see you. I didn't come for work, no sir. The first vacation I've had in I don't know how many years, and I came to see you. I promised, didn't I? So you see, I keep my promises."

"Well, let's say some you do, some you don't."

My private god is half listening to me—it's happened before.

There is also the other possibility: that I find all kinds of defects in any guy who approaches me with supposed attempts at affection. And I claim to be looking for love: all through these pages I'm looking for it. I don't even understand myself.

There's something that terrifies me in all this and it's loss.

(Loss is what terrifies me in all of this.)

Not loss of the other, which, after all, I've studied and noted very well, but rather the loss of my thinking parts, my neurons. The ones that store memories. And the other ones, the ones that process complex information, after having understood and accepted it, and then almost immediately relegate it to oblivion. Publicize it? No!!!

FILE IT AWAY

So here I am; tear me apart, all of you. I've always tried to write rigorously—or at least cunningly—and like a coward I've urged others to do the same—and here I am now sitting next to the tunnels of my rolled-up notebooks, writing as I've always wanted to, without resting, in a more familiar tone, with the intention of telling it all, without shame.

Writing everything about the other, for instance the disgrace, the absolute dependence and the fury at this dependence, the kicks given and received, by me, by them, in this man's world, frontal kicks and sometimes kicks right in the balls (if only they knew how to really earn them).

Fellow writers, this diary is not for you. Close friends, this diary is not for you either and anyway it doesn't matter. Oh, how scared we are of finding something out, of discovering some secret nook in ourselves.

I poke; you touch lightly, with your fingertips. I too would like to touch with my fingertips and call it a caress, but in touching sometimes I dig in the nails that I don't have, and I tear (tear myself).

I rip myself apart and at the same time I try to give the other a good image of myself, I try to be sweet and suddenly I forget. Or is it the other way around?

That attraction of the moment that I know so well how to exploit. An impulse that I generate and that soon turns against me.

The mottos we find in life. Recently in a subway station (when am I not in one?), I read some graffiti: "Why destroy?! Enjoy!" Something that I've been repeating for centuries, really, and look at the results.

A manual for how to relate to the opposite sex. Something I've meant to put together since I was born. Or let's say since I was at least three or four years old in the Plaza San Martín, when I would bring little cars to use as bait.

Do you want to play with me?

But then I cry out, every once in a while: I'm not playing, no, no, guys, I'm not playing at all. Enough of this putting in and then taking away, giving with one hand, and taking with the other. Giving and taking, in and out—leave that for more enjoyable activities. Or more entertaining ones.

"The man who doesn't know his own history is condemned to repeat it," an adaptation of Santayana's famous phrase. I found it on the wall of some office. Even walls shout to me, come to teach me things. I'm a sponge for knowledge, I try to absorb everything, and I do absorb—but very little of the nutritious liquid I've assimilated comes to me when I most need it.

Today I'm so off-center that when I combed my hair, I couldn't part it in the middle. I tried changing hairstyles, believe me, but that didn't work either. Duck wanted to see me with my hairstyle from the old days, with curls like before—the rather bellicose look of that photo that turned him on. I gave him that pleasure, thanks to the wig Celda had lent me and which appeared by magic at the bottom of a bag that I started poking around in, looking for something else. Served on a platter, the wig, and that way I was able to recover the look in the photograph, in other words, to travel to another moment of myself, and Duck loved the idea. That's what having imagination is all about, I tell myself. And then we started fighting, for some reason or another, and after a while, I tore off the wig.

Let's end this farce. In other words, I am myself in this precise instant, and to claim to return to yesterday is to unrecognize myself.

And who doesn't recognize myself more than me? Maybe everyone or maybe no one, and that's why I want to shake them up, so that they see me, not that they accept me but at least so they see me as I am. It can be interesting—you know, gentlemen? A real challenge. Something that not all of them want, because showing them changing, unstable faces doesn't help anyone. (That's why I too would have to learn how to accept myself in all my aspects and keep all of my photographs. However, I accept only a few images of my face and think I'm always the same; since I almost never see myself in photos of myself, I destroy them.)

And that's precisely why I tend to wonder where I am. I almost never find an answer.

Later I find a bad little poem with which I also identify:
"To be able to know her / it's necessary to compare her / from afar see her in dreams / And to know how to love her / it's necessary to leave her."
It seems the guy who wrote this mess was writing about his country, but in a spurt of true egocentrism, I look at myself in the mirror and I know that *I* am a land of exile.

May your right hand not know what your left is doing, or vice versa. May today's eyes not see what yesterday's hand wrote in this same notebook. A formula like any other, to be able to keep on living when perhaps the last thing you want is to keep on living. Perhaps what you're hoping for with all of this writing to the death is to stop time, freeze it.

Last night I dreamed something that left me thinking. (Today is a dilapidated day, a Sunday of *chiaroscuro*.) What was the dream?

I was a guest in some woman's house, and the husband, in a very friendly, brotherly way, gets into my bed. I don't reject him and I don't encourage him, but I think I'm happy. Then comes the judgment. Not a sound opinion, which I would eagerly await and finally watch arrive with pleasure, no. It's a legal one, filed against me, with my sentence implicit in it. They torture me for each moment of pleasure and I say to myself, it doesn't matter, some things get saved. The pleasure stays intact, happiness that's past was nonetheless happiness, and besides, there are places that survive and that were saved because they were the scene of some happiness, and so they remain sacred. Places, I think, and I think of the forest where I was happy (with whom?) and while I think all this, they torture me, and it doesn't matter at all, though I hear the noise and I know they've cut down the forest and that's how they'll finally succeed in defeating me. I'm an agent of destruction. I can't love because whatever I love or the person I love seems or is or becomes unpardonably condemned.

The Forest

To think that I never made it to Central Park with Duck. He wanted to go there but after a few steps I led him in a different direction. Why? Without realizing it I decided that it was better to go somewhere else, or it was just really cold or my boots were hurting me. Whatever. And later he told me: I couldn't do what I wanted either. I wanted to go through the Park with you and you wouldn't let me see even a leaf of it.

"There aren't any leaves—it's winter," I answered him then.

Crack. End of chapter.

The forest? A lot of forest with Théo, in the Palermo of those first meetings, or that pine forest in Normandy where we sometimes made love. A lot of Palermo again with Joseph. One night, lying in the field next to the lake, way too absorbed (and that's the right word) in each other, to the point that when we wanted to get up, we realized there was a car parked just two meters from our heads. Much Joseph in those city forests—hardly noble. A tender guy, Joseph, who looked like Gérard Philippe and was so sweet. Will all those men parade through this book? For now, we're in a forest. We. And I tend to be alone a lot in forests too. Sometimes with my dog Vanessa, me sitting under a tree, she scaring away the most irritating marauders. Another time, Vanessa and I climbed a tree, and sat on a really wide branch so that she too could know what the world looks like from above. Grouchy little bird.

Insight from today's date (and this is all happening to me because I got up early): I'm appropriating furiously, or maybe just recognizing myself. Whatever. The fact is that this is *my* place (anywhere I am). And I can't give it to anyone. Not because I don't want to, but simply because I occupy a certain space. No one. Not even my own characters (creatures). That's why poor Bella, in my story of her and the Ambassador, is a bit languid, bloodless. Because I can't give her all of me to make her live. And without my sap, what else can she feed on?

In a world of beings who don't exist, who self-destruct and erase themselves, perhaps one should make a valiant effort to at least draw oneself. Maybe that's where all the sex comes from—to feel real.

In the Subway

Submission perhaps as a form of self-recognition. A dream of the black pimp in a white raincoat. He's sitting in front of me reading a newspaper. He doesn't look at me, he gets off the train, he abandons me. Another one who doesn't wait for my submission or anything else. And then I'll be able to let him leave in one piece, no need to destroy him, or worse yet, destroy myself.

There's a man (loose in the middle of the train) talking about salvation. And then he asks for money. We all talk about salvation while we go begging blind through the tunnels. Very few are listened to. They usually don't give us so much as a penny.

Feathers and hats are the real objects that Duck left me. Love and trouble is what I add to these, because I feel like it. So that the story sounds good. And for it to end.

Here we are in the middle of rather archaic rituals, reinvented daily.

How unsettling, no? To find something broken in your purse, something that's been destroyed without your ever having needed to bring it out into the open, to give it some air.

February 29

This is the special day and I spent it messing around, not even giving myself the luxury of writing a bit in these pages, by hand, or even typing on other pages, not even the pages of memory. Memory, so often cursed and vilified. Just preparing myself for a party, just trying to soften my edges, which oftentimes jut out in spite of me, and then, at other times—more often—are filed down with the thoroughness of an artisan, with the love that someone sharpening a tool has. A tool, my edges? Sharp edges that perhaps defend me from something? But yes, maybe yes, you must admit that with a jutting prow, I'll be able to advance with greater freedom and less fear of the stormy waters of destiny—as my third-grade teacher would have said.

(Sharp edges, I think now, I am a defender of the cutting edge, synonymous with falling in love over there in my southern country.)

And that same freedom that sometimes races inside me and fills me with a corporal, almost corporeal, happiness. The same one that I referred to in the note I found leafing through my notebooks (submerging myself in that sea [*maremagnum, magma*] of paper that is myself). And the ma/ma of mother and the memory of the image that dazzles me when I'm about fifteen years old:

> My mother submerged in her own sea of papers, in bed and writing—like me now, only that I'm not in bed, I'm getting in and out of bed, not in a nightgown, but dressed. Getting in and out, incapable of staying in one place, always opting for the other, the further away.

Damn, I tell myself, going round and round the same thing, always the same thing. The mule used in those ancient chain pumps going around and around—memory. I can't let them take my place, but where is my place? It's a moving target. And now trying or not really, to occupy without even realizing it, my mother's place (my own old Mama!!)

And the old sentence unearthed:

To leave the mother behind, my one absolute necessity.

(This is a book of broken promises or promises that will probably be broken.) Then I complain so much, and I tell Duck for example that I can't stand his offering and taking away at the same time.

The good man should have a monument dedicated to him, after all this. He deserves it in many respects. What sort of monument? I know! I know: the gigantic carrot hanging from a crane that my friend Leopoldo Maler presented in San Pablo. The carrot:

a promise and a phallus at the same time, or better yet, the eternal promise of a phallus that's so difficult to reach, and most of all, to reach a happy end with.

There's the one who, I know, doesn't want to promise—which is why he lives always retracting, which is why he's going to end up like a raisin, all dried up (I'm referring to Pale Fire). Duck on the other hand promises that he will promise and then finally promises and later he doesn't remember a thing. Or he remembers, but only for himself, only remembers what interests him.

All of you promise, you all promise, and then you don't keep your promises, as that old woman poet friend told the men who approached her silently on those dark nights in Buenos Aires, whispering in her ear things like I'm going to lick you all over, honey, lick you all over.

Then I remember the affair with Jorge, that big good-looking guy who so skillfully employed his cock as a weapon of domination, who took it out when I most wanted it in, and tried to put it in when I wanted it out. Ah, but what fun nights they were, full of blood, sweat, semen, and other things, and what have I been doing with my life? A stage, a magnificent stage of exotic theater and that's why I felt so comfortable, so at home in the big living room where the orgies of Plato's Retreat took place—not at all Aristotelian, me, playing in the shadows of the cave where couples were fucking.

That's how my life has gone. Always down that road, not only the road of fucking, but the platonic one as well, in the sense of searching in the night for the one good man who can synthesize them all (I've got a bit of Diogenes in me too), and of course that's why you have to try a lot, and insist, insist, and not be afraid of aging, knowing that you can always keep trying, attracting, *seducing*. And here I am, brought back to same thing: caught in my own trap.

It will disappear, the trap, and then the situation will feel profound, coherent as it did once before, years ago, when I said, I think it was in Barcelona:

I'm sick of hitting my head against the wall. What I'm going to do is get rid of the wall.

It was an arduous task and I never went through such a period of vaginal aridity as those days in Barcelona, but perhaps there was a good reason for it: the elimination of that wall can only be a gradual process, and only now—some seven years later—am I seeing the results.

Seven years, it's time for the prosperous times to begin again, no? Seven years during which there were two years of analysis that are now and at a distance bearing fruit.

After the US, which country has the most analysts per capita? Argentina! You guessed it. I'm one of those people who've tried to find themselves in the spoken word. But (in the end) I'm one of those (and it's not the analysis's fault—it actually did me a lot of good) who believe more in the written word.

In a few words, I will summarize: Duck supposedly came to try to convince me to go back to Buenos Aires, that actually things there weren't so bad or so dangerous and all that, but he had the bad luck—or perhaps good luck—of arriving in the middle of the PEN conference, and he listened to me give the talk on censorship and human rights, and then, with the little English he knows, he understood that I wasn't about to go back, that I was better off staying quietly where I was. Do you always talk like that? he asked me. And I answered him without lying.

Maybe he felt irritated, maybe he started to see things he himself didn't want to confess, maybe he felt at that moment that it was useless. I can't blame him now, although I was indignant because he couldn't fulfill two of the three conditions that I'd given him upon his arrival, when he told me about his sad state of impotence in the last eight months.

If I cure you, I told him, if we take up again with that divine wind that once blew us around Europe, I'm making three conditions:

1) That you set your watch to the local time

2) That you throw your wedding ring in the garbage, since at this stage it's a farce

3) That you write me a certificate praising my curative powers

He loved these propositions, and for the first time in his life as a devoted traveler set his wristwatch on something other than Argentinean time, and for a while he hid the ring, the same one that he would put back on again so many times, unaware that he was even doing it, and at the most unexpected and inconvenient times and places.

You came to New York to cure yourself of me! I told him angrily one night about two weeks later. *I won't cure myself of you anymore,* he wrote on a piece of paper. That's the only certificate I got from him.

Dieter

I met Dieter dancing. The same day as the fight with Duck because he was still going on about the ring, lying, not capable of taking it off forever, hiding it, playing all kinds of dirty tricks on me. It wasn't time yet for violence, but I sure felt like smacking him. So I went alone to the last session of the PEN conference, those were exhausting days, and to finish up, we had that meeting that degenerated (or generated?) into a dance. That's where this fellow was, Dieter, a very interesting guy who was flirting with me, while another much younger and prettier woman was trying to eat him alive. Meanwhile, another man was trying—and was actually pretty suave, I have to admit—to eat me alive, but only having cooked me first, with a more elaborate approach. This

Dieter fellow took me to the dance floor in such a comical way, transmitting all kinds of ridiculous messages with his body, and I felt so free, and not just because my lust was already sated, but because Duck was out walking around the city somewhere, burning up in the flames of his own ring-hell. (He had been calling me like crazy and I was royally ignoring him.) And so, during that PEN dance, I was dying of laughter and humor and polyglotism with this really tall foreigner who looked like a stork (not to lose my bird metaphors), and who after a few hours of jumping around and sweating, suggested that we get out of there (flee the devourer who was already slobbering over someone else without taking her eyes off of Dieter) and go have a drink somewhere.

"No, no, it's cold. I'm near home. Let's stay here," I insisted, until I remembered Frida's Disco and then I accepted because this foreigner was the only one who would ever take me to that dive, which was just around the corner from my house—den of iniquity that it was, or den at least of the secret intention to sin. A place where sex was always—for good or ill—anonymous. So we went happily to Frida's Disco and I didn't have to warn him about the transvestites since they were marvelous and really looked like women, and the big-breasted enormous black woman who served us wasn't a transvestite but maybe she was kneading them all until the small tits they were so proud of grew.

"What have you been doing lately?" Dieter asked me.

"I don't know if I'm writing or living or doing both. I'm in this ping-pong game between a novel and life, and now you're a part of it all since I'm standing here in front of you. And I'm not sure if I like it."

That's what I said and thought forty-eight hours ago. Now I know I like it, I love it, and think it's the only way to incorporate the chill of literature into life (which is rather warm). Although I don't know if it's a trap for the man in front of me and a trap for me too (trap in the sense of trick, not the sort of thing you set up when you're hunting). I remember my only lover in Barcelona, or at least the only one who meant anything. Yes, Cesar, the one who, one fine day (and not exactly because he'd been spending time with me) checked himself into a psychiatric hospital, and before or afterward became for a while what he called an underground hermit, and then I lost him forever even though I'd already lost him some time before.

One night we were lying on the sofa looking into each other's eyes in the darkness, and suddenly he said:

"Wow, we're falling in love."

And both of us got scared, naturally, and I started going through my usual routines and saying funny nonsense meant only to make me laugh and thus avoid any sort of dialogue with the other—writing aloud, so to speak, for my own entertainment.

It's something that used to alarm me before, that schizophrenia, that duality of seeing life's most passionate moments as if they were happening to someone else, trying to get the best literary angle on them. It used to happen to me during fights, those soap-opera melodramas in which, to my horror, I've been the protagonist on more than one occasion; and also (oh, confession) to my absolute delight. Like that time a thousand years ago, with my ex-husband, when we were screaming at each other, very seriously, and I ran to the bathroom to be able to let loose crying, and I cried and cried until I discovered myself in the mirror with my hair on end and my eyes red and swollen and it seemed so hilarious that I burst out laughing, though without being able to stop crying with absolute sincerity, laughing and crying, until I got hiccups, falling apart, but underneath it all, happy.

It's this ridiculous feeling of happiness, coming from who knows where, that always saves me. The sense of humor and the ridiculousness of every human situation returns me to my axis. In other words, in the act of laughing, life wins the race, finally, against literature. Laughter as a vehicle between language and the body, the cunnilingus of life. But sometimes, no, we get serious, we worry and we break the spell.

We all have our Achilles' heels. When I start unraveling balls of wool, sometimes I find little tufts, the not-so-beautiful things. Like that anxiety that would take hold of me (then, then—what luck, it seems I've managed to overcome it), that the guy I'd slept with wouldn't call me the next day, or that he would take me off his map entirely. Because maybe there'd been nothing more than a good fuck, and maybe not even that. Stupidity or obligatory pride, believing that I had given—or worse, that they'd taken away—the best of me, my most private part. Without receiving anything in return. But in bed you both give and receive in equal amounts— what comes afterwards is pure bonus.

Maybe it's a shame not to see each other again, but this shame shouldn't mean that I've lost a part of my self-esteem or that I feel abandoned. That part of always feeling abandoned is losing its hold on me, luckily. Nonetheless, feeling that I've overcome feeling abandoned is also a bit of a trap.

Those were different times, and rather depressing men.

Now is the positive time, the stimulating time, like being with Dieter can be—now that Duck has ended up leaving with his ring on but his feathers rather wet, a disgrace to his species.

The Sunday of Seduction

Why are you looking at me with those mischievous, dreamy eyes? And I half-close my own. Why are you throwing me little kisses with those enormous lips? And I receive them, almost absorbing them. Why are we talking about what we're talking about? Is it because we're skirting the subject of sex, the love act, attraction, all those things, and I make jokes, sort of licking my lips, and you give me that look again in all its clarity and how do I respond?

"Stop this seduction!" I suddenly cry. "Let's get off this train that's taking us down tracks that are so well established and predictable."

"Stop the seduction?" you inquire, unconvinced. "Isn't that a little drastic?"

"Don't you see that it's rupturing our dialogue? We had such good dialogue before."

"This is the second stage, and it's inevitable. We liked each other the other night, and now we seduce each other."

"We were already seduced when we liked each other. This part is useless, reduntant. We're never going to communicate anything to each other this way. We're only going to be repeating what we already know—classifying it, limiting it—in order to avoid communicating any further."

"Do you think so?"

"I think so."

"Don't you think that our dialogue could be reborn—much improved, aired, free—after love?"

"After having fulfilled this requirement?"

"Perhaps."

"I don't make love in order to be able to talk afterward. I make love to enjoy myself."

"Good idea. Let's go."

No, we're not going anywhere. And I ask myself too, I'm not accusing you, why this game of seduction?—it's so sterilizing.

And I wonder, seriously, very seriously, why break up the game in which I've eagerly submerged myself more than once (i.e., see Michel), why try to destroy this fable that suits us both if after all we both know—I already know—that this is going to end in bed and that's precisely what we're both looking for. So my attempt to change the direction of our conversation is perhaps an attempt to take the reins, an imperious need to be in charge of the maneuver and to be more or less the boss of (or at least an active partner in) the present situation. (I would at least have some options, as I told Duck when he finally told me here in New York the real and most painful reason he felt obligated to disappear so brutally more than a year earlier in Buenos Aires. Look, you could have trusted me then, you didn't have to lie to me so completely . . .)

"Let's stop the seduction," I tell Dieter, "because seduction is a lie, and I've had enough of lies. Let this be what it is without any tricks."

And he, while driving his car through the darkest areas of the Meatpacking District, maybe in order to frighten me, but also getting near (I would find this out later) his lair, said:

"What should we do, then? Should I take you back to your place, or to mine?" (He's offering to go to his place, I think, great! At least there's not a woman there, that's already something.)

"Let's have a drink somewhere."

"You've destroyed something by destroying the seduction," you tell me as you make beautiful drawings on the tablecloth with the crayons put there for just that purpose—to unburden oneself.

"That was the risk I took, now take one yourself," I tell him while I write *Seduction* in light orange on the tablecloth. And I say, "It's not the same as actually having sex."

"I don't know. You see? You broke up our seduction to be able to talk and now we don't know what to say."

"Maybe there was nothing to say from the beginning."

That's what I told him while I was drawing a box to play tic-tac-toe in, but he doesn't play, no sir, he just paints over it with furious colors.

I observe and I keep quiet. (Duck said to me: yeah, yeah, you know everything. You know my deepest unconscious strata better than I do and better than anyone does. Congratulations. You don't even allow me the possibility of being elastic, contradictory.)

"There were things to say, and there was also seduction, let's not deceive ourselves."

"It's precisely so that we don't deceive ourselves that I started this complicated business."

(Damn, how stupid I am! I who claim to want things simple between a man and a woman. And just look at me now, complicating everything.)

And feeling that my body is shrinking, what a drag, and I'd been so happy holding his hand in Frida's Disco, feeling so free because my absolute conviction was: I'm not trying to seduce him, I just feel so happy being with this guy I get along with so well (and Duck flying low out there somewhere and what do I care).

Not now, now I've screwed everything up again. And Dieter, very understanding, says:

"Things are never simple between a man and a woman—and you aren't a simple woman to begin with."

And things turned out to be really good; it was nice and hard, really erect, and just at the right moment; and I was inspired to make a general critique of the penis, which, when it responds in the manner expected of it, loses all softness, and therefore tenderness.

But what jewels these very rigid, enormous cocks are! What pleasure with the Somber Argentine, when he undressed and all of a sudden before my eyes appeared that really enormous cock, always unexpected because so surprising—attached to that being who was so trapped by his own complexes. I would applaud with delight then, and the very somber Somber Argentine would be annoyed, even appearing offended.

And the men with little cocks complain, but I wonder if the ones with the larger instruments aren't in fact the victims of some sort of conspiracy of the small, since otherwise there's no way to explain the tremendous shyness (more like seclusion) of this sort of guy, who should really be more sure of himself. It's the same old story: the ones who do have something to show for themselves are the ones who are most insecure when it comes to showing it.

A child's game: one of the kids in school would thump on the desks with—guess what? Voilà. Punches sometimes come from other things than fists, you understand.

With Dieter, the second night we went out together, that is, Sunday night, in the middle of a bit of a fight because I had stemmed the tide of seduction, or at least diverted it substantially, he again took me through some dark streets full of abandoned warehouses. While I was thinking, "This guy is taking me to a gay neighborhood, and he's going to stop the car somewhere in order to fuck me right next to one of the parked trucks they use to turn tricks in," I made a pertinent comment:

"Dangerous place, this."

"You're with a man. You don't need to be afraid, really."

"I don't know. By the look of things, you can be sure that if they catch us around here, you'll be the first one to get it. Maybe the only one."

And that's how life is, and that's what these guys believe, the Great Defenders of the Cunt, I'll never forget that one guy, what a fool, a thousand times a fool (and I believed him for such a long time, and I suffered, I even suffered, my God). In the country of the Macho Men, the three-balled man is king. That fellow (an Argentine novelist to boot, with pretensions of being *un poète maudit*) would tell me: Woman must be the earth—I don't know what sort of earth, but the earth: the living earth, the promised earth, the giving or open earth. Rather Neruda-esque he was, to top it all off. And I believed him then and I'd suffer because I wasn't any kind of earth, and I would torture myself with this idea and so many other seemingly concrete things until one day in his parked car he started to tell me again:

"Woman must be the earth blablabla, and must blabla."

And I had to ask him in a flash of lucidity, which I would congratulate myself on later:

"Okay, then what's man?"

"Man is here to defend you. For example, if some mugger comes along right now, I'll defend you. That's why I'm here."

"Bravo," I exclaimed, and with that unusual lucidity, I launched myself toward other arms.

Now it sounds easy, told like that, but it cost me a lot of tears and loneliness. Nothing was as fast as it is now; I'm too calloused now to get scars from every little thing. Life has taught me how to shorten my bleeding and coagulation time.

Dear Alicia:

No, no, don't criticize good ol' Ugly Duck who got what he deserved and was my catalyst. He made all my anger—accumulated over years—come out, and he's making me stand my ground. It's a gift from God, or at least from Melpomene, the Goddess of Tragedy.

I've thought about doing something (else) mischievous: send him a brochure: SPA VALENZUELA.

A woman friend (friend?) used to tell me that Duck came to me like Gide would go to Tunis, to be able to find his own true skin but without paying the least attention to Tunis. I think it was something like that, yes, but not that much . . .

Even though I may never see Dieter again, I've already got everything from him that makes me happy. This story is complete now, I tell myself, although for some reason, mischievous as I am, I forgot my vest in his house. Papa Freud already studied this phenomenon to death. When I was leaving, I asked myself, am I forgetting anything? And I looked around and all I could think of was my necklace and my ring, so of course, I left the vest. Bulletproof? No, sir, a sequined vest, which goes with a certain necklace, forgotten in yet another house. I think I wrote about it somewhere under the title *El collar de la reina*, although I'm afraid that I'm not going to like its tone anymore.

All of this is a relating of events from a vaginal point of view, of events that perhaps don't *amount* to much. (Although I have been well *mounted,* that's for sure. When mounted, well mounted, I ask myself why I don't try to have *this* more often. And I answer that too much sex leads to an infinite tedium with sex.)

But what good times! What energy we had!

In his book *Do It!* Jerry Rubin breaks off at one point and says he's going to go and masturbate for a while and then come back—and I liked that, confessing an unconfessable act and with total disinterest. As if he (we) weren't already been committing the masturbatory act of writing our confessions.

I confess that I have lived, said the other; I confess that I have fucked, I say and what luck. The odor coming to me now from between my legs is mixed, it's my gift and the other's too, rather acrid, sharp, not entirely pleasant, but the best you can ask for on this earth.

So much sperm! I love it when I go to the bathroom and loosen my muscles and it comes out of me as if it was mine. A white gush, something with a life of its own. Though not all of them give it to me. And not all of them have so much. But this one does, and the one who was nicknamed—though not because of this—Pale Fire:

an erupting volcano that time we changed positions and didn't do it fast enough.

Damn! The quality of my orgasms has changed. They've become less intense, diluted. It's not terrible, no, they're more like a re-iterated pleasure now, one after the other. But the old kind was vibrant. And my friends wondered why the Lousy Brute drove me so crazy. That's why. Because with him I would attain unsuspected heights of orgasm: an extraordinary internal explosion that made even my hair stand on end. The hair on my head, which I have a lot of. But another question would be: why did I only reach those heights with that one guy?

Here we have another one of the mysteries of erotic life. Sexual chemistry, as they say.

The orgasms are real enough, but the phantoms are something else. I need to analyze why I am a phantom for Duck.

Write about the two zoological dreams:
1)   From a week ago:
A very big, hairy, white dog of some strange breed appears. Actually it's an unknown animal, not a dog, because its mouth is like a clothespin or a parrot's beak. And with that clothespin-mouth, it grabs my fingertips, and even though I scream and try to get away, I can't escape without leaving behind chunks of meat. Yet, I know I shouldn't kick the dog in the balls or anything like that because this is its way of making friends. And when it finally lets go of me, and lets itself be petted gently, I go to wash the blood off. My shirt is spattered with it, and actually I'm glad because it was like passing a test. A rite of passage.

Subsequent pseudointerpretation: that mouth with its teeth squeezed a little bit like Duck's, and I'm reminded too of that much repeated phrase of his:

"Well, after all, we didn't make a blood pact."

No, we didn't cut ourselves on our fingers and join them in order to join our lives. I wonder: Did he do that with his wife? Is that where all his nonsense about the ring that he made appear and disappear comes from? Lying that he had thrown it away, and then the impossibility of separating him from it even when things were going so badly.

Now why am I still worried about that? Duck has flown back home to his nest and now it's something else. A change of skin, and I change skin, and to the great horror of all web-footed animals, who are encapsulated, im*pond*ed, encysted, with stiffened joints, I transform myself.

So that's why this time with Dieter was so good. We met as equals, and every time he starts to forget it, I have to remind him: pass me the ball; you've let it bounce enough in your own court, now it's my turn. I don't know if he likes these sorts of situations, I'm afraid he doesn't. But that's the challenge. And he comes back.

If there isn't a challenge in an encounter like this, then I wonder why even bother.

The second dream is more condescending, and it happened yesterday morning in Dieter's falsely enormous bed (two beds pushed together which sometimes stay together and sometimes establish a clear dividing line). It's a short dream, precise, beautiful, and brief, rather like a hologram.

Dream 2)

I'm alone in the big bed with wine-colored sheets, looking out the big horizontal window that in the dream has a frame of thick, decaying wood. First I see some white feathers go by, which then become very beautiful seagulls. Some of them land just above the window and you can only see their tails, others land on the windowsill. Until one comes in, a bit afraid, and right away goes back out, and then another one enters and flies to my side, and stays there making a nest next to my left hand on a bundle of sheets and blankets. At first I'm excited, but when I look closely at it, I see it's rather droopy and I say scat! It's sick and surely came in here to die here with me. But at that moment the seagull stands tall and looks me straight in the eyes, full of happiness.

And I wake up to find Dieter on my left, grumbling in his sleep, and I wish that seagull were he, Jonathan Livingston Seagull.

In a while we get up and we're happy and we eat partridges or rather a bunch of delicacies he's prepared, and I say, you guessed it, there's nothing I like more than a man who knows how to cook. And he answers me, no, I didn't guess anything. And I don't know if he says it because being with me is a pleasure or because he doesn't want to let himself get trapped. I hope it's both.

Today I'm having a condescending day and I'm inclined to think, poor guys, they too have a heart. Not to mention that unreliable flagpole that they have to keep erect when it so often falls down and makes them miserable.

Once I said that I liked the word penis because it came from the verb *penetrate*. Now I don't know if it's perhaps the other way around. As far as Dieter's concerned, he gave me an authentic vision, a drilling vision (or sensation, to be precise) of what the gentle penis can be like as an object of domination. Still, I would have to amend his reading of Robbe-Grillet's *Jealousy*, which interprets the penis as the world of the white colonizer, who needs to impose order, geometrization, confronted with the vagina's chaotic and threatening forest, the world of the blacks. As though his penis was ever that clear in its intentions! Although you have to admit that the penis is a truly delightful form. Dieter's binary and simplistic analysis of the novel is likewise applicable to this other aspect of literature: fucking. An activity in which, thankfully, things are much less clearly defined.

I love writing this because now all the other has to do is give me arguments to fill up these pages. He doesn't even have to profess continued fidelity.

All material is valid and welcome.

A letter arrives from Alicia. Good questions, questioning the situation of this couple. Bad, bad, that she criticizes Duck so much, the man does have his good side (or did have, rather), otherwise I wouldn't have stopped that memorable night, at the bathroom door in the hotel room in Paris (or was it Nice?) to say that memorable sentence:

"I finally understand Alicia Dujovne's novels."

And Duck, who hadn't read about all those multiple orgasms and erotic levitations still understood me because my entire skin vibrating couldn't have meant anything else.

"I feel like a little red wagon is running through my veins," I whispered, and it was very true. That sensation of a red wagon kept running through my whole body, sliding through my blood a really long time. taking pleasure to every single corner, making me twinkle like the stars.

Who can take that away from you? Who can take away the generosity of a man who, after coming, instead of lying comfortably beside you, slides down to the foot of the bed, to go down on you and keep giving and giving, making you vibrate more and more?

It's just that sometimes I wake up from those delicacies (and those delicacies, do they ever last very long with a single person? Do they ever come back, like they came back that time?) and I think that such generosity can also be transmitted to other levels of life.

In which case I would have to say: stop the presses! And start to write the story knowing that there's no interruption. But the presses can't stop and interruptions are good accomplices of evasion. Now for example I don't feel like going down to check the mail for fear of having to mention it here and then both stories would vanish, the one about Duck and this very brief but intense one about Dieter.

I went with the red hat that Duck finally gave me (the same color as the wagon that runs through my blood after such pleasure) perhaps intending (but not admitting this) to once again become the man he was in those days of transformation and love.

With the beautiful red hat on my head then, I conquered without even wanting to a certain Andrés, Venezuelan jewel, who I didn't feel like sleeping with, not that day or any other, more from a lack of energy than anything else; or even more than that—from a lack of the mental stimulus that would have made such excitement exciting.

He did write me a beautiful poem though. I've harvested some good poems in my lifetime, especially during the times I was traveling. I set out as is my custom across the world, meeting men, and struck it rich with—often less-than-impeccable—verses.

What else? I'm afraid there are poems I never knew about because there were other poets always writing them for me and then another one who wasn't a poet but swears that he devoted himself to that noble profession because of me, because of being inspired, or however you want to put it.

Do I feel *fulfilled* by all this? Not at all. I'm no muse by vocation, and I'm only going to succeed in feeling fulfilled when *they*, the men, are the muses. All of the ones who passed my way, crunch, crunch, reduced to words.

That's why I keep those little boxes. Now I'm discovering why I've loved those little boxes. Duck gave me one with a heart painted on it, and I bought other ones. I found these notes in another notebook:

> *Against everything we've been fighting about, against everything we've been facing from the beginning, now this: the desire to pigeonhole them, put them in little boxes just to be able to take pleasure in something that has no movement of its own.*
>
> *Love placed in a box, whole, to whom should I give it? (Send it off.) Love dispersed, loose, a little for everyone. Give. Give. Without thinking of what might come back to me. (Retribution, recovery.) Completely whole, preserving me whole for a new love, a fearless love.*

"As long as I have fingers, I'll never be alone," someone said, and she wasn't referring to any lover, or to her fingers touching other skin, not even her own most intimate skin. No. Fingers to massage the fingers of her other hand and relax them to be able to keep playing the violin. Or: to keep writing—in my case.

Very strange things are going to start happening as soon as I give myself permission, as soon as I feel the courage to let the ties loosen.

Lovers

A man
A lover
Something solid that I've been anxious for
Something to put in my life
Intensity.
A blade

A man? Friend Dieter would ask, what's that? There are neither men nor women, just having a cock or a hole doesn't make things clear. It's been discovered that the biological message given by the body is quite different from the psychic message, Dieter says. These elements aren't formed at the same time in the fetus, and can very well turn out to be contradictory. Statistically it doesn't happen very often, but it does happen, as has been well proven, says Dieter.

And how are things in your case? I've listened lately to my men confess that maybe, given the opportunity, they would have "experimented." Who wouldn't, I wonder, but the question is recognizing where this golden opportunity lies, and if—when the moment arrives—it's still considered golden, and you don't chicken out. I myself let myself fantasize about it, but I know that's just what it is, a fantasy, so that no one is about to trap me in its reality, making my fantasy—which is so beautiful—peter out.

Marginal Notes

Sometimes we write things we shouldn't write. Sometimes we sigh for things we shouldn't, a thousand times no. Today I had to look for an address in my old Argentine address book and I realized that if a certain dark character of that time for some crazy reason appeared in my life now perhaps I would sigh and even be moved. Again! And then I say: with such a difficult past, who would accept my present?

And what if I'm like that unhappy aphid trapped in the anthill? All the ants suck and suck wanting to get to the last drop of my sub-stance, they suck and get drunk and suddenly, zap! All those blood-suckers are dead drunk and have no substance of their own and the anthill crumbles.

I don't want the anthill to crumble. I want it to change.

Narcissus

Like someone looking through the window of the bar, I look at the window. The guy who sees me from outside comes in to talk to me.

"I like you."

"Me too."

"You like me too?"

"No, I like myself. I was looking at my reflection."

*Poom. Another thrust parried. Bowling (*bolos*). They make you be hard, damn it; they make you knock them down. I have my own little collection of pins.*

What was or what could have been should never distract us from what will be.

The let's say very traditional story of fear of rejection came up, it came up many times. In a certain bit of dialogue as well, in that stretched out, impossible novel, which could be called *The Ambassador and Bella*, from a time when I was a little wiser and intuited that rejection isn't the worst thing in the world: rejection is a relief; it's getting a burden off your shoulders and getting on with life. The worst, the most terrifying thing is the encounter with the other and the various transformations that the encounter provokes inside you, and which disappear forever if the other goes away.

I prefer provocation to seduction for now. Last night, Andrés wanted to provoke me, which seems less stereotypical of his gender, maybe more juvenile and refreshing.

"I accepted your invitation to listen to jazz, but nothing more. I never claimed to be a cradle-robber," I told little Andrés.

"Never ever say that again. Never ever put age into the equation. That doesn't suit you one bit."

What a serious woman I've become!

Thank you, my good friend, not only for inviting me to participate but mostly for speaking in your seminar about Hermes and of the poet as thief. I feel much more comfortable in that role than in the role of spectator (expectant, the one who has expectations—hopes?). Yesterday at the jazz club with Andrés, I looked around (at people's attitudes) and said to myself: I'm not observing them from outside without getting involved, no. I'm stealing gestures, expressions from them. I'm involving myself. I'm a part of them.

Obsession is a form of observation that becomes infected, sickly: the compulsion to open up our notebooks and write there so that nothing escapes us is a farce. Imitating monkey. Real writing is something else.

Profound question (as deep as my throat): does eroticization feminize? Because in the street I happened upon a group of young men looking secretly at what were presumably pornographic photographs, and they were letting out little squeals and jumping around, full of an excitement that was not at all virile.

On the other hand, what is virile after all? What do we expect from men, the poor things?

This work, is it an autobiography or positive feedback?

Something of that really powerful sensation of being fully involved in the theater of life, of being on stage with all my body, my hands, feet, nose, eyes, and ears. Risking my skin, not like the spectator who's looking from the outside in. This is New York, no denying it.

Sometimes I drag myself through these crazy streets, sometimes I feel as though I'm levitating a foot above the ground.

Something about looking and being looked at, about the novel of the look and the wooden eye that Dieter found—because he knew how to look—in the middle of the forest. It was a real find and he says that it's his sculpture, now. Like one of Duchamps's *objets trouvés*. A piece of wood like a giant eye hanging from the wall of his living room next to another piece of wood vaguely reminiscent of a woman's body. He promised to give them to me before he left. Do I want a woody souvenir?

Now I finally know why I'm circling around and around this theme of the look. Something other than *l'école du regard*! It's because now I know that I have a neighbor who exists, who knows my name and therefore exists and his window looks directly into mine and in this world without curtains I know that he sees me and has seen me when I read, write, am in bed, those kinds of things. *No es nada lo del ojo*, as they used to say in my country, in my adolescent days.

Damn, damn, the number of places you can only go to with a guy, and then only the few guys ready to take me there, like:
The old Palacio del Baile, in Buenos Aires.
The old Palacio de las Flores, on the tango weekends, in Buenos Aires.
  And here: GG Barnum's, transsexual bar, and the memory of the uncontrollable panic of that one guy we named the Magnate when he learned that the person dancing in his face swinging her black skirt and showing her boobs and making him sigh wasn't a Colombian woman, as he himself affirmed with total certainty. No, and Marta corrected him with a pause . . . it was a Colombian *man*!

In GG Barnum's the danger isn't from men harassing us women but rather from the confrontation with one's own undefined sexuality. The Magnate experienced it firsthand without understanding it and was struck down with a horrible headache and we had to leave the dance floor. Now even breathing has become threatening to some of them. Not Dieter, fortunately, in spite of having his nose broken or maybe because of that. (I know, I know, and you know too . . . Papa Freud knows, *et voilà*, everyone's happy)

What a drag to have to cut off the flow now. Give me fifteen days like this!!!!!!!

And then what? I'm going to feel totally abandoned. Because I'm living my romance with my writing now. And I love it. I'm not even remotely alone when I write. Is that why I write, I wonder?

Like someone who is drowning in a sea of words and suddenly can open the floodgates and let out the flow. A beautiful ejaculation that can last for months.

I come back from S's seminar where again we talked about the poet as thief, among other things, because s/he produces symbolic value appropriating facts and people. I hope that's true for me too.

We talked about enigmatic desire (where does it start?) and about betraying it as soon as it's named. We said that for Lacan an ethical act is one that is in accord with one's desire. Desire that can't be named or given a number. We talked and talked and also acted. There were those who, without noticing, acted out their desire. And I understood S's fierce aggression towards the beautiful romantic woman (aggression that, in the last seminar, turned me against S because I felt him to be disagreeable and intolerant, and which helped me treat him with a certain indifference the Saturday that he invited me to walk around Soho). The beautiful, devouring, romantic woman, trying to eat him in one bite, playing with some yellow flowers and some half-smoked cigarettes. And I carefully observed: devouring is characterized by a lack of humor and fun. Especially fun. So necessary and so absent in human relationships. Whoever devours engenders an intolerable anxiety in the other, and even for themselves.

From there I flew to the memory of seduction, and the fight I started with Dieter.

Rainy Saturday

Where is my enthusiasm of yesteryear? Is this what people are referring to when they talk about maturing? What a bore.

Dieter finally called to ask me to go to the movies tomorrow, with all kinds of misgivings, as if I were going to eat him, but in any case proposing the movies and something afterward (a movie that lasts seven hours—how could there be time to do something afterward?), and I was happy, but with a skeptical aftertaste, thinking what a lie that he had been calling me all week as he claimed. Where have all the good old times gone, back when I didn't get all wrapped up in incredulities, when everything seemed simple and vital, like that July 14 in Paris, for example? That really crunchy bite of chocolate, that almost blue skin that the night before I had seen close up and in the moonlight?

The story of Seseko

I had waited all day hoping to see him, floating on air, tearing out the hair on my legs with my fingers so that I'd be softer, sponging my feathers. Floating on warm (hot) expectations. And all that for what? To let myself be dragged beforehand to another party, a most sinister party—solemn, I would say—attended by a man who had arrived there with another man and who came to my side to flirt blablaba in French. And I blablabla answered him in his native language and we told each other a bunch of intelligent things that I didn't even register at the time—thinking as I was of hurrying to the dance at the Marais firehouse, and of that black man's young arms, so that when the man who was just a voice offered to take us to the dance, I went along and happily, pointing like a weathervane, in that direction, without knowing what winds might still blow me off course . . .

Because a traffic jam caught us just at l'Etoile and looked like it would never unjam. People were even dancing on top of their cars: a true Sunday, Quatorze Juillet. So for the first time I deigned to turn my head and really look at the Frenchman, and discovered that he wasn't half bad—like that, in profile. Actually, he was really handsome, and when we finally arrived at the dance an hour late, I decided to stay with this adult, intelligent white man and leave the call of the jungle for some other time. I've had time to regret denying myself that chocolate candy, after having desired—still desiring—it so much. In complete possession of the body, of enjoyment in movement. That Parisian Quatorze Juillet, I chose the word over the body: I told myself that it was better to be with a guy who understood me verbally, even if later, erotically, nothing happened. I told myself that and I deceived myself, of course, but not completely, as usually happens, because it's one thing to spend a horizontal night in blue sheets and quite another to wake up to a white and distanced morning. But over the course of several encounters, Pierre was nice enough to inspire my only intellectual porno story.

Orgasmopierre

Pierre is my lover of the highest caliber
(and when I say—write—caliber, I THINK "caliber")
Now, when I think/thought Pierre is my lover of the highest caliber, I was writing this (mentally) and not fornicating. At least, not as much as I believe/d myself to be fornicating.

Where is Pierre in all this? Pierre wraps his leg around me, turns my head to kiss me, and I begin sliding my mouth down his sternum, his belly button, and even farther down while I'm only thinking: Pierre (like that, indefinite, as though he wasn't making me turn my whole body around, looking for my crotch to kiss in turn), and I think (I mentally formulate): Pierre is my lover of the highest CALI-BER. And I add, caliber *in all senses of the word—*

   a)   *because he's the most skillful*
   b)   *the most well-endowed*

Another question: when I think (thought) Pierre . . . etc., am I making this statement in comparison to all the other lovers I've had in my life? Am I really comparing or just affirming that in this moment Pierre is my lover of the highest caliber? Of the latter, there is no doubt; we're not in a round bed although for all the movement there is/was, you would think we were.

Pierre is not a delicate guy. Neither is he sordid.
Delicate—sordid (?). Are these even antagonistic terms?

He has a special quality all his own, able to control himself as long
as necessary and only to let go when I can't take any more and cry
out that I'm coming.
Pierre is my lover . . . *am I thinking that as I write or as I fuck?*
I suspect it's all the same act: simultaneous, my dear Watson. Even
if I don't like it.

> Amante: m. mar. Cabo grueso asegurado en la cabeza de un
>   palo o verga *(third definition)*
> Calibre: m. Diámetro del cañón de las armas de fuego. *(first*
>   *definition)*
>   (*Pequeño Larousse Ilustrado*)[1]

I could write about how he asks me to pronounce words that don't
sound good to me in his language but do in others. "Où veux-tu ma
langue?" he asks me.
"Au con . . . God, that sounds terrible. Ma craquette, horrible. Ma
chatte . . . ?" I shut up.
"In my pussy, mi concha, la mia figa . . ." The gift of tongues (and the
generous gift of his tongue) paralyzes my tongue, and therefore para-
lyzes his tongue where I most want it. Damn. Literature is killing me.
AND WHAT AM I DOING BUT MAKING LITERATURE?
I'm fuck-ing.

---

1 Translator's Note: The word "lover" in Spanish does indeed have this third,
nautical connotation: the thick cloth attached to the head of a pole or yard (in
its nautical sense), while the word "caliber" can be defined as the diameter of
the barrel of a gun, in both English and Spanish. We take the author's point.

Yes sir, now as I write this

And before? Also, surely,

and also in the restaurant while Pierre is biting my finger, caressing the palm of my hand, which I surrender to him on top of the table (altar). Red tablecloth, oysters, the delicate torturing of the live animal in its shell, detaching it with little forks ad hoc after pouring lemon over it. Then sipping the juice which is pure sea water, pure passion, while he sends me messages with the tip of his tongue that my entire body registers, trembling. So, I know myself, and there we are indeed fornicating (the famous telefuck of my older writing, so hornyyyyy!), and, well, nothing is anything if it's not literature. It's just that after a while, we're out in the street again, floating through this exterior space back to my lair and here I am stark naked, standing on the bed, and he buries his noble French face (with his hair combed back and wearing a tie—he looks like some kind of secret agent), his noble face, I say—no: face yes, but it's only noble in its expression, his lineage invisible (because he's some kind of count or something). Pierre de . . . burying his face in my (noble) crotch.

A question in the margins about Pierre in a tie:

CIA or its local equivalent?

WHAT DO I CARE?! I shout inside and it leaves sort of a hole in my lungs—Pierre, my dear man, take advantage of that hole to get inside me better—Pierremyman, impossible to get inside me better than you usually do, what you've done or will do, it's just that, when will you understand Spanish, man? Man, manly, cock, gigolo? I've had my doubts, will have. But it doesn't matter one bit right now with the way you're moving inside me, with the way I feel you moving inside me.

Theelectricityrunsthroughmefromthetipofmyhairtothevagina, frommytoestomycunt: in other words, orgasm is like an ink stain

Literature   Literature   Literature
It expands, it grows and grows and grows and disconnects.

But it doesn't end here:
1)   *it's repeated three more times during the night*
2)   *there are a lot of caresses in between*
3)   *there were so many things beforehand**
4)   *and there will be afterward*

*beforehand:

> *Pierre saying, I'd like you to get on
> top of me and rape me. Like this . . .
> Me saying (sitting on him), That's great,
> deeper, move like that, that's great.*

*The same as always, bah, seen now without the raw emotion, com-
motion of the moment, only words now to be narrated. The same
as always with the logical variants of time/space/mood/meet-
ing, and especially with the almost inhuman potency of Pierre.
Pierre=stone, let's not forget, and his tenderness too, which doesn't
appear on paper, first because I would have to go get more paper to
be able to keep writing and secondly because it's not easy to write
when Pierre starts kissing my face, and then puts his hand you
know where and he takes my hand and places it on his sublime
erection (again! Mein Gott!!) and then I let him write me with
his wise fingers and I stop making literature because my left hand
is much happier than this right hand which wields the pen. But I
don't stop thinking*
Pierre is my lover of the highest . . .

Enough already, damn it, ENOUGH!
(although you can't deny the evidence either)

You have to remake yourself daily, and that's what words are good for, sometimes. You don't want to jot them down, you don't want to repeat them, you want to store them up for yourself and nourish the secret.

How strange. I think that when I stopped the seduction with Dieter, in one fell swoop I ended the magic. Now with him it's all very straightforward. Get to his house, have a drink, undress, each of us on our own, and off to bed. Then, luckily, things get away from him and he turns into an affectionate guy, at least for the time it takes to fuck and a bit afterward, looking at me with that sated expression (I respond to that look, why deny it). Maybe all that is what made me think of Pierre.

Let's see, let's see; I think these barriers are crossable, it's just that there isn't much time left. Let's see—I have to remember that brief dialogue about the devouring woman.

And why not? I had to ask, oh innocent me. Why not accept things as they are and let yourself be eaten by the woman who after all made man, why not let yourself symbolically reenter the same way you came out? And (of course, stupid me) I told the joke that's so antifeminist and politically incorrect, about the overprotective mother:

A young man at the right age, a bit past it really, and a mother who threatens him every time he goes out at night: "Be careful, son, those loose women who take any man they find have teeth you-know-where." And the boy is careful, and the years go by, and at around twenty, when he can't stand it anymore, he finds a delicious blonde ready to help him out a bit. "Look," the blonde says to him, "I'll open my legs and show you. You'll see that there are NO teeth." So they go ahead, and after the visual inspection, the blonde asks, "So are there any teeth?" "No, of course not," he answers, "with the gums in that state!!!"

I think I told that joke before accusing Dieter: Yes, devouring woman, but castrating man. Castrator of women, not letting them be themselves, not giving them respite. Yes, he accepted (or threatened), that's just how it is.

These encouraging talks take place in his house, in his temporary house, which he has managed to personalize nonetheless with some things he's bought to add to his collection of African art. There's an idol from Benin that always catches my eye—when I'm not enraptured looking at, let's say, another idol. But this one from Benin is an anthropomorphous piece; in other words, it eats men, as women do if we're to believe the owner of the house and all those really manly men who are supposedly walking around out there. From which it can be inferred that my Duck has perhaps a bit of the feminine in him, and that may be precisely what attracted me to him. Because lovemaking with him was gluey, enveloping, letting me swim in a warm sea of trust. Everything is open and permitted with Duck, and it's another dimension entirely. Not that I don't reach another dimension with a guy like Dieter—that's what orgasm is all about, finally—but with Dieter, you can't forget the verticality and the hardness. Bravo for what that's worth, as far as virility goes, but, what about tenderness—which comes from softness?

And back to the same, eternal conundrum. The search for rigidity in tenderness or vice versa. At the beginning of my erotic life I had it, and that must be why I keep searching for it. Only then it wasn't accompanied by the sense of the specific quality I needed; who knows what ingredients are needed to make the dish complete. Duck *à l'orange*, Dieter *au jus*, Pale Fire *mijoté*.

I think I'm going to devote myself to abstinence for a while, like I told poor Tom who extended his hand without much hope and was rejected, to his great relief, or no? And I'm going to devote myself to the reclusive life simply because this is turning into something so intense, anatomically speaking, Dieter amazing me each time with his weapon (weapon, where do I get that term, so *Memorias De Una Princesa Rusa*?! Per Bacchus. Will we spend our whole lives using sexist terminology, as if there aren't other words to describe a cock in sublime erection?) (again, that stretched skin, as if it's going to burst, again those balls, crushed against the trunk, raised by the skin stretched to the maximum, yum, yum. What are they feeding these Europeans to make them so erect?).

Lacanian, they are. The phallus as signifier, or better yet, as significant other. A gift that Mother Nature gives us ladies from time to time, but I don't know if I really need it now . . .

Have I told you that Duck's dick is quite hairy? That's right. Hairy. Something monstrously glamorous, delightful. Well, it's not completely hairy, but there are hairs up to the edge of the prepuce. I called it Pipé, in love as I was; it was really rather sublime, but he was embarrassed to death of it. Before knowing me. So many repressed things, so uptight before knowing me. Corseted. And then afterward, he let loose, but only a bit, maybe like going for a walk around the bay, returning soon to the protection of the port, a bit disheveled—in every meaning of the word—and rather agitated.

I think I'm telling this story, centering it indirectly on the story of Duck, because once there was love. It was a very intense love, but with the same capacity to slip through our fingers and leave us empty handed.

Because Duck came back but love had already gone, and then what? Only the imprint, a fossilized print. I don't want to lie to myself. Although I know what's happening, and that the wind could fill my sails once more and change my direction, I think there's something that's closed, that's over, that I need to narrate in order to get it out of my system.

Mein Gott! Is it like using a bidet? In this case the expiatory flow is of words and I say and say: this is my path to wherever it wants to lead me. And don't contaminate me with betrayals. I have (I should have) enough strength to accept the truth whether I like it or not. Generally I don't like it, maybe because any complacent truth sounds more like a story. Also, every truth is full of possible other truths that I don't want to hear—for example, like Pale Fire coming to tell me he's with someone else now. Fine, he screws up, but I don't want him to stop.

"I'm sick of all these men who feel so superior," I told Rosario referring to Dieter, perhaps unjustly.

"As if the ones who feel inferior are any better," she replied, pragmatic as she is, and I think I know to whom she was referring.

Damn, when will one show up who's just right?

I'm going to try out chastity. Because, seeing how indifferent I was to these recent events, which are now in the public domain, I could easily fall into promiscuity, and that would be very boring.

Those admirers I don't happen to like always upset me, because to fuck you have to choose, no doubt about it, and how many people do you run into that you really like? My average is about three a year, which seems pretty lucky as it is. This year is only just beginning and I've already found the first one. I have to be careful—I wouldn't want to run out before the year is over.

Last year was exquisitely prolific: Michel in March, Vince in June and July, Pale Fire from mid-August on.

Repeats don't count. Only new contributors. But you have to keep the repeats well-oiled so that the great motor doesn't stop.

And now complete calm for a while.

A certain Chucho has landed from afar; we knew each other once. He's arrived with his sails full for who knows what reason but I stop him before he can take off, telling him about my austere plans. You're taking a sabbatical, he says. That's a nice way of putting it, I answer, and I make his saying mine.

I write things, I lubricate them, but it can take a good while before I've managed to internalize them.

The hunt, a game, Zen archery. Whichever it was, LUCKILY I've finally arrived at this ideal place of not caring. Buddha be praised.

I'm finally achieving my goal after all, of putting my lovers in little boxes, or between the lines, so that I'm no longer obsessed by them. At least some of my lovers, the last ones. I beg the forgiveness of those who don't fit. Their stories were also surely beautiful, but distance has made them fade for me.

But not always. Sometimes it's a question of skies:

And the magic of Bahia? And oh, Playboy of the coke snorters? Those stories of love or of pseudo-love or of trying to catch love's thread, of cavorting wildly in strange beds trying to pass through the other side of the mirror and know more about love? Let's go backward and forward:

Backward: Those moments of my first enormous disappointment in love. Not because he left me, no—that would have been clear and concise—but rather because what left me was love itself. An emptiness difficult to fill that stayed forever in the pit of my stomach. I got married full of love, or maybe it wasn't love, maybe it was just enormous horniness? And a few years later there was that beautiful being, looking almost like an angel, loving me (yes) but also exposing plenty of defects. At times stingy. And me? Feeling totally and absolutely trapped—no exit. The only escape: suicide. A bullet in the head or jumping from the eighth floor. Anything that would blow my head open. Endlessly fantasized scenes, with all kinds of changes in the plot. Until an attack of sanity came over me; I was sane after all, then. Instead of killing myself, I thought, why not kill him? In any case it would be a sort of deferred suicide, albeit with a bit of hope.

Well, instead of living out all these stories of death, I managed to get myself a trip alone to Rio, with journalism as an excuse, and from Rio I worked my way to San Salvador de Bahia, my secret destiny.

That must have been the beginning of my professional globetrotting in search of the wise word. Falling so low sometimes that I had to ask for advice. And the later creation of seven hundred and twenty wrinkles, mountain of a woman, smelling of goat.

I wonder why I never stay to live in those ziggurats, why I barely skimmed over Bahia and stayed only a few months in Tepoztlán that time when I rented the house on the outskirts of town. Tepoztlán has, after all, as it should, an enormous stone phallus, completely natural, marking the crossroads, at the entrance, corresponding to its mythical position. They call it the Cane of Tepozteco (the local god), but they don't fool me: short and stubby, with the little trees that bloom during the rainy season, it makes me reminisce . . . about certain things.

Later I wonder if New York isn't the ziggurat of this millennium's end. Aren't I now living in a place sacred through antonomasia? Simply because all imaginable madmen converge here and because tenderness is here turned into imagination, and not the reverse, as usually happens?

The most exciting thing about this ziggurat is that we are all—now—contributing our little grains of sand, creating it. Not stumbling through the streets with dreams of past races but rather leaving our own dreams hanging here, bringing along all kinds of personal vibrations for the creation of its mystery.

I leave all the sperm that has passed through me in New York,. The hundreds of millions of spermatozoids dampened by my juices, I give them to the underground sewers of this city of the living, to the living blind sewers where the blind alligators go marauding.

It's very simple, and I'll explain it because I don't want these truths to be taken as metaphors or symbols of something ephemeral. The underground New York alligators do exist; they're alive and kicking, but blind. With the usual desire to astonish their neighbors and take in unusual domestic animals, the good citizens of Manhattan would buy baby crocodiles, a rarity. But the poor crocodiles were stupid enough to grow until oh! they're not sweet little house lizards any more, and start to turn into voracious monsters—a rather serious matter. So plop plop they end up in the toilets and from there naturally and through all the shit they land in the sewers, and since they're amphibians they survive eating all kinds of filth—just like my cats of death—and the absence of light makes them blind after a while. There's my pseudoscientific clarification.

Did I say I leave the sperm that's passed through me? That I *have* left, I should say! Let's not forget that I have sworn abstinence at least for a few pages. (And not because I lack opportunities. Here opportunity is the last thing that's lacking.)

Pleasure in disgust. Now I'm researching that subject, from the literary point of view, of course, in certain writers' work. At the same time I notice that I've only let myself experience it very few times, in writing as well as in life.

It's the moment when the midwife is showing my mother the placenta covering my daughter and said:

"This is what's richest in vitamins. It's because I'm always in contact with placenta that my complexion is so good."

I do not have a good complexion. I'm afraid that placenta has never been my strong point. And not because I don't want to; I'd like the lake I swim in (remember last night's dream) to be a warm and viscous lake—no! actually, I don't want that at all. I prefer water to be crystal clear and slightly cold. Tingly. Remembering the disgust I felt the first time I got in the tropical seas on that dreamlike island, in that paradise of Paquetá. It was like getting into a bowl of soup. Bouillabaisse, let's say, but still soup.

I prefer cold water. There's a lot that's masculine in me; that's perhaps why I feel a connection with men who have certain feminine characteristics and despise them at the same time (the men). Another part of me despises machismo, so what to do? And especially, will I ever find someone to end my days with? The couple, not as something closed like a cyst, looking at each other and mutually reflecting each other, but rather as company, in solidarity, looking ahead, advancing. What a pretty pretension, and what a tacky sentence.

What can I do in this telling of facts that are far from being facts? Actions yet to be taken, perhaps, or more likely undoable/unseizable. I can do nothing, and that's what I'm doing because to write is to give a concrete dimension to that nothing, swimming between the white coral reefs of an idea and suddenly—nothing, only the deep, vast abyss underneath that awakens fascination and terror at the same time. The never forgotten vertigo from looking into the abyss that you have to respond to somehow and it's usually with fear. Writing is the desperate dread of facing the abyss under water, one more stroke than what's needed, and the escape can turn out to be fatal. The terror makes you lose the rhythm of your breathing; in the disruption, you let go of the tube of oxygen that you were clinging to—when the natural thing to do would have been to answer the call of the abyss and let go of your cowardice . . .

Everything that's still to be said, everything that you can say and you don't want to, or rather everything that you'd like to say and can't, your mouth sealed shut, your hands tied. Is love yet to be said? Eroticism and death, our only engines.

Where does the writer end and the character begin? Or vice versa? Where am I, acting out my own masks—seduction, which is after all the great mask? Letting everything go, written down, in an infinite number of notebooks, and the same in life.

A mini-scene that I'll give to Bella, but which is mine, and I'll reproduce it here to cheer me up:

Eyes of Water

You are what I would like most to see and don't dare, he told me once.

The messianic thing grabs hold of me sometimes, and when they tell me something like that, I usually believe it. Because it's a big deal to be an ideal for a man, you have to risk it, though few succeed, right? So that I, not that I'm a saint or anything like that, but rather daring, yes, and to those who notice, bravo for your perspicacity, but still, goddamn it, they get frightened.

(As if I never ever ever got frightened.)

Dieter told me what, very literarily, he defined as his most beautiful love story. It happened on a trip, as the most beautiful love stories almost always happen, and maybe that's why I'm on a perpetual trip, so that these things keep happening to me.

When Theo came into the party where we would meet, he asked the friend who brought him, pointing me out, "Who is that woman? I'm going to marry her!" And that's how it happened, like in the most beautiful stories people tell you and seem so wonderful in the telling. Or like in fairy tales. But since the words *The End* never arrive at the best moment, fairy tales have ample time to deteriorate, in life. And thus the purity of the story with Dieter, since it only lasted the span of a kiss between two strangers.

I too have kissed a stranger once, just like that, because I felt like it, but never out of love: when there could have been love, I ran away. How horrible. I ran away.

Trap. That's not what I was talking about, or maybe it was. Something that impels you to take the other person in your arms, to lose yourself in the other. Also losing myself in the arms of that other lover in Paris, the famous man, crossing the bridge like in a story by Cortázar. At one end of the bridge, the sound of other people's passion, at the other, him, waiting for me, with the door unlocked and headphones on. The music he listened to, that he heard because of me, what was I for him? So much attraction circling us, so much feeling so close to the other person. It was a great love and somehow I threw it overboard. I threw it overboard just for the hell of it; I forced him to escape me out of fear that he would escape me after all.

One night in his bed I huddled against the wall and confessed:

"Now I know how some men feel like running away afterward—right now, I feel like running away too. I feel like going through the wall and disappearing, letting the earth swallow me."

I think he understood me. We had beautifully reversed roles. He waited for me to be ready for his dick that was like a sword; he prepared baths for me, he would tell me:

"This is like a dream. Something I've wanted for such a long time is suddenly happening and I just let it happen naturally, as if that's how it should be!"

That sentence sounded a bit cloying, so it distracted me from the obligation of believing him.

I never told Duck that he ruined my most beautiful love story because he arrived in Europe just in the middle of that other romance. When the time came to tell him about it, he didn't deserve it anymore. Although, thinking it over now, maybe it was my most beautiful love story precisely because Duck ruined it. It would have been sad to have had the protagonist ruin it for me instead.

What nonsense, as usual. My most beautiful love story, at least in the last few years, was the one I lived with Duck. We sure did do our best to shut that one up in a box and limit it to the time we had in Italy, France, Spain (if there was indeed unity in time, the places multiplied correspondingly). It was very beautiful because of all his transformations, as if love had made another man of him. Adorable, adult. Every woman's dream. And every novelist's: a beloved of flesh and blood!

I think the moment has arrived to tell the story of that meeting in Europe, to put it in front of me and look at it from afar. But each time I try, the narrator of stories in me gets diluted, and I get more interested in reflection rather than action—let the action take care of itself.

Is this a masturbatory attitude—like a recuperation of myself? To remember my own integrity. The current can circulate from your hand to your genitals and through your entire body back up again to your hand. And it's an answer to the fear of feeling needy, totally dependent on the other person for pleasure.

And the hand that receives the vibration writes.

Coming to, recuperating, making oneself whole again thanks to renouncing or rather rejecting, the revitalizing power of rejection.

Never again, never again any more of what I wrote in other places.

Maybe that's why Duck's story is slipping through my fingers and leaves cracks where so many other stories that have nothing to do with it pass through . . . Maybe because Duck's story isn't dried skin yet: it's alive, viscous, slippery, rather threatening and s-h-i-n-y. In white with just a few colored feathers, or with the colorful tones of the yarara snake and the silky skin of the boa constrictor? Maybe with rings like on a coral snake? Yes sir, ANNULAR and ANNULLED, as in wearing a ring and at the same time cancelled with the gesture I use in writing; even if it seems to go up and down, it's actually the straight line of an erasure.

Something in me has to break (out). There's something in me that should be born. Something that needs to be pushed out. Struggle. Give birth to it. A force. There is a force in me that wants to explode and I don't let it.

Inherent in all of this? Self-deceit. The notion that the storms to be narrated are external. Rich atmospheres. Human beings struggle against the elements or against other beings, as if the elements and the enemies weren't also—and especially—internal.

In this precise case, it's about the internal enemy, so let's take my old fury out for a gallop! Let the dogs bark. Let's stop traffic

116

and in the middle of the street let's build a stage and then get on it. To give the others back their faces. Or no. Let's go through a park.

Another One

She's walking through the park with the wind in her hair, when the other appears out of nowhere. A young boy with identical black pants and his face totally painted white, a mask upon which, inexplicably, her mask imprints itself: her raised eyebrows, her startled eyes. She smiles timidly and he gives her back the exact same smile in a game of mirrors. She moves her right hand and he moves his left, she takes a big step and he takes one, the same way of walking, the same gestures, cadences.

The game of projects begins—projections. Fantasies like washing the other's face and finding her own face under the white paint. Or mating with him as a slightly awkward way of completing herself. Or letting him go away and being left without a shadow.

Vain projects while the other follows her through the park, reflecting each one of her gestures. Getting closer and closer to her. The same expressions. Until he crosses without any warning, without even meaning to, the two-foot abyss separating them and takes her place. Forever.

In other words, now, again, caught in the morbid world of transexuality via writing, the temptation of androgyny, the Yin and Yang in me, when I'm allowed the luxury of going out in the street to confront reflections.

But enough of stories. Confront the novel. Not the one you're making of your life at each step, but the one that you've been trying so assiduously to finish, lately: *The Ambassador and Bella.*

Months ago I woke up in Pale Fire's bed and thought that the novel was definitely going to be a novel about love—but where is love? Where is Pale Fire?

Rhetorical questions as always, or maybe just displaced, because who knows where love is, but I do know where Pale Fire's gotten to, wandering about, although now he's far away.

Today the vampire in me has awoken and I want to suck them all dry. Suck my fingers, that is, because the food here has been quite juicy (in a language dish, the sauces make all the difference, and I feel completely at ease in this area of cooking).

At ease. Legs wide. Broad ass. Someone once told me: "This can't be just the work of nature. The hand of man has to have intervened." The hand of man? No. Nobody's hand. But then again, yes. But more the eye of man than anything else.

It's just that I'm not really happy with my big butt. Although I'd better accept it since that's what I have. Thus the self-portrait I made for Burt Britton, for his collection: a mass of curls and underneath, two concave waves, like an ample, very rounded W

A self-portrait for *posterity.*

I think I mentioned my fear of needles, and my feeling that, in order to defend myself against them, I had to gain weight in my ass. What I've never stopped mentioning throughout these pages, however, are those other injections, with a needle of flesh.

And to think that at one time I proposed to write a defense of the phallus—poor thing, I thought at that time, a species threatened with extinction, if seen from the feminist point of view. (Inasmuch as much the women who are dying to receive it are fewer and fewer, as compared to the number of women who painstakingly crush it—even if, often enough, these are one and the same. Poor, innocent rod.)

You have to distinguish between the Phallocrat and Phallograce—meaning the divine grace of the phallus. Thanks for the phallus, and its inherent humor. Anna Lisa at least laughed a lot when she first saw her father naked. The one who developed a bit of a complex because of this was her father. Though he didn't need to, in that sense.

I don't know why I'm adopting the literary style of a certain comic who really fucked me over, once. Not his style, him. In that sense precisely.

A beautiful guy as far as his exterior, and also as far as his humor, I have to admit. He approached me one day with the usual misplaced fearlessness of the very shy:

"I feel like kissing you."

Ah, how delicious! I licked my lips, because I had been noticing this guy, and he had been looking at me too. So, since we were at a house in the country, we left the party and went to a dark corner to kiss each other like crazy. No, I wasn't fifteen years old. This happened about three or four years ago, in the south of the south (though I was still fifteen in a corner of my heart, of course). When we finally returned to the party, there were hardly any guests left, but there was a lot of the wine that he kept drinking before, during, and after dinner, so that when we finally got to bed—oh what fools we made of ourselves in front of our hosts!—he only had enough vigor left to make a few promises of love and to talk about "our meeting."

Somewhere I wrote about how the freeways separated us in our crazy return home the next day, with a guy driving who thought he was the racecar driver Reutemann. But that's deceiving myself too. It wasn't the freeway or the wine. The great interceptor—who refused to share our enthusiasm—was what separated us: old master phallus, in whose honor I claimed to want to sing an ode in *illo tempore* . . .

How frightening, ladies and gentlemen! How frightening for all of us to get together, to really meet each other, even if only for a short while (the measureless time of an orgasm, which is so brief, as I think I wrote somewhere or other).

But really, how frightening. They move inside and outside, brutal penetration or impotence. I move trying to appropriate them or force them to flee. And then, at a prudent distance from each other, we sometimes emit growls that we call dialogue.

Man as Grenade

In just one night he told me so many yeses and so many nos, constantly contradicting himself. Every word. Now I remember that night and its not very original contradictions and I open the dictionary haphazardly (like others do with the Bible) to find the solution, and I do:

> *GRANADA: F. Fruta del granado que contiene numerosos granos encarnados de sabor dulce/Proyectil ligero (ex-*

120

*plosivo, incendiario, fumígeno o lacrimógeno) que se lanza
con la mano//Bala de cañon[2]*
(Gentle projectile then—the second meaning. Explosive, incendiary. A cannon incarnated/made flesh. Tear-producing fruit that you throw with your hand. A bullet with a sweet taste.)

Incorporation. The appropriation of what we spoke of last time. Now I'm going to S's seminar with this notebook. I have to get what I can out of it and recognize that the master himself seriously risks being incorporated into these phallic files (phascinating fantasies, filed phantasms).

Do what cats do, like the Efficient Cat.[3] I prefer them when they purr. S, the master, seems to be one of those who purr, a clever bastard when no one contradicts him, and this semester, at the beginning of his seminar, I was able to witness with a certain satisfaction that he had taken off his ring. I can no longer see a man with a collar on his finger as just a tame little dog.

Acquisition and Control of Fire

I take notes to appropriate them, in some fashion. After all, in the last seminar we spoke about the poet as thief since Hermes stole the lyre from Apollo. Moreover, the question was posed:

What kind of truth does art embody?

Answer: A general truth that the reader/spectator can steal, that s/he can appropriate in order to gain access to his or her own truth.

---

2   Translator's Note: No single English word has all meanings of the Spanish, giving us "pomegranate," "grenade," and "cannonball" all at once.
3   Translator's Note: Refers to *El Gato Eficaz*, one of the author's books.

Today the subject is Prometheus. If we must acquire fire it is because it is not ours (it is outside us, and in another time). S maintains that, according to Freud, in his first encounters with fire, man peed on it and put it out. (Something he keeps doing till this day, I think, but I'm careful not to say it).

Man begins putting out the fire through fear.

The man who responds to fire (aesthetically), who doesn't renounce, carries the fire on his stick and ends up being burned.

S: The renouncing of satisfaction attracts desire.

The mythical instance of the stealing of fire is, for Freud, equivalent to a nonspecific act (a desire), the gesture that lets us acquire fire is the renouncing.

The ethic of fire is the ethic of desire (an ethic always related to eroticism).

(Art is not an aesthetic but rather an ethic because it doesn't aspire to awaken only a distant and admired, necessary, contemplation.)

Impulse is not desire; impulse wants to be satisfied (peeing on the fire).

The gaining of desire is not a blessing (and the renouncing can lead to desire, but there is no guarantee because the renouncing can also be repulsion).

Prometheus in a feminine position. All men who want to acquire and have control over the phallus (fire) must pass through a hysteric (feminizing) phase, S affirms.

Women's traditional role has been that of guardian of the fire.

There is no return once the fire has been stolen. (You can no longer put it out.)

The second step then wouldn't be to put out the fire but rather to destroy the desire. Desire is destroyed bringing everything to normality, a natural state (Prometheus's punishment as the cycle of seasons).

Basically, desire is indestructible (surrendering oneself to destiny, to fatality, to indestructible desire), and that means that analyses can NOT cure desire.

(All the better! I say, but the master isn't listening).

As usual, one listens to the story when the story is already over.

Occupying the Place of the Other.

Hasn't this been, and doesn't it perhaps continue to be, my search? To play with fire, masculinize myself in some form. Or perhaps it's the other way around: I masculinize myself because I want to occupy the place of the other who is playing with fire.

I prefer the first version. It resembles more what I was in my long childhood: tree climber, tomboy. Appropriate the phallus, definitely. That's where we were headed. The woman ends up not envying the penis because finally *all* penises can be hers.

I'm only interested in writing, in spite of my headaches that I still haven't succeeded in alleviating.

The idea of the oyster in its shell. Above all and especially from the Argentine point of view: the location in a confusing place, genitals as the here-place of everyone, the nerve endings of all our emotions vibrating precisely there, in that ambiguous, dark zone that I myself refuse to know completely. They can make us really cute little drawings, simplified and even symbolic like the ones that come in tampon boxes. They can tell us all about the labia majora and minora, clitoris, vulva, vagina. All cold scientific words. We ourselves can utilize all the slang words: cunt, hole, pussy . . . and we still know nothing, we still haven't named any one of its dark recesses. From there to using the great metonymy and saying that women are confused and ambiguous is just one simple step; the big step they all take without at the same time accepting that women are deep, humid, and warm. WelCUMing. And then on the other side of this same step, its other face, entering the realm of the insecurities and confusions of those who by their own definition should be clear and geometrical. In other words, the males, the great terrified ones. That's why I understand Pale Fire better each day and love him in spite of his cowardice. He can't live with his insecurity and at the same time somehow admit it. Maybe that's precisely why he designed his ex-wife a wedding gown that was incredibly romantic, full of lace. And he wanted to design the rest of her too—which he did. And his erotic daydreams? Have a bunch of women strung along his dick. The great universal male. Damn! How insecure he was! If only I could reproduce those conversations we had when we were still more or less together and he was trying to break the tie (the leather strip that we both wore as a collar), remember his similes, those metaphorical comparisons always with objects, because, truly, we are always objects for men. I was a package for Duck ("It's as if I'd been given a present wrapped up in a package that I didn't have the courage to unwrap!") a glass of wine for PF ("In these kinds of things, you get involved without even realizing it. It's like with wine: you drink the first glass, and then another, and another, and you're drunk before you know it!").

Nobody recognizes me where I really am. Always paying the price of lucidity, damn it. The little bit of lucidity that I've managed to put somewhere (as if it were light), and suddenly I'm blinded. This should be the book of exile.

Dream

I wonder what last night's dream means. I was teaching in a high school where they're taking students away from me, where they leave me only one or two in an enormous room, and they're not listening to me. And they accuse me of having spoken to bastard children, maybe even the children of prostitutes, because it seems I showed them a video adaptation of my first novel. Then I'm going to swim in an enormous pool that's there. And I decide to swim all the way across, and I start to swim with incredible freedom, entirely up to the challenge, and I swim and swim, and feel that I'm moving forward so well even though there's some brown junk like earth floating in the water, and further ahead there are little plants and a bog at the end. But I'm swimming so well that I want to keep on going even though the water ends before the pool-lake ends. (like the Nuñez one of my childhood, although it didn't seem so dirty then). So I start walking because it's impossible to swim. I walk back along the side of the pool-lake but there are a lot of cruise ships anchored that don't let me get back to the water. Then I find the ladder and I climb in again, careful not to put my face underwater, and I swim back thinking that the swimming is doing me good. But at the same time the little water that's getting in my mouth tastes like oil, although I exhale as hard as I can, and whatever benefits I might hope to enjoy from all this swimming become very doubtful.

On the one hand, a woman who for almost two years has been trying to write a novel where reality and fiction can be included in equal parts. On the other, the woman who is living this reality and who is washed over by waves of fiction because, what else can be done?

At this stage of the game I think I could elaborate a Theory of the Abandoned Husband:

Every husband tries to make an object of his wife, for his use, pleasure, disgust, or whatever, and when she leaves, he suffers doubly: for his wife's abandoning him (betrayal), and for the loss of this object. That's why, generally, men are more desperate after a separation, when practical sense would indicate just the opposite.

Women can be left penniless, homeless, but they can struggle to rebuild their lives. Men are left without their illusions, and that is what is intolerable.

No, no.
What's intolerable is being the other's illusion. His fantasy.

Does it make me happy that every two or three years Théo sends me the news that he would marry me again? Did it make me happy that Duck would come in search of my love? Not at all. Because I'm not really a part of either of those expressions of desire made by the other. Or maybe I am, but it doesn't interest me. I prefer staying home in my own cunt, counting hairs.

And at other times, I used to envy love. I would envy those women who were unforgettable for some man.
Now I know:

a)   You never envy what is out of your reach. You envy what you could have for yourself if you only made a little effort, but you won't.

b)   That isn't love anyway.

What is love? Seeing the other as he or she is and accepting him or her? Nonsense. For that you have to start by accepting yourself with all your own defects and weaknesses (these are notes for a pusillanimous self-help manual!).

A slippery dream in which Duck and Pale Fire are combined. Duck arrives, handsome, thinner, with his face covered in freckles (marks of sin?), with an inner confidence, the same that he acquired in Europe and which was lacking on this last trip, and he shows me the marvelous photos he took last time—with subtle, superb colors thanks maybe to some filter. And the photos of us? They're like gigantic slides on folded cellophane paper. I don't like the fact that he's given them less importance than the others but, heck, they're pretty too. And he says to me:

"I'm going to stop writing and devote myself to photography and drawing. That way I'll seduce a lot more women, and only with a pencil."

"No, not with a pencil," I answer him. "With your pipi, your pipi."

And the dream about the man, which I see more clearly now?
I get out of an elevator in a hospital and run into a huge guy in a wheelchair. The man complains furiously:

"They just operated on my foot and the doctor told me not to put my leg behind me and here you go pushing it back with all your might. You're going to undo all the good the operation did!"

I try to say how sorry I am and somehow get away from this mess and all the people who've crowded around, but I can't and I'm even sorrier for the guy.

I stay next to this man in the wheelchair, and help him go here and there without anyone noticing that the guy is shrinking until at the end of the dream he's become as little as a doll, and I'm carrying him in my arms and then settling him in the chair, which has gotten enormous and has a ramp leading up to it, and I feel profoundly sorry for the man when he tells me that his wife and son are going to go live in the US and no one will come visit or help him. But he tells me all this without complaining, just establishing a fact. And he tells me that it's the second time in a month that he's changed his shirt and he doesn't have any more clean ones.

I wake up just when I'm considering washing his tiny dark green shirt.

It's been years and years since I washed a man's shirt; actually since I washed anything, clothes-wise of course. Maybe the last time was that very remote (dark green) shirt that Ch. left in my house so that he could somehow stay in my closet. I washed it just because—it was already clean. Did I wash it to be nearer to him, or to take out his smell?

Give, give, give. Give information about intimate occurrences. Has it become my obsession, this mania I have of throwing my life at other people, like a big bundle? Bundle or dart. Thrusting it into the skin.

A line of thinking that I believe belongs to everyone. And an engine that propels me, many times fueled by happiness, by the acceptance of and wonder at little things.

Late last night in the sordid square of Astor Place in front of the subway, that gentle music coming from far away, the sound of a flute always seems to get to me on the deepest level. The snake awakens death in me too—all coming from the manchai-puitu flute—but it was really sweet when the flutist came nearer, blowing that long, stretched-out whistle penis with all its holes through which a semen of notes gushes and bathes us.

How to give the happiness that the flute player on a New York night gave, and how to even consider living in another city where playing the flute isn't allowed, especially in the figurative sense.

I feel as though I've been twirling around like crazy all these years. Going from here to there, disorienting myself. And suddenly, in one of those twirls made haphazardly and almost blindly, I find myself here facing the true road: my own. The opposite of poor Dante in his dark wood. Now it remains to be seen if the good road produces some good work. It's producing this inner peace and I'm grateful for that, and it's producing the yearning to tell all. To go back, to leaf through notebooks, write down how I got on this road.

The vote of silence is not my vote. Nor is the respect for linear time. When all is said and done, we are this accumulation of time and words.

Yes, the unconfessable effort to create a paper person and to struggle against pretending not to understand. In other words: understand as much as possible, and especially never be disinterested.

An Afternoon in Washington Square

To be anonymous for a few hours. Sitting on the grass (in patches now. I remember when it extended like a carpet, covering the enormous flowerbeds in green), drinking some carrot juice right out of the bottle, waiting for the moment when something that's hovering around will strike me: a Frisbee, a ball, a skateboard, an idea; or for someone to recognize me. This is a dangerous place, almost the NYU campus, in the vicinity of the New York Institute for the Humanities and other such job-related sobrieties. A really old couple goes by, she flirtatious and standing tall, dressed in sport clothes, completely pale green from her head to her toes, from her socks to her small Swiss hat. They must be Irish.

Nearby a radio is oozing hard rock. Far away, at the other point of the diagonal, far, far away from the great circle of the fountain still without water, some jugglers are making their pins dance in the air to the exact rhythm of the music that I'm listening to but they can't hear.

This park world so filled with people nevertheless has the placidity of a direct contact with nature. Human nature, in all its varied and extravagant splendor. Today the pianist of a single note has dragged his piano out anew, putting it directly under Washington's Arch, scanning the Twin Towers from afar; today my favorite transvestite all covered in different colored wool is crocheting a new cape, sitting on the same bench as always, in the arbitrary but no less reliable skating zone—today is a day of incredible skateboard pirouettes. How do they transmit their messages to one another so that they all come together at such harmonious, secret meetings? Another day it will be rollerblades making decorous jumps, and another, who knows what, and that's why I come back again and again to be dazzled by something new.

Moments of learning, of taking. Taking without trying to apprehend, without the voracious intent to retain. The role of hunter no more. To no longer be the net, but rather the butterfly. Invert roles.

Burning disjunctive: to take the bull by the horns or the cow by the udders?

After an exhausting tour of lectures at different universities and cultural centers, going halfway across the country, I'm beginning to enjoy the strength of the spoken word versus the written word. The truth is I prefer to think writing rather than think speaking, but suddenly the idea of thinking aloud traps me because it's like offering your live thoughts to others. Only, at times, the poor thought is more half-asleep or dying than alive. But it's worth trying, so that's why I changed the title of my talks, modifying them as the days and locations went by, and putting together new puzzles like a form of writing mentally, on the road. Maybe these are merely excuses to justify my innate disorganization. Like the excuse that I found to justify my untidiness: whenever I have to look for whatever got lost (papers, books, pencil), I'm actually putting my ideas in order. And sometimes, with a bit of luck, I find something that I wasn't looking for and the search therefore becomes invaluable.

I remember when Alicia and I wouldn't say the word lecture, because these were a burden we weren't anxious to assume, instead deciding to call them Claudias. It was much easier to say, "I have to give a Claudia somewhere." It made us feel freer, with fewer commitments, less attached to formalities. And now, putting together these journals, I think of that memorable tour with Claribel Alegría through England and Scotland. They took us from one city to another, from one theater to another to read our works. In Oxford, for example, we both believed we were talking to a black, empty theater, it was so quiet, without a single audible breath—it was like Kantor's *Dead Class*—but at the end, the questions were astute and pertinent, and we knew that no one would ever listen to us with such devotion again. But even so, Claribel told me as we were on our way to the next meeting: "I feel like a trained seal that has to repeat the same acrobatics one more time . . ." Adorable, admirable Claribel! Since then we've called ourselves "the little seals."

My vision is getting blurry and I don't know if it's because of the bad light, my age, or the subject under discussion. I'm inclined to think it's this last, so I'll try to change the subject as quickly as possible.

I breathe deeply, gather my courage, and again take up the puzzle of being a writer.

Writing is a completely different matter, although now writing is also full of holes and injuries. The other issue is the realization that writing takes me to the fringes of an anguish that is so unbearable that it's better to run away and get involved in something else, something else however likewise curdling with the anguish and the guilt of non-recognition. That's precisely why the moment has come to let loose, really let loose!

A lot of Skidmore College, a conference about Cabrera Infante, Pepe Donoso, and yours truly, a lot of PEN and New York Institute for the Humanities, which were and are—absolutely others' recognition of me as a writer. Now it's my turn to do the same. Accept myself (in continuity, like a line that's progressing without the hiccups of piecework stitches) (but . . . every line is a succession of points, don't forget, especially don't forget the points, even though what's progressing are years!) or explode.

I should add, "as a writer," thinking perhaps of extricating myself from all the other stuff, from my necessary self-recognition as an independent, self-made person.

But perhaps recognizing myself as a writer is the most difficult part. Along with it, somewhere or other, comes a very hidden, very primitive sensation of killing the mother. Especially in my case. It will simply have to be done: kill the mother that we all carry inside. Like the king of the Golden Bough. Killing the king, killing the father is man's obligation. And women: Electra, Clytemnestra (get more into this).

To get out from under the mother, I've written about it somewhere else.

The sensation, for these few days anyway, of not needing a man to protect me should liberate me from some of the pressures. For these few days anyway, there is the possibility of a local guy who could and seems to want to protect me . . . I have to see how much I like him, how much I can accept him without destroying everything and how well our chemistry works together. I think it's pretty difficult, if it weren't for his measured but constant interest. On the other hand, when have things ever turned out easy for me, eh?

Battles badly digested keep floating around in my interior lithosphere. Freud swallows it, Elaine de Beaufort told me, and she added: it's very important to keep the reason for rage safe. And that's done by writing very clearly from the beginning about the event that started it going. Later it's enough to reread that paragraph to relive the whole scene and what followed . . .

I've been writing it for a while now, and what I have most of are titles:

- The Ark
- You will Caulk it on the Inside and Outside (Or: You will Cover it with Caulking)
- Chronicle of Demons
- The Book of Bad Love
- In the Name of the Game
- Dark Desires and the Others
- A Street Walker

Titles that say everything that needs to be said. This way, nobody has to write anything.

And love. I think I wasn't going to talk about love anymore, I intended to bypass it. Not completely forget about it, no, but circumvent it somehow, incorporate it by omitting it. Never by forgetting it.

My first night with S when I finally accepted after he was perhaps already tired of trying. And he was unable to live up to the friendly circumstances.

That's what I get for going to bed with someone I should only have shared a table with, a round table, or, at the most, a couch.

But he is a man of principle; I'm sure he'll be capable of winding things up as best suits us.

And now I'm waiting for him to call me; I hope he won't turn out to be an imbecile, that he won't disappear after the—let's say—interruption:

"I didn't know about those lateral effects of grass," I told him.

"Lateral, that's the word," he agreed.

So we fell asleep that night holding each other, and woke up as strangers. I called him yesterday and he sort of growled at me over the phone although later he apologized. Don't think I'm going to call you again—I already showed you my goodwill, now it's your turn.

Days later he asked me if I was mad at him (or something like that).

"No, quite the opposite. Now I feel more affection for you."

An appreciation of human failure, proof that we are not machines. The tremendous charm of the fallible (a word that everyone will realize derives from phallus).

Beginning of the Species

I approached the perennial plant of the woody and elevated trunk that branches out at more or less floor level and stretched the part of my featherless biped body that goes from the wrist to the length of its fingers in order to collect the edible organ of the plant that contains the seeds and is born from the flower's ovary.

The reptile generally believed to be of great size encouraged me in my difficult project which was soon and resolutely accomplished. Then I urged the male of this species of two-handed mammals belonging to the primate order and possessed of reason and language to begin eating the plant's organ. He accepted my proposition feeling whatever is felt by a creature experiencing pleasure.

Few things have a name, for now. I think they're going to call what we did a sin. If they let us choose, though, we would know to call it a thousand better and more enchanting names . . .

So the plan to stay on an ascetic footing with my professor friend and confessor went completely to hell, though not without a fright, God knows why. Or else, perhaps even God doesn't know, but in the depths of my little soul, I do: because we already knew each other pretty well, because we'd been circling around each other for quite a while, if during very isolated periods, because with him I would have liked to have something real and I didn't have the courage to say so.

Although I don't know if you really have to say anything—do you have to speak words, or can you just let them ooze out of your skin? (That is if they ooze.) Saying them is a risk, of course, but necessary to be able to enter into the hollow zones belonging to what's been said. Where you find the ineffable, or at least the unsayable.

Why don't I ever believe declarations of affection? It could be because of my own doubt. Not insincerity, no, but always doubt in relation to the other (is *this* the one? I always ask myself, and I can't decide). Or no. It must be the other side of my own inability to speak.

Apprenticeship of Silence

As if things were that easy, as if a poem were able to say something in a single thread, and prose on the other hand were able to weave a plot and darn together a difficult, reflected reality.

Saying what isn't said, at what moment of my childhood did I learn the official language of silence? Or better yet, at what moment did I catch the vice of not being able to express what I feel aloud? Later came the more or less heavenly sensations, the encounters—misencounters—and I couldn't say a word, not I love you, not kiss me here where I like it.

An extremely important moment because useless: the one when the guy shows up who talks nonstop about himself—which is another, more elaborate way of not saying anything. These guys talk and talk, offering everything without listening to anyone. They talk not to get trapped in the silences; they talk just to talk, and they talk and weave the most beautiful stories that any mind could invent, but don't know how to dialogue. Then they happily go to bed—with someone or without—completely satisfied with a job well done, without even suspecting that the real conversation is still to begin.

Later, one of the really taciturn ones shows up, the kind that look at you with deeply grim eyes and make you feel like smiling, just to be silly, but not even then is he able to or does he decide to feel like saying what he feels. He can only stretch out his hand at certain moments and caress your face. He can sometimes—barely—express his contentment with a sigh or a slap on the rump.
He can't say what he expects either.

*But he can at least look you in the eye and express so many things
that way—say I love you with a hug.*

*And afterward—or more like during—you are mute, unable to utter
a word, like kiss me now and I don't care what happens later.
You can only halfway formulate an invitation—a half-question and
a quarter of any kind of demand—intimate expressions that offer
much more than they demand, that leave you open and vulnerable.*

*Thanks to some twist of human nature you learned to be silent, and
now this:
Demand that others change themselves without recognizing at the
same time that without a mutual transformation, love is not possible.*

What I haven't learned nor am I learning is how to draw the line—
to say, that's far enough, we've gone far enough: stop.

Will I learn some day? This journal (spiral of itself) is testing
me, to see if I can indeed draw the line through the years and find
myself again in that line.

It would be like limiting yourself to a telegraphic message: some
sleight of hand Stop a more or less deep kiss Stop a look Stop
maybe before before Stop

A trap. This isn't the message. The message is other:
If I keep muddying things up, I'm never going to see clearly. I'm
never going to wait for the waters to calm enough to be able to see
to the bottom. With the waters of desire calmed, will there even
be a bottom?

I'm always stirring up the waters, giving them one last shake, clouding them, clouding my eyes with desire, clouding my sight, not see-

ing any farther than wanting to be embraced, to be cradled, to cradle, to submerge myself. And finally trying to curb desire without managing to completely. Aloud with Dieter, in a muted voice with S, frightening myself. Escaping through some invisible tangent, but always accepting. Acquiescent. Open. Open for others who close themselves to me, or pierce me, or overflow into my hands (water between my fingers, fine, warm sand; me open, but perhaps not enough, accepting a form of fear halfway down the road).

I know that I want to stop and at the same time I don't want to stop. I know that with almost every man I'm with (and who is with me), I tell myself for a few instants, this one, yes, this one is a solid branch and I'll make a nest there. I say, this one, yes, I say this one solid branch and at the same time I jump onto the branch, I shake it, I nibble at it, I find a thousand defects in it until finally the few straws (oh! oh!) that I put on it fall to the ground and are scattered by the wind. And once again, I'm flying from here to there without a nest, searching for some local baker who's waiting for me with the nest already made and with freshly baked bread. Nice and warm—as warm as possible.

Having slept with S (and slept is the right word, although we did kiss like crazy), he makes me feel like someone who's left her secure platform and has jumped into the void. A guy whose company I can't seek out now, to talk—if tangentially—about my problems. Even his seminars are changing—now jealousy has reared its ugly head. I want him all to myself, with his intelligence intact (is this what that famous devouring is all about?).

Today I'm going to see Dieter, back from a long trip. Today I have to write my new lecture on censorship and nevertheless these other stories are obsessing me. I hope to be able to talk to him, clarify things.

I wonder if I need an analyst and if that analyst is S—even though now I can't tell him anything.

Why do I keep jumping into the void? Why do I endlessly repeat my joke from when I was twelve years old:

Diving headfirst into a pool when there's barely a foot of water there . . .

They give me a foot of water, and I dive in, damn it all.

I envy Dieter's Pierre Cardin waist, in other words his confidence in being handsome and so deserving of nice things, his self-sufficiency. An extremely intelligent man, and yet I don't envy his mind. With S, I envy (it unnerves me how much) his ability to invent, to organize while inventing, to tie up loose ends in order to arrive at a conclusion.

A guy who seems so inexperienced, mamma mia! And there's an age problem with S (which I've always had: I always felt older than most of them) and that feeling of not being on the same level as them. Is it a competitive spirit? An unclean, competitive spirit?

Maybe now I'm waiting for S, for him not to be a jerk, for him not to make a run for it without even having succeeded in finishing his first assignment completely.

"I didn't know about those lateral effects of grass," I told him.

"Lateral. That's the word," he agreed. And we fell asleep holding each other, under a lot of blankets, only to wake up later as strangers. I called him and he sort of growled at me over the phone, although he later apologized.

I'm sure not going to go after you again, again. I already showed you my goodwill; now it's your turn.

I tell S that Phillippe Sollers once told me, referring, of course, to anything but the possibility of my sleeping with him, "The sexual act ends up killing dialogue." We're not going to let that happen to us, are we?

During the seminar, S says: "Women are the great other, the great foreigner."
  I object: "For you. But not for me."
  Some other woman insists: "For us, men are."
  S: "No. That's a modern idea. Archaically, man is alone, and the stranger is the guardian of the fire."

(How great, S is as intelligent as you are, and with no sense of abstraction. Personalizing the Other, one could say.)
And besides, how dare you try to shut me up instead of fucking me!

Luckily, and in self-defense, my sadness turned into anger, a feeling that's not very compassionate but much more productive (if not generous).

What can you do with men who don't dance? Why get near men who don't know how to express themselves with their bodies, move their pelvis? At least with Duck I know that I awoke other movements in him. Other waves. In spite of the distance and his absence, that man is mine. I made him, in more than one way, and I know it's true that without me, he won't find himself again, like he said. It's just that I'm not his here and now, I'm not his sacred space, the place where he can really develop his eroticism. He's still inside his barbed-wire shell, which I managed to untangle so many times, but so many other times just stuck me.

I had that miracle in my hands, and I opened my hands when he came back to me, then turned my hand upside down and let it drop. Should I have kneaded that clay one more time? The last time it happened so naturally, involuntarily.

Almost without intending to, I've put myself on a diet. Do I feel like erasing myself from the map? Disappearing? More like wanting to feel good and be able to dance across the world, move house—as I'm always doing these days—with lightness, not weight—dragging myself from one place to another without knowing where to land. No. Lightness and indifference. Like a feather.

Time. I'm always wanting to shake people up, accelerate time. I'm right to do it now, feeling as I do that only few years are left to me. But as that sensation has been with me for a long time now, it's become a habit, something that alarms me and soothes me at the same time.

Actually, I think I'm waiting for Dieter to call me so we can repeat the other night, Wednesday night: Dancing, walking, eating mussels—so like vulva (and he meticulously lining them up: >>>>. "Very artistic," our waitress told him). Me talking about Bahía, about the fear, the magic, about Candomblé. How did that subject come up? Ah yes . . . throw a white flower to Iemanjá in my name when you're in Puerto Rico by the sea. And that other miracle: discovering that you can cross all barriers and there's no danger at all when there is deep inner security. But it has to be something so rooted, so profound that it's not a question of will but rather of impulse. Can faith move mountains?

Some other time, I'll talk about Bahía again. Did I write about the cocaine playboy? These anecdotes become cut up, flat, from having talked about them too much and having revised them in the process.

Home again, my new sporadic home, Dieter naked, on his knees on the platform/bed pointing his splendid penis at me:

"Do you like it?"

That color, that glorious violet color more like vulva than penis, something so sweet (and here I'll ask for help from Alicia to describe that smooth purple delight). Help to describe it, not to touch it, no, not to admire it. I do something with all the lights on that other times I've done kind of in secret, almost hidden. I lift my index finger slowly to my mouth and get it really wet with my tongue. Then I run my wet finger along his penis, lubricating it, caressing it with spit like from a snail. Several times like that, in slow motion, looking at it with eyes full of desire, not with modesty or shame. Then I put my finger in his mouth, for him to get it wet, and I run it along his penis again, communicating with each other like this, revolving around the phallus like Lacan says the human race always does. But the phallus Lacan talks about isn't here, and this one is—and how—even if we might call it by other, more common, much less solemn names.

And then I don't remember. Not the moment of penetration or what happened or how we died together. A strange block, although at the end extremely satisfied, I get up from the bed to wash myself because I'm soaking wet and don't want to stain Cathy—the soft, silky comforter that was lent to me: a very suggestive gray, a gray that goes so well with his purple cock, although at that moment I didn't think to contrast them.

If Dieter calls me now I'm going to say: I'm thinking of the color of your cock. Even if he doesn't expect a woman to say such things. Actually so little is expected of women in terms of sex. Just that they open their legs and shut up. I open my legs, yes, and I shut up for a while although it might be good to say certain things at the critical moments. I shut up perhaps because I learned to fuck aboard ships, and the ships' partitions are so thin, so revealing.

I really do have to thank Théo for that, among other things. The respect, the delicacy with which he took me the first time. Love. Why later did we have so many fights over the other stuff, the domination? Maybe Théo was basically only masculine, and I took his attitudes for personal aggression, not the generic kind.

And being so inexperienced, I couldn't understand it; and he being so young and arrogant, he couldn't control it, and so we kept butting heads.

Today I feel like forgiving, under the guise of love. What's happening to me?

To conserve this state, this feeling. Like when I went back to the high bed with Dieter, and he had already wrapped himself up in his sleeping cape, distancing himself from me and embracing himself, and I'm trying to take him out of that invisible cape while he's grumbling a bit.

"Help me get back in the mood," I begged him. My body's mood, more like.

"That deserves a kiss," he said and gave me one. Why don't Dieter's retractions seem as aggressive to me as Pale Fire's? They don't awaken in me the same desperate desire to flee, to leave the bed in the middle of the night.

Of course, this was *my* bed. And I have to admit that PF's behavior wasn't the same in his bed as when he was a visitor.

Something to remember about Dieter: he arrived with his bag and inside it, a kimono that fits him so well (and kimonos play a certain role in this story), and his shaving kit and vitamins and even photos of his country house in Provence. And he says:

"I'm a snail. I bring my house with me."

And I remember Salomon Resnik who always said that you shouldn't uproot yourself, that you should take your roots with you wherever you go.

The hard apprenticeship of self-protection, so different from vulgar cowardice.

Dieter protecting himself, not wanting to get involved in something sentimental. Maybe. He's right: he's leaving for good in twenty days. I should be grateful for his barriers. Although the last time he showed the same tenderness as on the day we met.

Steps backwards. The result of swimming against the tide. Because it's all very well to go against the accepted norms, but it's not a question of BACKING UP. I read in an article on Doris Lessing:

"I think most writers must have to start very realistically because that's a way of establishing what they are, particularly women, I've noticed. For a lot of women, when they start writing it's a way of finding out who they are. When you've found out, you can start making things up."

And here I am, after more than twenty years of making things up all the time (not that I mean putting make-up on them, disguising them) and I need to—finally and only just recently—write my own stories perhaps in order to know who I am and especially *where I am*. Once again, what a find! Luckily I tend to forget all this weight stuff and gallop happily around my worlds, both exterior and interior, country and city.

And this is a city that doesn't skimp on worlds; this is a city that gives them to you with open arms, throwing them in your face— the most diverse kinds of worlds—and poor you if you are distracted for a second and you don't juggle them as they come at you, intermingled and exultant.

I should sing the praises of all these confluences that offer me the gift of being everywhere at the same time, and of course I never stop doing so. The silly thing is that when I sing, I don't write: I frolic. I levitate. I warble. I howl at the moon with happiness.

In my part of the Village, on foot, I can walk through the whole world. Gastronomically, visually, with my nose. I do it all the time. I know how to pick out the remedy for whatever situation I find myself in. Am I very agitated, confused, do I need calm? I head west. Do I want an almost demonic intensity? East. North to be able to advance toward the world of tomorrow, south to put myself instead into art, Italy, China, into the sea, into surprise. I walk, and walk, and walk. And I recover my joy and I don't write.

Some day I'll write an ode to the two cities I've really loved in their respective moments. The Buenos Aires of my adolescence and very first youth, the New York of the '80s. They offered me their secrets. Paris on the other hand didn't succeed, or more like didn't want to bother. An Argentine myth that I skipped over, that I lived from the inside, at the beginning of the '60s—maybe that's why.

For now I just write down what I regret. Blank paper like a handkerchief soaked with tears . . .

Many times I've found myself out of my element in situations that are too important.

Who will give me back that desperation to grasp the meaning of Beckett's manuscripts, strewn all over Francis Warner's rug in Oxford, and me knowing very well that it was vital and not even managing to be present mentally? Who will give me back the bubble baths prepared with such devotion by the person who was so important to me at the time? Who, who will give me back everything I've lost, what I knew I was losing as I opened my hand to let it go or as I spoke the sentence calculated to scare him away?

Passion is a smack given in order to unsettle me.

I need laughter. I also need—now—a really clear line. To avoid escape through association.

To not go to bed with that guy looking for some kind of support or company, but only because I feel like it. Why S? Why not J, for example? They're all the same jumble, the same mix.

I know that with Dieter something happened this last time we saw each other. I know it. Does he? That moment when, already far away from the car, I turned around to say good-bye and there he was, lingering, staring at me. Or when he offered me something in his house as a souvenir, and I didn't know how to ask for anything.

And the idea that I should be the one to give him a going-away party. I'm sure he'll tell me something on that last night, and I'm already going to know what it is. From the first night I spent with him, waking up feeling that this wouldn't end here, that it was just beginning.

Enter into the other's universe, into what they tell you they have, and then what they really do have. Because for myself, here, I hardly let myself have anything at all. Perhaps my motive is selfish: I want to be a passenger, not the captain of the ship. I don't want to absorb them into my house. I want to invade other people's houses.

I'm only just being born. Although I'm no longer young, like Macunaíma.

And I'm always trying to insert myself into some myth in order to feel supported, that I exist, since reality doesn't support me one bit. Or does it? Maybe I'm doing all this work because the other stuff seems rather opaque. Or inaccessible—which isn't the same, but they have a family resemblance. Like those grapes that are usually green.

Why try to understand? Why want to join? The things people say when they mean the opposite.

The price of a certain form of clairvoyance that doesn't explain anything anyway (doesn't *clarify* anything).

Now, instead of creating my fictional beings and trying to understand them, I'm trying to understand real beings and sometimes even create *them*, and then, to complicate things even more, I try to incorporate them into my fiction, and everything becomes a great big boring mess.

The end of this tumultuous month and also of this experience of writing if today I give it all I have, and very carefully.

I'm rotten from having discovered gunpowder. With each step I rediscover gunpowder and what's worse: I rediscover it for myself when all along I already knew about it in some deep and secret place inside me.

I must admit that I've just discovered a book that amply replaces (as far as my own growth goes) anything I could write here. *The Dialectic of Sex* by Shulamith Firestone. She is proposing a sexual revolution, which is perfect for someone named Firestone, but Shulamith?

Male writers are so lucky. Without this constant need to rebel, to fight in order to establish their position in the world. They start from an established situation, from a *fait accompli*, and from there they can just snoop and analyze and build all they want.

But I'm not going to complain. No. Better to rescue my rage right at the beginning and give it a good shine without falling into a simplistic hatred of men, whom the unforgettable Greta once said with a sigh, are so well made!

In some ways I'm more a gay man than a woman: men never stop being an erotic object for me. And a beautiful penis is a work of art, no doubt about it.

Given that S and D threatened to come see me, I can toss a coin and maybe even not let it fall and choose PF instead (he came back from a trip yesterday and made me go running over with the keys to his house, which he did *not* need, and received me very affectionately). But I realize that I've already filled the album with little figures. Enough of playing musical beds, as Erica would say.

Interesting symposium, with a few *crises de conscience*: there are ghettos and there are gay/tos, both equally exclusive.
    The specular image leads back to the speculum. Speculum as a mirror that opens possibilities of looking inside, taking the vagina as the other face of you-know-who (equidistant and inverted: that is, concave for our various convexities).

Pale Fire very gallantly comes to help me solve some problems in the house, and actually does very little, promises more, and talks about his position in relation to women:

"I'm not in a place right now to be able to commit. It's as if I wasn't hungry. You can put the tastiest dishes in front of me, and—nothing happens. But the next day I could be dying to eat them." (Recognition on more than one occasion of perhaps missing out on something important.)

"Oh well, your loss," I answered him. "And no more deceptions please."

Dieter called me at 1 A.M. in the middle of some unbelievable noise.

"I'm in a restaurant, celebrating after my lecture at Columbia," etc. etc.

"You're calling because you want to come sleep here."

"What on earth are you thinking? What a bad opinion you must have of me, such terrible thoughts! As punishment, you won't have your reward."

"*My* reward?"

"Well, our reward. I'll call you tomorrow. Bye-bye." (In a singsong voice.)

"Don't be a jerk."

"Bye-bye." (In a singsong voice.)

"Bye."

I got angry, of course I got angry. What does he think, little golden dick? If I called him in the middle of the night, I'm sure he'd get mad. Why didn't it occur to him that I could have been with someone else?

The next day, he called again. Oh Dieter, *la Récompense*, little golden dick! I exclaimed. And he apologized, that he hadn't realized how late it was, etc., etc. And I was thinking that this could be an awakening as well as a disillusionment on my part: what at other times I would have believed was passion now I read as invasion. Or simple lack of courtesy.

I told all this to PF (and Margot, who is visiting, thinks I should have kept my mouth shut), and PF perhaps understood and kept his cool, staying with me when Dieter came over to bring me his new book, just out of the oven (this baby he shows me—the one of flesh and blood he carefully hid), and to say that last night he'd been drinking before and after the lecture, as I'd probably guessed. Of course. And PF, waiting patiently for the other guy to leave. But at that moment Margo and Cathy arrived, and the parade of people began, culminating with S showing his true colors, defending war and IBM, all multinationals, etc. Disgusting. Which he tried to excuse (later, when we were alone), and his confession was that he was really afraid of me, which seems to be a fear of women in general. Anyway, I didn't tell him what I thought about all his bullshit; instead I climbed upstairs toward the bed for a fleeting, but rather soulful session with him.

Before that, S talked about his ego, that he had suffered by putting himself in situations that he couldn't control (too much fear in the atmosphere). And why are we afraid? I asked him. Instead of answering me, he talked about his trip to Paris, about meeting Lacan (personally through his secretary, as Bustos Domecq would say), something which should have strengthened his ego. He said that he didn't know anything about the relationships between men and women. He didn't know anything, look at that, and who's the doctor of psychology here? Why so much Freud, so much Lacan, and so much intelligence then? I mentioned the threat of devouring, sort of in self-defense.

"I for one wouldn't dream of devouring it, but it would be nice if you'd let me take a little bite," I clarified.

"Why not?" he accepted.

And afterward, re: my complaint about men:

"Yes. Men are a real pain in the ass."

"Mainly for gay guys," I remarked. But perhaps I was mistaken.

One day I told José G:

"I've had it with men. Enough already. I'm not going to worry anymore: I've completed my album of little figures."

"No," he said, alarmed. "No." (Of course all my good friends have a great time hearing about my amorous misfortunes; only *I* get kept awake at night). "Remember when we were children," José insisted, "remember the little Kelito figures in those long ago chocolate candies of our childhood; the album was never complete—the toucan was always missing. You can't finish until you get the toucan."

My personal zoo is pretty complete, actually. My collector soul has emerged once again and here I am forever in search of that big disdainful bird (because whether it's one bird or another, it always ends up being more or less the same thing, no?).

Today I've decided to fall in love. In other words, I will invest my affection—but not all of it on the same bet. I will diversify my game. I'll put some tokens on that tropical island where there's someone who doesn't even remember me but who was so sweet, and the rest of the tokens I'll put around here, in this merciless and beautiful city, but I'll put them on many different options and that way I avoid, for now anyway, doing what I should in these cases. I won't put myself—as a certain friend did—on the roulette table, crying out, "I'll bet my entire body!" No. I'll save myself for other, more appropriate occasions. I don't applaud myself for that.

Relating then to the conversation on Thursday with PF: the only bet that is worth making is on looking for the impossible. Not love. Maybe. No. Because love, blind as it is, can make huge mistakes— I would know!—rather, we should look for understanding. Look for a good relationship, not jumping from one to the other to see what happens, but rather simply rejecting all the bullshit from the beginning. Not letting the humiliations happen in the first place, not accepting anything that hurts us just because we want to get something (least of all a good fuck).

And today I was thinking: if the relationship between men and women, or the relationship of any couple, whoever they are, is a power relationship, then I don't want it. Because if I win, I lose. Who wants the defeated one at his or her side?

As it's the age of oral sex, each time there's an ad in the subway with a woman's face in profile, some guy draws a dick in front of her mouth, complete with balls. But this question of oral sex isn't so much about sucking dick as it is about talking. It's time for us women to talk about sex, brazenly, in full flesh, very fleshy.

How interesting—at the round table the other day Margo referred to the mouth that talks and the mouth that gives birth. I spoke about absorptions. Two sides of the same coin?

I live, so to speak, lost in the supine confusions of style. And not only of literary style—lifestyle as well—and this even though there's no doubt that I've been loyal to myself in more ways than one, however you look at it.

It's just that the need to be drawing everything line by line is wearing me out at the same time that it's keeping me going, keeping me stimulated.

What luck, ladies and gentlemen. I'm running on fumes that nonetheless go to my head. This strange and vital way of getting at the propulsion behind *what it's all about.*

Yesterday I began to die. Today I'm still alive.

I have to start slowing down, letting loose to be able to test myself at each step, to be able to gather my strength.

The problem with loving a man is that it soon doesn't fit anymore—not the man, love. I feel too much love for everything that's alive: stones, rocks, mountains, rivers. Too much love, which makes me vulnerable when I start to expect everything from just this one being who's put a mark on me (who has branded me) with his embrace. There is too much love for those who get near me, the homeless, the strangers, the flowers, the insects. (Who sat on a bench in Mexico City—on Paseo de la Reforma—for half an hour, observing a caterpillar? It was a beautiful blue and orange caterpillar and I left it on the bench after observing the flow of its juices, leaving it intact, compassionately—to be squished by the first passerby, perhaps.)

Who observes and observes? I travel in the subway and I observe the adolescent, nothing but hair, who suddenly takes out his turgid marker, substitute for the phallus, and draws a heart and some letters, secretly, lost forever among the thousands of other graffiti marks. He writes, I write. Both of us, surreptitiously and rather afraid—only he's risking more than I do and writes less. Where does the value of graffiti lie if we both cross the bridge at the same time? He could write more, and I could write better: are these terms antagonistic? We keep crossing the bridge in broad daylight. Very soon we delve once again into the dark tunnels. We retrieve our masks. In the tunnel's darkness he will once again be, because of his name; he will draw a heart and repeat himself anew.

I will return to being just another anonymous human, malleable and unrecognized.

Today I went looking for the new figure. The toucan. None pleased me so I will keep looking, as I should.

I did buy another notebook, like this one, only green. Remembering about notebooks. Doris Lessing, *The Golden Notebook*. Virginia Woolf who in her diary writes that she couldn't go on if she didn't get a certain kind of notebook with a hard black binding of which there were few in London (and she was in the country) during the war. Margo, the college notebooks she prefers. The much-lamented Alejandra Pizarnik and the little Uruguayan notebooks she liked so much. Mark Strand who proudly showed me the ones he had bought in Italy, very beautiful and stiff (a bit like him), to start his novel in; this while he gave me his love stories about estrangement to read, and I made him touch my notebook with his soft calligraphy: touch it, touch the notebook, since you're never going to touch me (because you don't have the nerve or because you don't want to?).

Tomorrow, theoretically, Dieter gets back, and he has two days left in these latitudes. Do I feel like seeing him? No, not really. I don't feel like seeing anyone in particular since nobody is willing to really give me a hand.

All the other stuff is the surface of the depths I claim to be in.

Moments of pulling myself together again. Putting myself in my place. I thought that Michel was coming because I received a letter from him, and yes, he may be coming, but with another woman. How could I expect that he would have waited for me all this time? And yet, why not? As if I couldn't compete with the other people who are already here. Suddenly I thought: Michel is the only guy I feel like seeing because he is simple, because he doesn't complicate my life.

How about that.

Today I found an old sentence of mine: "Men only think about one thing: their mom."

Heberto Padilla, Pablo Armando Fernández, creating characters. Ángel Rama. Emir's stories about *gaucho* literature. Stories that begin with a joke and end on a more serious note. ("I'm from the place where the Battle of Masoller that Jorge Luis Borges talks about was fought.") I'm from Melo, the land of the *gaucho*, etc., etc. Some people start out by imagining themselves as fictional characters, and end up believing it.

From imagining to believing, just one step.

Conflict: If I'm here far away from Anna-Lisa, it's to get the most out of it, professionally, and on the contrary all I want to do is shut myself up in a corner and write all this that has nothing to do with my profession, or my achievements, or even with real literature.

I can't find the toucan to put on the cover of the new notebook, and maybe it's better that way. It's not about finding the toucan, it's about the search.

End of the red notebook. End of the chimeras? They try to stick you to the wall with a pin, to freeze you. And they nail you. And trying to get away, you leave bits of flesh on the wall or on the pin. Bits of skin that still feel pain.

What good is all this? How can I use it?

Like the other afternoon in Kingsborough with the myth and the Puerto Rican professor who talked about having known Evita because he worked for the CIA, looking for political prisoners in Argentina. What? And me, feeling drunk, as always when I'm on the outside of something that I think could interest me.

The dominant ideology.
Vallejo demanded a place for man.

I don't want to be vulnerable anymore—no more handing myself over, letting myself be crushed.

Dieter hasn't called and it's his last day here. Will he leave me the pieces of wood, the ones he calls his statues that are really *objets trouvés*?

Dieter says he is a snail. Carrying his house (photos of his house) with him. Robert Graves talks about snails: if one snail eats another, it inherits its memory. Incorporates it. It must be not to lose his memories that Dieter resists being devoured. Yummy little snack. He opts instead for going away without having shed a drop of the other. Retaining his own juices. That way, I save them for tomorrow, he said laughing. Mistake: tomorrow you would have had more: using it makes you produce more.

He also made a slight, insinuated complaint. Michel weighs on you, I told him; the other guy I told you about who was also relatively young, doesn't he weigh on you? Michel weighs on you because of your blue eyes. Everything that is transparent takes up too much space to be tolerated.

You make me uneasy, he said.

And since when is tranquility good for a poet? I answered, quoting Graves in my way.

Counterattack. The hourly, instantaneous, moment-to-moment reconstruction of myself. Drawing myself by hand.

Dieter, before returning to his country, comes back in order to leave me not only his pieces of wood, but also cabinet (the cramp-iron is for me, I won't share it), his nuts (the edible ones that you have to break open, not his own), and several other things. He arrives full of affection and charm and leaves me his memories. His pieces of wood. His lights, the candles, the only copy he has of his book. As offerings. The good-bye is short, the absence long, says Atahualpa on a record I don't have and would like to have had Dieter listen to.

I fall into romance with such felicity, with such phallicity.

What am I saying today? Luckily something very different from what I'll say tomorrow.

You gentlemen! Just an accident on the road (or changes in my mood). Men like mirrors. Only now do I understand. I thought I was seeing myself in them just as a reflected image. Now I know that I use them as reflecting material. Some are concave, some convex, and there are some who give me back little threads of light that I then deny.

Run away? Never: it would be like stagnation.

The snail fabricates its own spiral and grows. Men spiral into themselves and diminish until they disappear.

I know. Or I don't know. It would all be the same.

Nothing can fill me as fully or importantly as my own solitude. Happiness. That's it. In each meeting with someone new, I start losing myself, and when alone, I find myself.

And the security of being so comfortable in my skin during sex? That also. But it's too fragile a security as far as securities go.

Am I perhaps interested in searching for a sure thing, a lasting love?

Dieter really pouted and suffered when Barthes died—such an un-expected death. Later I suffered too. Now will we both suffer in our different parts of the world, or have we grown apart in that too?

The sole wisdom of Duck's notebook: having only suggested, named something that I know about myself by heart. A name for each thing even though they're my own things. The proper name.

Will I understand my own handwriting? And if I don't understand it, what does it matter? The only thing that matters is the power of the already written word.

Do you understand me? Maybe only a poet could understand me, and I've never liked poets.

Dieter returned to his native land. S was swallowed up by the earth. PF is still friendly and distant.

Erase everything and start over?

Another one is wandering around near me, and confesses:

"I was raised by women. It was years before I realized that they aren't the ones who decide everything."

"They aren't?" I ask, and lose interest.

Come Back, Solitude, All is Forgiven

Now we don't even have solitude. Where has it gone? Sometimes some tango evokes it and I remember the times when there was solitude and I even miss it. There's no solitude in New York, or in Buenos Aires, or in Tangiers, or in any of the cities where I learned the hard way about being alone. When you lose solitude, you walk around with your ivory tower on your back, or more like a cheese sandwich inside a glass bell. Protected, yes: the bread doesn't dry out and the cheese doesn't turn into cardboard, but what about contact with the air? I wonder if that contact with the air called solitude—which dries and uses you up—isn't necessary to be able to commune a bit with others.

Me, you, him; and the space of solitude between each one, configuring the vehicle. The link.

Without that sense of solitude I'm lacking now, there can't be an "us" either, because the distance—real distance, not as in "distancing"—lets you gather strength and then jump. A true meeting.

Something like finding your place, and all the resistance along the way. Mine too. I have the pieces of wood and I put them in the perfect place. The day after Dieter's departure (rather touching good-byes all around), Pale Fire came over and put his own works next to them, to complement them and perhaps to distract my attention.

Now I go up to my bed above my (ex) men.

Sometimes I daydream about Dieter. Something different from nice romantic daydreams. Something that was left floating, something immanent in front of the sea. A lot of let's say civilization around but also boats and seagulls. Why?

Because the sound of the sea is the same everywhere in the world next to the sea (the same). Because the smell of the sea is the same. Because of me. That's why I close my eyes and my dreams flow together. All just for me and all just as sweet.

Janet's house in Carmine Street that I'm subletting had (has) three of my essentials, things that I've grown very attached to lately: a Montblanc pen that I'm borrowing now, a filing cabinet that's just howling to be filled, and a little pencil sharpener machine. So nothing stands between me and writing!

Nothing, and least of all this sensation of being *la Machi*, a witch doctor, *la curandera*, the one who helps. Ms. Repair, bah. An acceptance of being single, but also of being near others.

Who built the barriers? He put down some sticks (less than he would have liked) and I put down others. Meetings that link to each other. If his appearance, Dieter's, had occurred at another moment and not so soon after the return of the web-footed bird, would I have reacted in a different way? I was under attack then by the themes of seduction and deception, all in the same bag. And maybe that's what tangled Dieter up somewhat. Well, nothing's in my hands anymore. In my hands, only the Montblanc that fell out of the sky and my new realization of being *la Machi*. But this is a secret that I'll develop, without giving it away, somewhere else.

I'm being Squeezed

New notes from the world underground.

I get on the subway and know, even without its being clearly defined, that I'm entering the world of writing. These cars have all lost their sordidness thanks to the enormous colored letters spray-painted on their exteriors. Fortuitous letters, incredibly elaborate: true works of clandestine street art.

Inside the subway car too there is no end to writing, scribbling. There are names, signs, curses. And the boy in front of me, with his eyes painted pink, puts his leg over his (male) friend's leg. He's not writing, or is he? Tracing a love story with his body.

The one who writes is the other one, over there in the corner he writes when he thinks no one is watching him, takes a big fat marker out of his pocket and writes his name really clearly over the other old scribblings that are now somewhat effaced. *Sam*, he writes. *Sam.* I look at him out of the corner of my eye and he doesn't care: we're accomplices: I too write. His lines are black and firmly traced, mine are red and have their own special slant. His thick marker as a phallic substitute. My thin marker barely marks, okay, but it produces a good flow of red ink from its tip.

Which of the two of us belongs more to this underground world? Which belongs better?

We both write about the same character. It's just that Sam can't continue his narcissistic, repetitive work: too many people are getting on at the next stations. They're even pushing me down the long seat—they're corralling me. I'm now next to an old woman drawing her own characters on little slips of white wrapping paper.

It's a good exercise—she feels the need to explain to me. My models are free, she adds when I'm already almost on top of her papers because of the crowd. Luckily she spoke to me in English—I don't want anyone to read what I'm writing in Spanish. So many people who know hw to rd Span I'm surr by Hisp abbrv—being squeezed—1man—yes—1 man almst on tp of me—can't see his face—my rd hat conceals it—dt let him rd these wds—he's coming nearer—pushes hat bk—he's tall—gts closer, 2 close—his zper almost tching my mouth—shd I bite him? Push him? No, I lift my pen—better a really visible red line on his light pants—yes—and now I can write freely because nobody can see what I'm writing. When we got to Forty-second Street, the man got off, terrified and speechless, and the rest got off after him, in a hurry not to miss their trains to the suburbs. Sam has gone, and I continue on to the Village, and run out of ink.

I say to myself: your aunt isn't here, to know the streets you have to walk the streets—not claim to study them on the map. To know men . . .

And it's the same with words—you have to know how to shout them, shake them, in order to know about words. It's necessary to shake words like dice, grab them by the tails until you find the rest of the sentence. The ultimate wisdom.

Now I don't know if writing this multiple diary hasn't been a mistake all down the line. The production line, yes, putting in all my insights, my small discoveries and perceptions outside myself, confining them to paper and separating myself from them like someone who wants to shake free in order to finally forget—though forgetting isn't the worst that can happen to us in this world. Forgetting ourselves, our intuitions, perceptions, insights.

I'd already written it down on a previous occasion: To look for equilibrium in others is to hunger for the absence of oneself.

And then of course I had the dream about the little dog, all wet from his own diarrhea, a wound tearing through his flesh in front of my eyes. But I find the magic potion to cure him, a mixture of gringo ointment and the *Clinal* of my childhood, and the wound gradually stops bleeding, leaving only a tiny bit of blood.

Waking up, I realize that I am or was that dog: having wet the bed.

I'm finding so many canine allusions in these journals.
Like:

1. Like someone's dog. Being obedient. Wagging my tail.
   Not always but sometimes . . . poignant. Because once
   I was obedient. Other times I wasn't so obedient, but al-
   ways wagging my tail. My backside. The rear, as they say.
   The tail. As if that was such a small thing.

2. Why do I have to live with a dog who watches over my
   every slightest gesture and endures all my awful taunts?
   This question could be shortened to: why do I have to
   live? With my tongue always hanging out and with the
   suffocated expression of someone enjoying herself.

3. It's a dry impulse, without membranes that offer any
   resistance; it's the fleshy drooling of nothing, the green
   agglutinant of a blossoming vegetable. I live with a dog
   and like a dog, but with so many buts and why and hows.
   Although most of the times I read a question mark in the
   dog's eyes, framing the whys and the how and the when.

4. My dog's eyes recriminate me and I throw her a kiss as if
   a kiss could fix so much of my wasting myself on other
   stupors. Today I'm happy, what can I say, and my dog's
   eyes fade and decide to ignore me. What foolishness—I
   shout getting into bed—so much foolishness over nothing more than the uncontrollable amazement caused by
   some chance contact! The horizontal, howling dance, that
   music that emanates from each one of our pores. He's already left and now I'm alone or perhaps not so alone because my dog is waking up now and starting to howl. She
   too, howling, as if in our memory.

So many things have happened, and so many internal transformations. But before anything else, since we're walking through zoo-dreams, I'm going to write down what I remember about one that also left me wondering, a few days ago now, left me identifying with the animal, as one should—

I was walking with María Luisa Bastos in a small garden and in front of the gate there was a big mother owl with her wings spread, feeding pasta (later I thought they must have been worms) to her enormous baby who was lying face up, fallen from the nest, with one eye injured.

The right eye. Upon waking, I wondered why—if I'm going to identify with the owl's daughter—I had this eye thing and not for example an injured left ear, which would have made more sense. But lately my headaches have been giving me neuralgia on my right side. Look at me, still depending on my mother to feed me!

Chronicle

I was invited to San Francisco to a big poetry festival. I accepted, delighted. After all I came to New York to fulfill a contract, one semester, which was extended, but always with the idea in the back of my mind of moving to Northern California as soon as the opportunity arose. San Francisco, the beautiful city that was so talked about in the '60s; Berkeley, those dream places. I didn't even think about what I'd actually do at this festival, me the self-confessed, convicted prose writer amid a hundred or so poets from all over the world. Read stories, they told me, don't worry, there must be some reason why you were on the cover of

American Poetry Review, they told me, without knowing about the shock I myself experienced on entering a bookstore to buy who knows what and seeing myself there in full view, *in vera efigie*; I turned and ran out of the bookstore before anyone could recognize me.

In Frisco I was supposed to read before or after Miłosz, Kenneth Rexroth, Richard Brautigan, and all the rest, and only José Emilio Pacheco as a fellow Spanish speaker. Of course, when the moment came, my head was bursting, and the organizer of course offered to read a few lines for me, adding insult to injury, poor me, no, no, I said, I don't know what effect that could have on me, I better just do it and that'll be it. It came out all right. Anyway, cocaine or no cocaine, headache or no headache, who can even remotely compete with a recital like that of Amiri Baraka/LeRoi Jones, for example, an unforgettable show because he sings, jumps, dances, howls, shouts—whispering a long poem that I can't describe as good: it's dazzling. And since we're on the West Coast, where paths cross, the very American Rexroth reads sitting in the lotus position to the rhythm of samisen and subtle drums played by solemn Japanese musicians while a Japanese woman poet reads to the rhythm of the saxophone and drum and almost loses her voice trying to impose herself on the anarchy of this jam session.

I come back from beautiful Frisco having made two decisions. First: I prefer New York, unreservedly prefer it; next to this explosion of a city, belly-button of the world, all other cities—not to mention the Californian ones—are like painted cardboard.

Second: to accept a challenge that's been hovering around me for a month.

Playing Hide and Seek

No. I'm not where you're looking for me. You count to a hundred, I hide somewhere difficult, and you lose your patience. Whatever your name is, however old you are, and whatever color your skin is. And me? Where am I in all this? Where do I usually hide, hoping not to be found and not having anyone find me? I am the real hidden one—it's not a game for me—and they are simply inconsistent,

Joe

Dear Alicia,

This letter is an attempt to contribute to what we could call our files on better understanding the male of the species. You tell me stories, I tell you stories, and one of these days, we'll be able to put something together, the two of us. Nothing is lost; everything is transformed.

Imagine this: some time ago, I went to a party, and sitting on the floor chatting with someone, suddenly I raised my head and, oh New York miracle! Up above and staring at me was a beautiful face with very almond-shaped eyes, very, very long almonds, a fine nose, high cheekbones, an afro. It seems I took a while to react, because the young man (only twenty-eight years old, what can I say) immediately got down from his chair and started talking to me. Newyorican, he was, strange, friendly that night, and verrry enthusiastic. It was around April. He called me a bunch of times, came to see me, and me playing hard-to-get, fearing I'd catch something. And not from racial prejudices, I concluded, but rather from social (I have to admit) prejudices. A guy from the Bronx, after all, from the ghetto—

a poet, yes, but not that much of a poet, who revealed himself to me little by little: he left home when he was eight years old, living in the street and in different institutions and correctional facilities for minors where he naturally learned all the tricks and horrors and tried all the drugs—he even stole cars. And at eighteen, he enlisted in the army to go to Vietnam, married a prostitute there, brought her here and they had a son—he got in some program to quit drugs cold turkey where they cut off your dose of heroin just like that and you turn blue and desperate and suffer unto death. But he survived pretty much unharmed. Problems with his mother who doesn't love him and you wonder why not, sporadic presence of a little brother: a very corpulent and rather fierce kind of giant, who, here in my house, would be unable to stand up in the attic, which is really my bedroom, where the ceiling is precisely two meters above the floor. Here, okay, not a big deal, but just you meet him in one of the dark alleys this city is so well furnished with you'll be scared shitless.

My Joe—what other name could he have?—appears every once in a while to claim his pound of flesh, with the utmost elegance I have to admit, and me denying him, he offended, but always coming back, luckily coming back each time I thought he would until, zap! My dream of having an affair with a black man became reality.

He's mulatto, and that's why he has such fine features—a Cherokee grandmother to boot, and there you have his high cheekbones, and I won't tell you how delicious he is . . . I went to San Francisco and found myself with all those poets—Ferlinghetti, LeRoi Jones— who had traveled so many miles' worth of experience and if I measured their words, my head would spin. Why did they invite me to read, me the black sheep among so much local poetry? I can't explain it, but I'm very grateful. Especially since, when I came back, one evening Joe told me, What you need is a husband, and me, be-

ing a wise guy and quoting the feminists, said, No, no, what I need is a wife.

I know you understand me, Alicia; what we need, jewels like us, is someone to take care of the house and things while we bury ourselves up to our ears in writing. But a wife with a penis, of course— only just phallic. Anyway, he understood too and said, I'm going to be your wife, and there, boom, I succumbed.

And it was a marvel, honestly.

Afterward I wondered why I'd been wasting so much time with white men these past thirty years or so. Because this guy really does trust his body and his skin is dark caramel colored, and so very sweet. He doesn't run away from showing affection like others around here we know so well.

That's it for now. It'll continue in the next installment. Hugs and kisses.

As you can appreciate, Joe is excellent literary material for me. And I hope to be acceptable vaginal material for him in turn.

Now I know I kept him at arm's length for such a long time so that he would see me. At first he only saw himself reflected in my eyes when I discovered him and thought he was so beautiful, the night of the party. If we could know something, beyond simple perception, if only we could know—but there are no manuals. We'll have to make the rules up as we go along, one by one, in the flow of life, as well as break them.

If I start writing Joe's story now, with all this time ahead of me, when, when will I dive into and submerge myself in my novel? The novel will come when it comes, but please let it hurry.

I want to talk about Joe because, yum yum, he's the most delicious thing that's happened to me in years, and if I really am experiencing a change of attitude toward men, that's not going to stop me from marveling at them. Especially when they reach that degree of beauty, of tenderness, of glory.

I became a mother at twenty. I could have been a mother at fourteen if I'd been interested in something other than climbing trees. Tomboy, they used to call me then, as well as cowboy, because my friend Tunchita and I wore jeans all the time. Yes, we were already precursors in those days, and very iconoclastic for the time.

Only for me to have been your mother—at fourteen—someone would have had to come between us: your father. A handsome dark father, darker than you in order for us to give you that glorious skin color. A young father, a lot younger than you are today, an intense father; and me climbing trees like Calvino's Baron, carrying you snugly and securely, tied on my back, stuck to me.

I prefer the way it worked out: how you're stuck to me on those nights when my bed is the tree, high up in my loft. Today.

There is a wooden ladder with nine steps to climb up to my bed. On the landing I put the big-penised idol I brought back from Puerto Rico and from a supine position I can only see its wooden cock, horizontal and a bit shaky because of the spring that holds it up. I retrieve the image of this morning, when I saw Joe descend by that wood-colored stick, erect, so crazily beautiful. The next time I wait for him down below, open.

Look at this! How details overlap. Where everything is related and in agreement. Maybe that's why I want to write all these stories of romances, of impossible love and non-loves, to finally get to the marrow, to the internal threads, to the plot that unites them all and forms the central intrigue of the novel. Get to that nodal point, the conducting thread.

So now I see the cause of possible mix-ups in the culmination of all these encounters and running around. In other words, on Sunday we took off on an excursion to the Bronx. Joe wanted to show me the tough neighborhoods of his childhood, tell me his story *sur place* like the Peuser guide.[4] But his places weren't there anymore, and he was diluting himself among the fragments saying, We used to live here when I was seven (and it was only an enormous pile of rubble on some corner), around here was my best friend Charlie's house (and it was a vacant lot). Like someone back from a war, poor Joe, and seeing the earth scorched and nothing growing. Dry empty lots covered with rubble, not like the tree-filled lots of my country, not even that. He could only perform one real homage: peeing into the air, from the top of a stone staircase, to perhaps try to delineate precisely where his childhood house had been. Shaking his penis right where he took off his black nanny's underpants. Exhibitionist homage to his first experience in love.

And the long walks under the burning sun, in the middle of such desolation. At one moment, I touched his arm to transmit a brilliant idea to him: since he was sick of having a tattoo that said Mom, no less (he'd been missing his mother when he was in Vietnam, but here now, so many years later, as he'd repeated so many times to me, it just wasn't right): If you're sick of it saying Mom

---

4   Translator's Note: A book full of information about Buenos Aires and later, Argentina's cities, roads, train schedules, etc.; anything you had any doubt about, you would look up here.

here, I have an idea, I tell him, and he breaks away from me furiously. I only wanted to propose that he underline the word upside down, and add an exclamation point: wow! Then it would be and wouldn't be the same.

But Joes gets furious and the walk ends just like that, all hell breaking loose.

I realize a thousand years later that I chose the worst possible moment to suggest a change. What can you ask of a man whose childhood neighborhood has disappeared, whose past has been erased?

Joe comes and confesses to me, They used to call me Lobo. The Spanish word pronounced in English has a nice ring to it. Lowboe, not bad.

The bad thing about wolves is that every now and then they go out howling with the pack. They sit on the steps of boarding houses and drink beer out of cans in paper bags to hide them from the police on patrol, their wolf mouths drooling with hunger, and they say they're talking about life but really they're checking out the women who pass by, while life—the bitch—is passing *them* by.

Depressing perspective of the urban wolf.

So now I'm a wolf tamer. Domesticator more like. And I had dreamed of brandishing a whip, saddle in hand.

They say that when my grandmother became a widow, she began using a whip on her seven sons. It would seem that I inherited this fascination with whips. I would like to be a wild animal trainer but fate doesn't usually put wild animals within my reach—only a puppy, or some other animal who likes to put on airs, but with little consistency.

That's why on certain occasions I start lashing the air furiously. Lashes of blind fury and many times I hit and punish myself without meaning to, too distracted to be careful.

Joe sometimes recovers his untamable nature and while waiting for his orgasm, gives out a sort of death rattle. A Beethoven chamber music piece that he can't manage to finish, always on the brink of sounding the final note. One more turn of the screw, a few more shakes that seem to be the end, but no, don't you believe it. Then I start getting the hang of it and begin the concert again with some piano solos.

Later I realize that he has feelings all right, mostly of self-pity. He makes enormous efforts with me, is tender and good and makes breakfast for me and all that, but then there's suddenly the threat of rejection. Everything he's had to put up with in this life, all that he can't be or do. Write your novel, I tell him, but the problems are too immediate and he gets furious not having his latest whim satisfied on the spot. Like a little boy. And I tell him, enough, enough, go away. And he goes away and later comes back and I let myself be tempted again because he's so soft to touch although not always soft on the ears.

And soft to the palate? Oh man, no!
    I have to learn now how to talk in the negative, black, like we've been talking in this house recently. You are *bad*, woman, Joe tells me stretching out the *A* a lot. Which means I'm good. Today, anyway.

Of all the rear parts of men, I'm most interested in their necks. I never would have thought it, but there it is. As much as their hands, for instance. And I realize that this habit of appreciating the hairless backs of certain men's necks comes from long ago. I noticed another man's neck, years ago in Buenos Aires, and now I can't help staring at that line, so pure, so perfectly vertical on Joe's neck, made with a plumb line.

Heidegger says, if I've read well the little I've read, that the essence of truth is freedom. It's worth keeping the opposite in mind: without a profound truth—that is, without self-deceit—there is no freedom possible.

Sometimes I get very solemn like this. What are you going to do? Especially when others envy my mobility, my life, and I know it's enviable and realizing that weighs on me.

Devoting myself to transgression isn't easy. Or better yet, it's not comfortable, peaceful. I've entered into a vaguely Manichean struggle between good and evil and feel that I'm the very center of that struggle.

Sometimes you accept the game of seduction because it's the only way of being alive. But as soon as you're really alive, the seduction game becomes unbearable. The joy of being a woman in these times: not letting yourself get distracted for a single minute. Like living in New York: don't let yourself become frightened or intimidated, taking refuge in the warm and sleep-inducing comfort of habit.

And once again escaping him, again and again. It's not that Joe doesn't respond to my demands. One way or another, he does— sometimes at the wrong time. But then he makes demands. With silent screams he demands something I sometimes know how to give him, but at other times I refuse to listen and shut myself up inside where the screams reverberate louder and louder and all my membranes vibrate. I go away and I call him. He comes and sometimes seeing him come from far away makes me want to run. Not when I have him near. Very near—his eyes in my eyes—I turn to liquid. We penetrate each other so deeply. We penetrate—in other words we are integrated into that other reality, which is desire.

My dream last night: a very white Joe, looking a lot like that Wolfgang in my Paris adventure. Or maybe it was Wolfgang in the dream. He refuses to clean some wounds I have and don't know where they came from and I'm hurt, offended. And now I think: Wolfgang is called Wolf, logically. And Joe, Lobo. I begin to understand that I can't just shake him off of me; he's like a tick. He already has some of my blood. He is a part of me in the—symbiotic?—way I'm a part of him. Something of each other always stays, something of ourselves goes with the person with whom we've had very close contact. How many transformations, how many new beings will we become with each one who rubs up against us? Moreover, each one of them—and me too—are already made up of everyone who has passed through us . . .

Damn, I've lost track of the dates of everything, burying myself ever deeper in my ostracism, not wanting to see or call anyone and at the same time feeling like such an oyster, so *other*.

What I get for identifying so much with my mother and staying in bed more and more to write. It's very easy to write a diary and forget about real creation.

I would just like to note this: why did I stand so much shit, so much cowardice, from D and PF, who hardly showed a gram of tenderness? I've found all the tenderness I'm looking for with Joe, after all. Is it because there's not a profound intellectual understanding? Although there is understanding. It's just that, of course, we don't speak the same language.

All the same I'm going to write about what I like now. That skin so smooth, that luxurious male. Deprived of everything. Not owning a single thing, not even a pin (but very carefully ironing his feathers). He is a pure male, he is a big, affectionate feline, tender; he's the one I've been looking for and who fit in my hole. I know he can't be for me, but I wear *for me* like a hat. Because I know what he is. The famous toucan? His beak is just the right size, not too small, not too big—completely harmonious, like someone from my country said—and his skin is dark more from silk than feathers, as if they had sewn it onto him, without folds or wrinkles or even a gram too much, or any bones protruding, or anything at all unpleasant to the touch. Just that skin stretched to cover his muscles like hunting animals made for caresses. Caresses, caresses. Such a sweet mouth, that color between my legs, hair like steel wool, warm mouth sometimes cold tongue, the cold skin of that black, unfamiliar hand reaching the secret. The body. The language. The scream that can't be held back. The volcano. I am the subtle stimulator, I give to receive, I navigate through what some people call love and others out of modesty don't give any name.

But enough of verbalizing! Now I have to flip the switch—maybe turn off the little light we have—and penetrate the darkness to see what's happening there (I'm something of a Nyctalops, you know—I see best at night).

What else? A few days have gone by since I wrote the above and I know that something's missing. Maybe it's something I don't want to confess, or maybe not. Maybe it's something I don't know yet and that—with a bit of luck—I'll soon discover.

Three Desires

Melanin-filled desires
Dark
With smooth skin and
Shiny eyes
Three are left now
Because the best has been fulfilled
—or perhaps it's the best just because
It's been fulfilled—
And as everyone knows, desire
That is sated
Becomes something else

One is jumping rope in my memory
Forever
Shiny with oil
The other forever looks blue
Under the French moon
Of a certain July 14th
The third
Is still changing
In my memory
Seems alive

We write each other letters.
I dreamed I didn't want to lose him
And I can assure you that I didn't want to.
I lost him a bit further on
Because of one of the usual confusions.
I didn't lose him for good, like the other two.
I didn't reject the encounter.

One is jumping rope in my memory
Shiny with oil
Smiling and getting prepared
For the fight.
I must have looked at him
A little longer
—it happens to me in these cases
I don't know how to hide my gluttony—
Light weight
Loosening his muscles
Warming up
They're like water flowing underneath
That dark skin.
Water and earth, this man,
And sun inside.
That's why I wish him luck
In the ring.
Good luck
For what is not going to be
—promise not kept—

Before

And after
The fight.

He approaches me after the fight,
With a champion's halo
  One eye bruised
His face a bloody mess,
The fury left behind
Gentle again, he invites me for a drink.
I decline:
I don't want to dry myself with the towel
He had to throw to the competitor.

I never finished this supposed poem nor did I write about the "best" of the desires, but it's obvious that my passion for blackness comes from way back. Now, since the third desire is ongoing, I can't write about it yet.

Mexico

The yearned-for vacation—but also a yearning for what I'm leaving behind.

Friday, a trip to the market in Toluca and to Isabel Vlady's town. Wonderful. The story of her sister's sister, a professional water taster, no less, married to a Mexican cowboy.

It must be my penchant for eternity—no less—that makes me want to write everything down, compulsively, as if responding to some kind of command. Or, as Kundera says, an absurd attempt to take in all universes. It can't be explained any other way. Immediate fame doesn't interest me, actually it scares me. If not, I would do something about the book of stories I've already written, instead of insisting on giving all my time, concentration, and energy to the novel about the Ambassador and Bella that I can't seem to write.

Now I'm once again in Mexico, and my life seems to be divided like this notebook, divided into sections in which I write down loose ends while I poke around in the story of the Beauty and can't seem to take off on this flight stuck on the runway. I have everything so well put together, following Raymond Queneau's instructions (did I write that down somewhere else?), chapter by chapter, a well-developed intelligent story, but then, of course— I'm not Queneau, not even Zazie—I try to start everything before I've even read what I've planned, to see if I can find my voice, my breath . . . which don't come out as ordered.

A miracle has happened. A surprise, because that's how miracles work. I've been offered an absolutely marvelous house in the southern part of the city, the high part: splendid garden, pool, dogs to keep me company and servants too to keep me company and to whom you might say I owe this stroke of luck (*aubaine* in French seems the appropriate word, since I'll be in the house of some very dignified diplomats, friends of my good friends the Wimers). In essence: I've been asked to make sure that the cook, the maid, the chauffer, or the gardener don't bring their whole families up here to stay while their employers are away. Fine, I'll take possession of the place. I'll become a lady again. A lady writer, even, if my novel finally feels like flowing out of me as it should. And if not,

182

well, I'll have a different game to play. Why insist. In this beautiful house, I will enjoy my vacation, being in the same city where my daughter and her boyfriend live, my wonderful friends here, the sweet consequences of accepting that my time as a writer has been brief and that now I am a lady professor. I will enjoy my deserved rest in August (there are three good things about teaching, Susan told me: June, July, and August), I who never went through grad school—only the sidewalk in front of that old café, what was it called, on calle Viamonte, where we all hung out—am now an adjunct professor of grad students. In English, no less. I should be satisfied. So here's an ULTIMATUM: if tomorrow the novel doesn't take off as it should, I'm throwing away the more than three hundred pages I've already written, and I'll change professions. I'll follow Darcy Ribeiro's advice that every four years one should find a new job.

My dreams last night were so literary that I still have hopes of advancing with my novel. The Scotch party, full of all kinds of ingenious things, and that other dream that's indirectly connected to this one, since I tell it to people who are with me as if it were something real, naturally: a writer who in the dream is a friend but whom I don't recognize when I wake up has a hydrocephalic son. The writer is sick in bed, on a stormy night and can't take him to the local witch doctor's healing ceremony. Someone offers to take him but we know that they'll get lost on the road. So all the women of FEM magazine, including me, go looking for him in the beautiful storm, with its warm nocturnal colors, and through luxurious hotels and various nooks and crannies, until we finally—I think—reach the healer and the son, but it's too late. The boy dies and the writer writes a story in two days telling the

183

story, and in five days the book is already for sale and it all seems scandalous to me. I don't know why this reminds me of the story of the hermaphrodite in Fellini's *Satyricon*.

A River of Words Will Flow

[Today, September 2002, as I put together these diaries again and try to reestablish the sequence of events, I feel it necessary to clarify that the much-mentioned novel about the Ambassador and Bella was aborted, and the day after the dream I wrote about here, the second day in Ingrid López Cámara's beautiful house—and I will be eternally grateful to her—the story of the Sorcerer began to flow out of me like a river, and became the novel *The Lizard's Tail*. It flowed so freely, so crazily, that I couldn't stop writing it, and so my notebooks only contain the occasional little trickle in their margins, outside the novel, milestones on a badly marked road traveled all in one go, until reaching its end.]

You would think they're applauding, but the women in the market are just making tortillas. Flop, flop, their hands loose.

A minuet. What we want to do with what we call life is a simple minuet. One step to the left, another to the right. Turn. Now the other side. Lose your direction. Find it again. Walk backward, forward, and carry on.

I don't know if love is a pure passion. Disinterested. Or if it's self-deception. That's it. The only pure passion (of purity) is passion.

184

I have better things to do on this day, I wrote down on some loose piece of paper. For example, to be alone and forget my cravings. A simple ceremony that just consists of not feeding my memories anymore.

A little bit afterward or a little bit before, which is all the same, the theme of gluttony struck me. Concerning Joe at first, but then the gluttony grew and I became omnivorous and knew that I would swallow any and all material that would feed the novel. I am an antenna when I'm writing a novel, and everything's food for me! And back to the leitmotif. This singular attraction to the dark ones. Why then have I always devoted myself to the light ones, so incredibly UNtransparent?

Dark desires and the others, the ones desired by me, men who don't know about tenderness.
And the other desires.
One of the recent desires, perhaps the main one or the most goading:
The desire to tell all, not let one word disappear.
Hunt the language alive.

The isolation of the texts, the fragmentation of the body.

Five pages a day and today I haven't reached my goal, yesterday neither. I think yesterday neither, I don't know how to tell a story with a lot of characters anymore, I get mixed up, and I've lost the humor of the opening pages. What a struggle.

Days have passed, I don't know how many; I don't count them anymore—now the writing fever has me by the short hairs. Of all the impossible situations I've put myself in—with writing, there's nothing else going on in my life right now—I manage to extricate myself the next day. My five pages a day are no longer a desired minimum, but rather a maximum: if I continue with this gush of words, I'll start to repeat myself, to get sidetracked, and this should not be a crazy text, but controlled, rational in its apparent irrationality. Galloping on a short rein, I wrote somewhere else—my credo, in a certain way.

Cuernavaca. A rest from the novel. When I've managed to create a good scene, I decide to rest the Chinese way, writing something else. A diary. What luck. As if these notes were something else. But they don't really make a diary; there are a thousand gaps, there are defections. There are also defecations, called shit in the vulgar tongue, but this is a *doing* problem so it's more defendable than any *NON-doing* problem. What's left to write about, on this sublimely tranquil day, are last night's conversations, the anecdotes the ladies and gentlemen threshed in the very long rural after-dinner discussion. Since we're in Mexico, the necklace of anecdotes that was being threshed mixed up the theme of politics with the theme of necrophilia, and now I'm getting ready to make a list so that it doesn't contaminate my novel. It's all a bit too close for comfort.

1. The really, really drunk guy whom his friends put in a coffin with four candles. When he recovers, he never forgives them. His own buddies, it's inconceivable. He'll never forgive them. Even though they were praying and crying!

2. The guy that was gored by a bull in a friendly, almost homey bullfight. The poor guy lost his most precious equipment. With no hope of a normal life, he became a seminarian. In the seminary, he had a cataleptic seizure and woke up in a coffin, this time for real. Then and there he knows he has to change his life. So he adopted a young puma to get closer to the wildness that injured him. Everything is fine until, following his new inclinations, he also adopted some young beardless youths for his more human pleasures. The puma suffered an attack of jealousy and wouldn't let anyone get near him.

3. The dead guy. The truly lamented dead man whose wake is attended by his drinking buddies. When the late man's family leaves to rest, his buddies take the cadaver, make the locals open their cantina, and put it on the bar to toast him. You can't leave us without drinking one last drink with us! they say to the man who has already left them.

What isn't apparent in all this: fear. Better to cradle it in your arms, take it up gladly, and return to the novel, where it shines in all its splendor.

[And as a palimpsest of my stay in Mexico, one small anecdote that I'm sure is a key, or at least wants to tell me something. I'll try to be brief. For the month I stay in the house, writing, writing, seeing friends rarely, everything works fine: I'm prepared delicious meals, Anna-Lisa comes and stays overnight sometimes in Ingrid's younger daughter's room, and we swim a lot. I write in the main bedroom because I was told that the elder daughter's bedroom, which looks onto the front and which I had chosen at first, was locked—her orders. Everything fine until the last night of my stay when I wake up in the middle of the night hungry and leave my room looking for a bite to eat and I see to my horror those shapes running for cover, and I know, like a flash of lightning, that I've lived a whole month in an occupied house, when I believed I was alone, multitudes were growing, that the families did indeed come and install themselves in the locked room, coming in through the window and taking possession of the rest of the house when I, the illusive foreigner, was dreaming sweet dreams to compensate for the nightmares I was writing while awake.]

The exercise of freedom is an exercise of renouncing, of not incorporating. You are less free when you most want freedom or when you most need it. When you most desire it? In that respect, I'm fixated on Joe. He is the seat of my desire. The bad thing: when I claim to be the seat of his desire. Sometimes I am. Maybe I am more than I suspect. He always comes back. Will he always? For now, I receive a few letters, sweet, minimal, with drawings. Unexpected. I want the other thing. For that I have to

Return to New York

And yes. Here in my own home, Joe has moved in with his television set and everything, although less with his actual human person, and I call him on it and have a fit and later I wonder why do I love him so much? What can I do all the time with a presence that doesn't take up more space than one hole or maybe two? He fills up the hole of adventure with his interposed person. I realize that I'm expressing myself with aquatic metaphors all the time, and not only in the Sorcerer's lakes. Also beaches, ponds, the river, the sea. All of it just to talk about human beings, yet I feel that I'm completely on target—aren't we around 90% water?

Another association:

Iemanjá

I've long invoked the Yoruba goddess of the sea. Sometimes I open my spiral notebooks and read them to find treasures and the worst is that sometimes I find them. Not always, but yes sometimes, and there are even big surprises, things really forgotten:

Punta del Este, December 31, '76
Today is the day of Iemanjá. A different day, the one celebrated in Rio—not Feb. 2, which the people in Bahia celebrate. Anyway I know that it's in some notebook or on some piece of paper, but these things never really get lost—there are always some threads hanging from somewhere—there's the story of Barcelona, when I did the purification thing and went to Sitges at dawn and discovered that the little mermaid statue had been moved.
Today I also did my ceremony, but much simpler. I just picked three white flowers and went to throw them from a jetty that appeared out of nowhere somewhere on Mansa Beach. The waves took the daisies out to sea and thanked me with a friendly crystalline splash, like a lick from a dog. That was it. Pretty good for such a gray day. Of course the sun came out later at dusk and here I am on the beach, before bathing, ready to greet '77, which begins at midnight, with a heavy dose of joy and the spirit of adventure.

This evoking of times lived in Barcelona comes to me from years ago, as well as the "pilgrimage" to Sitges, which I find in another very worn notebook:

Stories like clear spiders, pale ticks could come out of here as long as I don't let myself get invaded by pity. Something rather valuable for me could come out of this and I wonder why I want anything, and what does valuable mean. Maybe only bubbling question marks will emerge: ??????? The open question not upsetting anyone, not pigeonholing anyone or turning a corner with an air of wisdom. We are unarmed and seeing incorrigibly what is beyond our senses when everyone should know that what is beyond our senses offers nothing to be seen, only to be intuited. With intuition, solider things than time can be managed, the unfortunate ideas of those who have learned not to try to understand but rather to accept whatever happens.

Now I realize that by traveling all I've done is play with time, give it free rein to go as fast as it wants—as if this were a benefit. One more benefit—looking for it doesn't mean that I deserve it.

Simple vocation for the obscure dilettantes of the sea where the water absolves me. In other words:

an entire week trying to purify myself, searching, not a drop of alcohol or any other substance, meditating and muttering an awkward prayer or two. Iemanjá time and space. What is Argentine. What is hard, what is sought and not found, what is hidden. More like what is Brazilian, what is tender in me, what is secret. Smokecandleincense, the whole night smoke candle parentheses purification with the fish and I beg you to take away everything bad in me may you absorb it into your scaly fishlike unencumbered body, body of Iemanjá made living and now deprived of life, staring goggle-eyes veiled gelatinous rainbow-hued hardblack opalescent/silent pale staring black goggle-eyes rainbow-hued gelatinous hard hard eyes, pale succubus fish, found forgotten in the ice. Waiting for me, little tender silver and pink fish, little by little taking on a too weighty role in my mind, in my head, too much for the little fish who is transformed by my face my shoulders my chest, exploding inside its paper, decomposing in front of my eyes if I could see it, by my shoulders, my back, my crotch, my legs, little fish absorbing all the evil that's been in this body, all the evil that inhabits it. After the bath: ablution, purification, baptism, and enough of the symbol of Exú (appeased now) and fully assuming her amulet, the goddess of the sea's, (ah, Didi, if only you were with me . . .) after the white clothes, after having purified everything with incense, the time of the pilgrimage unfolds under beneficent signs: the train, going through the town in the solitude of the night, the auspicious appearance of the vacant lot before getting to the sea (a place nobody goes through and especially not me, the ideal space to throw the little fish and its burden of evil wrapped up along with it), and getting to the sea, the first fine rays of sun in such a dark sky and the shining cathedral. A jetty and an awakened sea, not the usual sleeping one, and advancing into the sea in between the waves I can see the day dawning, Feb 2 dawning and singing to Iemanjá closing my eyes to penetrate the secret better. A gray dawn, first, a sea of liquid lead tame one minute for me to throw in the white flowers I've brought for Iemanjá, and the fear of seeing her rise from the waves and then walking to where I do find her, a peaceful, smiling, full-bodied bronze mermaid, in a place I didn't expect her.

The truth behind the mask. The tedious, scrupulously and minutely cautious truth that feeds the, shall we say beauty, of the literary text (the mask): I want to keep it. Keep the writings that narrate the steps before the making of the text, or, better yet, those that narrate the tedious, scrupulously and minutely cautious anecdote that will lead to the tightened text.

To see beyond.

I'm coming home after the so-called performance of Leopoldo Maler with his own sphinx molded in ice, which was melting, and I think about subjectivity, in all that we had to give—what we voluntarily gave—for this to be an enriching experience. Let's call it that. Art, at such a level, requires such a committed participation. As well as certain encounters and circumstances. In contrast, others (and I think of Big Sur and about that moment when we discovered Emil Wright's house with Miller's ghost. And all the other stuff, all of Big Sur like a capsule of life in a single day. Thanks, Kerouac). A person definitely ends up reaping whatever he or she sows of added value.

Last night's terrifying dream. The full moon.

I thought Joe always came back with the moon but he arrived a day early. Wonderful, I have to admit, but afterward with the full moon, terrifying. I am a killer, he said at one moment of the night, just like that, and I took it literally and finally wrote his story—cold turkey—but I haven't stopped loving him because of that (with this restricted love that we're permitted lately). "The Word 'Killer'" is the name of the story.

Joe comes over and confesses to me: *They say I'm cold-hearted,* and I both find myself and don't find myself in that *they,* since I'm accompanied as usual. He knows that the accusation has a lot of truth in it and comes to me for help, to me no less, I who must also be his accuser, from time to time.

They say I'm cold-hearted, he says, but my heart is not cold. I have feelings.

And I, the person writing this, who isn't here to gather evidence, I hear the tacit questions: How to show such feelings? What can I do so that others know not to singe me too deeply? What kick can I give my feelings so that they finally wake up and flourish?

I don't know what to answer in my new role as teacher of gentleness. Giver of tenderness.

My first lesson of gentleness: make him draw. He draws rounded forms, slightly intestinal and morbid. Do I then recall my mystical experience with the fat intestine? Do I put myself in the ring? Not at all. I remember the experience but I don't tell about it as I observe him delve into a colorful drawing that includes me, and includes the novel I'm writing, and everything becomes phallic, intestine-like. Joe is almost naked, with a towel around his waist, a kind of loincloth that doesn't cover his private parts at all. His cock in front of me is almost a declaration of submission, since it is resting, defenseless. This is true masculine nudity and not the other. The other is pure bravado (with apologies to his honest face).

And here I am today, teacher of gentleness, and I can't even stretch out my hand a tiny bit to touch that tender gentleness of his. If I stretch out my hand, the cock changes, and becomes imposing and rigid. It dominates. And as we all know gentleness is a game of softness.

Now it seems that Joe was around too much for my taste. I started another argument. The unconscious reprisal on his part bought him a night in jail for carrying a gun. He wasn't using it; he was caught with it poking out of his back pocket. And they call me, no less, to vouch for him and confirm that he's a good boy. It's not hard to do, on the phone, and they reassure me that everything's all right and let him go. Good thing they didn't call my office at NYU, although in that university infinitely more worrisome things happen every day. The campus isn't in the Village for nothing. No. And sometimes my students and I go drink wine when we feel inspired and our writing is flowing. My writing workshop is from eight to ten thirty at night, and almost all the students write like gods—we selected them with a magnifying glass—and I feel that it's enough for me and I go back home to Joe happy, reenergized on Wednesday nights, and since he saw me dragging myself to class in the morning, he doesn't understand the change, or the energy that other people's writing gives me.

Joe too gives me his new poems. Some of them are beautiful and strong, like him, but he doesn't let me comment on them. He tears them away from me although later he forgets them on the table and I respect him and don't photocopy them or copy them to have them with me always.

Joe takes up his drawing again. A slow, fine work that he's been preparing for a while now (didn't I bring him colored pencils from my last trip?). Drawing, his hands are occupied (I don't know about his mind), and he doesn't get distracted.

Some day I'll talk about the burdens, about all the situations, the relationships, the feelings that become burdens. Joe shows me his old photo album. His photos of girls, naked, some soft-porn pictures, and I laugh and appreciate them, but secretly, I'm burdened. I accumulate more little grains of anger that will explode later in some argument, at the slightest provocation. Or the *best* provocation.

A worthy passion, anger—when it's not contaminated by any damn self-pity, that is.

As a response to everything I was writing before, Joe has now disappeared. Has he disappeared forever, erased himself? I won't move a finger to get him back, even though I know that on one level I want to. Only on a tactile level. A high level if you bear in mind that you get to my bed by climbing ten steps. He left one day, pissed off, as if I had thrown him out, and actually, there was some truth to that. He took his television and all his clothes, and left his squash paddle and his notebook of poems.

He came back in a week, celebrating, he said, for having gotten the job he wanted as a tutor in a reformatory for minors in New Jersey. Actually, he came back to fight and to tell me off since I hadn't gone after him last time. I don't know. Lovers' quarrel? And the next day, he was back in the house, fucking me like a god. And then? Swallowed by the earth. Which I hope (or not) will regurgitate him in time, before I go on tour again.

The Rights of Women over Ducks, Chickens, and Other Domestic Fowl (Except Roosters)
(and their implications in domestic life)

1. The right to pluck their feathers
2. The right to hit them over the head with a frying pan
3. The right to chop them up
4. The right to eat them raw
5. The right to shit on them from a higher tree

The right *they* don't have is to disregard the abovementioned in light of a better proposition in the chicken coop, or worse yet, the whole zoo.

I didn't remain graphically mute all this time, no. All this time I toiled away with the Sorcerer and did dedicate something to Joe in my writing. Now that he's distanced himself, I'd like to dedicate more to him (look at the rest of the texts around here), tell everything. At least the fears, their intensity, some anguish. Luckily, no more anxieties—have they gone from my life? That would be splendid.

Joe. Sometimes I felt tempted to make a novel of his life story. Maybe with a bit of my own added on. The fantastic thing about sleeping with someone is being able to enter another life, but damn! What a life, in this case! Going there makes me panic; there are zones that are just too dark. Vietnam, drugs, his criminal history, which he talks about with a certain delight, although many times I thought he must be exaggerating to fertilize my little novelist's soul. If he knew what I'm writing now, he wouldn't bother! But he doesn't read Spanish—the truth is he reads very little. What I consider important that he read. *Res, non verba . . .* not even written.

You can't walk through these streets; you can't even stick your nose in them. Now, immersed in Joe's story, trying to figure things out, I go out to buy coffee, that's all, and what do I hear? The howling of a voice, black to top it all off, emanating from the depths of some alley and hollering: Can you tell me what I have to do to be safe? Or maybe they said *saved*
Or maybe *sane*
And I wonder if it isn't the voice of my own conscience.

I'm feverish, sweating. What can I do to save myself, to be safe, to be sane? Or, all but the last one! In spite of everything I feel brave and generous and I want Joe to come back, even though each time I'm more aware of the danger. The mirrors. For some reason, I've just gotten up and have begun carefully cleaning the bathroom mirrors. Am I trying to erase his image? Some ghosts will stay forever. Some marks. The memory of Joe going down the steps from my bed to the floor, naked, so burnished. And me sometimes leaning down from the really high bed to ask for a kiss and him stretching out his arms, grabbing hold of the platform, raising himself with the strength of his biceps to give me the kiss (not like other kisses, not even on the same level!).

Mirrors have so much history, literally—far beyond the uses Borges put them to—so that when the adorable Nestor decides to have a welcome-home party in the apartment he just sublet while waiting for the ideal loft—diplomats can give themselves these luxuries—I decide that something has to be done about the damn mirrors that cover two walls of his living room. I come prepared to play a game I learned on the subway. I take along really thick markers so that we can each make our own graffiti and give this place a more human air (or less human—the multiplication of the guests in the mirrors is unbearable). So we all start painting and scribbling enthusiastically on the smooth, silvery, easily erasable surface, and Susan decides to repeat a then-recent gag she's seen in some station:

God is dead, she writes, and of course signs Nietzsche.

But it doesn't stop there. Underneath, with another color and handwriting, she adds

Nietzsche is dead

And signs God.

I've traveled to San Juan, Puerto Rico, for some lectures, and would like to have swept my bedroom, my room, my estate, I would like to have left everything tidy there. Not the disorder I left instead, not the fight with Joe.

So I'd already filled my album with little totems, eh? Well, well. There was another besides the toucan . . . the Wolf. Just the one I was missing. And that I'll keep missing. As long as I don't stuff myself with food. My demented attacks of actual gluttony are probably expressing other hungers. Other anxieties. But I feel really great in spite of everything! This is the best moment of my life. Maybe not the richest, but certainly the most enriching. Illuminating.

Back just four days now, and so much has happened. I even have to recopy this last page, crushed by the brutal Puerto Rican humidity.

Puerto Rico had some other things besides humidity that I should write about so I don't have to submerge myself again in my novel and all the trouble of getting back inside it. Return home and to Joe, who supposedly was calling me like crazy to say he was sorry about the little fit he threw before my departure. And here I am taking pleasure, amusing myself once again in his tenderness. When he shows it. But I've told him clearly that I won't receive him if he comes to me without tenderness.

I need Joe (?) to be able to put things in their place. Even though I've just discovered that he has that look in his almond-shaped eyes, elongated and dreamy, because he sees everything out of focus. Is that why he hardly ever reads books? Or does he see out of focus because he never developed the habit of reading? It had to happen to me! But when he touches me . . .

The Crystal I See With

Each new man is a new optical focus, a way of looking that we put on. Riding on the bridge of our nose, this man colors our vision and personalizes it with his personality, whoever he is.

Now I see everything Joe colored, I look for his likenesses, I reread Cortázar's "The Pursuer" for my seminar and I feel Joe in it and want to incorporate him into my system. My digestive system. Voraciousness, food, it sounds like an I Ching hexagram. As always, the gluttony of living itself lives vicariously, through others. Recovery of the mirrors.

I look and look at him. Sometimes he comes near me gently. His face comes near. I get nearer to it, and it's only a photograph—as if it wanted to kiss me—I want it to kiss me. How great to have him here in my hand like this, although even better would be having his hands here with me. How great that he gave me his long torso so that I have something to sigh for. And how great that I've sent him away so that I have time to sigh and not give him the chance to hurt me.

The deepness of the wound is usually in direct proportion to one's vulnerability, and I am vulnerable. I wound so, I love so. I wound and I love at the same time, attacking and defending, I too have skin: I am a drum and I resound with the blows that they give me and that I give them and which are never physical. He plays the drums like a god. He plays the drums and I vibrate. I'm a drum, once I was a piano, a flute. When will I be the whole orchestra? A combo at least. Actually, I'd like to be a baton.

At times, I have the baton, and then I lose after some exotic juggling, like when I try to be on a drill team. There goes the baton, flying through the air, and I watch sadly as it gets farther away, knowing however that sometimes it comes back to me, even falling on my head.

The Breath

I couldn't sleep because of a certain fear, maybe called solitude or maybe it has another name, but there is fear here too. And the night advances. Few hours remain for me to rest and recover, and the stories I read to relax don't help, actually they unnerve me, and the night brings its noises and its unknown perils and rancor, so I change the stories for a novel I've already read more than once, and reread several pages: "Talita slipped down beside him and began to cry quietly. 'It's her nerves,' Traveler thought" . . . and he goes to get her a big glass of water with some lemon juice. Always consoling, that Traveler, the other face of Oliveira, always so wrapped up in himself.

And suddenly I remember something infinitely calming, so fine. Joe, after the intensity of love, lying on top of me, pushing himself up with his palms, doing push-ups, and starting to blow on my face, my breasts, very softly, very tenuously, like the sound of a gentle refreshing flute, and I fall asleep, slowly fall asleep in Joe's arms.

What I would like is one thing, and dark desire quite another. I wonder why my dark desire has so much pigment, is so abundant in melanin.

Love is what's left after having satisfied your gluttony. I'm now submerged in a heady sea of gluttony and believe it's love and that's how I treat it. With a certain surrender and at the same time always licking my lips. What delicious love, what great satisfaction, what succulence; that's why I've distanced myself: the better to eat you with, my son. The better to nurse you, and for you to suckle at me. The taste of honey in your mouth, baby teeth, chocolate skin, your tender smoothness, your smooth wonder: crunchy like tempura.

Let's see why we have a premonition of so much stagnation. So much drawing that the hand grows tired. Written exercises, conversations, writings of a hardly ordinary explicitness. And playful. Playful, yes, and unbridled. Tell everything, don't try to hide anything anymore. If he has dark skin, then look for lightness. Try contrasts. While he fantasizes about being a strip teaser and shows me all his moves and I laugh and laugh and he rubs up against a tree in the park, pretending to be excited, a rather false sort of masturbation but maybe not completely, and I split my sides laughing, that stuff liquefies me with laughter. Liquefy me, like the tears of grief when faced with myself, unable to fully accept abjection when it's offered to me like that, so innocently.

Innocence can be a key and lost innocence the other key. And in between, this absolute indefiniteness that keeps us wobbling on the edge of an abyss. There's a step to be taken, and I don't dare take it. It's a step inside, deep inside. Of renunciation—not of gluttony. But maybe of affection.

Incapable of love, or actually something much more coarse. Incapable of showing love.

Dieter's fleeting return and what I thought would be understanding was after all complete misunderstanding. I told him about some chunks of my life during his long absence, and he told me that he would like to go to *that* place (Plato's Retreat), but I'm not in the mood. I would have liked to have an experience like that but I never did (Joe). You're too sharp, you see too clearly, etc. Tacitly, everything was said: I wasn't in the mood, I'm not in the mood, and you're too much for me, all those stupidities. And he told me that I have the mark of Cain on my forehead. I was already reproached in that hermannhesseian way, disguised as a compliment, some other time. I don't buy it any more, put that way. I had thought that this kind of lecture would no longer have an effect on me, even coming from such a delicious male. But it did. Galloping headache the next day. You have the mark of Cain, I've been told twice, so far apart, so clearly. Now at least I'll have to reread Hesse, as if I had nothing better to do!

A pertinent question:

For a headache, is a bath with Epsom salts or a bath with Mr. Epsom better?

If I is another, as the poet so wisely established, this other would write about me. And I would write about her, alternately, and once in a while—or else never—we would know who's dictating and who's holding the pen.

She likes to be alone and also (well) accompanied; she likes to travel the world and to stay curled up in her bed making herself write, dreaming about writing, telling herself that it would be better to go and bathe and stop getting annoyed.

It's in the bathtub where sometimes her best ideas come to her, and these ideas then get diluted like soap in water. Maybe that's why they're the best, because they make suds and wash, but this sort of hygiene isn't good for anything.

I would like to be a sensual, fascinating, sophisticated, solid lady, but I'm full of cracks where disproportionate currents of air flow through. I live disheveled.

What I don't dare devour (and is devour the word?), I swallow one bite at a time—but the food's too heavy, and there's a serious risk of choking, being tongue-tied.

On February 2, Iemanjá sent me her son Joe and I don't know if it was just to play a joke on me, because she's been taking him away again at night, and I don't like that.

In a world of magic rituals, how does one live? And how does one live (how do I live) in a world where you have to make up all your own rituals, one by one?

I told Iemanjá on the first of the month: if you think your son should come back to me, let him come back, and if not, then let your waters take him to other coasts.

On the one hand I hoped that Iemanjá would take him, just like that, to other coasts: I thought it would be easier. I wanted not to know anything more about this man who's tormenting me— albeit in moderation. On the other hand, I hope he comes back, although maybe it would be better if . . . I told myself. And he came back.

In other words, I said: if Joe wants to go, then let him go to hell and if not, let him come back, but a little bit gentler, no? And if I said that to the sea, to Iemanjá, it's because I have the habit—I have so many habits—of looking for intermediaries.

And it works. The object of desire is once more within our reach. And the metaphor as always ready to become flesh.

In the middle of all this my strong monthly hemorrhages are a vile conspiracy: *a river of blood will flow*, I started to write and then hemorrhaged after almost the whole novel was done, the novel which for the moment has around twenty equally valid titles. I only want to write down the psychosomatic shit here. I had to almost finish the novel before I realized that I myself was acting out Don Bosco's old prophecy. I had to have a D and C and hear Joe tell me, well, if I died he was going to miss me but he was used to it, he'd seen a lot of people die in the street. He was scared, I immediately translated, but not without applauding his merciless indifference.

Now I'm seeing Manhattan from the "front" end, closer to the bridge. I'm returning from a vicarious maritime experience. Mystic is the name of an ancient, beautiful port town. The sea, whale regions, those kinds of Melville-esque things, the lands of Eugene O'Neill. It could be the opening to another text.

My life seems to be full of memories of love . . .

I miss a certain quality of light in Buenos Aires—red and yellow lights, lost in the mist. I do return home, at least once a year, but it's not the same. Arriving in Ezeiza is a bit tricky, like walking on embers. The guy in customs scratches his ear and I think it's some kind of signal to take me away before I pass to the other side and am walking on Argentine soil. I walk through the streets a lot and think I'm being followed. Something takes me back to the times when I would visit friends who had sought asylum in the Mexican embassy, how I helped Stella go back to her country, or before, when I worked for the magazine *Crisis*. In any case, the situation hasn't changed, quite the opposite, it's stagnated, and there I am in New York making all kinds of accusations and having published what I've published and I wouldn't put it past them to have it out for me. But still I go back for short periods, and now I worry about Joe too.

"I don't want you to go back to your country. They'll kill you."

"But when I had to go to the hospital, you told me that it didn't matter to you if I died, that you were used to it, that you'd seen a lot of people die in the street . . ."

"Oh, but this is different. It's violence of the State. It's not a natural death. I don't want those military sons of bitches to kill you."

Ay, little boy!

To reassure him, I send him a few stories in the mail; that's the kind of reassurance he deserves.

Consumer Society

A scraping sound like an elevator door suddenly shutting: a guillotine. While he is our prisoner we have reserved all sorts of hellish sounds for him so that he won't be able to forget his fear, so that he won't stop asking each second what's in store for him.

He waits in silence, desperate, attentive, turning his head this way and that without being able to verify anything. Sometimes we put a bandage over his eyes, sometimes we leave him in the dark, tied up and muzzled, and we move with the utmost discretion around his room, although not with complete discretion, just enough for him to intuit that there is a threatening presence around him. We could kill him with fright or simply make him go crazy. He deserves either one of these alternatives, but we don't put them into practice; we aren't sadists, no sir, we're professionals.

We feed all our prisoners regularly but always in the dark so as to disorient them, keep them from seeing what they're tasting. The scale of the various threats employed should be calibrated wisely. It's an art. We just hired Martorelli, the well-known sound-effects man for the National Radio, to produce the most horrific noises. Now our work is going better, and whenever we take off the muzzle, the prisoner cries out in terror, giving us invaluable material for future sessions.

In the torture chamber we've installed a quadraphonic stereo system that's a real jewel. Our equipment needs get more complicated each day, and therefore more expensive, but that doesn't matter to us because they seem ready to pay. Our proposals have been proven to be of the highest efficacy, and don't even cause the subject any real pain, if you look at our work objectively.

We don't leave a trace. If things keep going like they've been going, we'll be able to apply the laser, soon, which is a marvelously

*precise tool, in many respects, as well as other glories of advanced
technology. You could say that these upgrades are pretty much in
the bag already, since the number of top executives—officials or
otherwise—who require our personalized service is growing daily.
They too want to know what it's all about. They want to experience
themselves what the others won't live to tell about. They don't want
to lose out on any experience, and we are here to satisfy all of the
demands of the market.*

In the corner café, so typical of Buenos Aires, the word "horror"
sounded in unison, doubled.
What from, why? I can ask this now and invent an infinite number
of satisfactory or poetic or terrifying answers. What I'll never be
able to relive or invent is that sudden chill down my spine and in
the air when all the customers in the café heard the word and its
shadow, and recognized it for what it was.

What a vocation, this—I'm the one who writes sitting down and I
can't help but write. It's out of fashion, they tell me, it shouldn't all
be written down, they insist, enough, they tell me, we don't want
to hear about it anymore.
   But I have to keep writing, in spite of it all.
   It's because I come from so far away, from the depths of time. I
was born in Mesopotamia, and I'm here to honor memory.

The Dreams about the Return to NY

How to reconcile the two dreams of last night and the night before? And especially how to reconcile them a) with the talk about Argentina that I gave yesterday at the Institute's lunch and b) with tenderness or at least the search for tenderness?

1st dream:
With a man (white, very young, who apparently was an old friend); at first we began kissing in a friendly way and then with more and more enthusiasm although still with a lot of tenderness. Then the rather frightening decision we both make, but especially him, to begin an erotic relationship. I'm afraid because he's much younger than I am, he's afraid for other reasons that will be revealed later.

He (although now he's someone else, more mature, tougher) has a cock that's bursting apart as if from some kind of internal pressure, or rather like those mangoes that are peeled and put on a stick and sold in the streets of Mexico. In sections but helicoidally. I try to gather up the pieces and stick them together with saliva to give his cock the cylindrical form it should have. But this man separates the sections again. He says that its sensitivity is inside, not in the external layers. I tell him no, that sensitivity is transmitted from the outside in. He lets me try, touching his cock, trying to gather up something that opens outward like a flower of flesh, petals of flesh, although it actually reminds me of a carnivorous plant. It's not naturally like that, I see, but has been cut with a knife—vandalism, a mutilation, even though there are no pieces missing and they all are still stuck to the . . . trunk? I'm gathering up all the pieces, very carefully removing the air that's left in between as the man prepares some kind of complex and precise chemical apparatus: "Just in case you don't succeed," he explains. He puts together a rectangular aquarium with some water that's heating up and some colored capsules that spill red and blue liquid into the water. I think that it must be some strange drug, and that he's going to abandon me by taking the drug. Suddenly on the side of the aquarium with the red water a very fine glove of transparent glue swells up and remains there like a warm, palpitating hand and I realize that it's a masturbation machine and I feel relieved. And I think and say that this won't be necessary. I feel confident (I know that I've triumphed on other occasions). Even though the final result of my thorough reconfiguring of his cock is only the white, transparent outline of a cock, with little bags on the side for balls.

2nd dream:

We're in a big group of very serious people (like my mother's old writer friends) in a place that's like a cemetery or a morgue but not at all depressing, just natural—and we walk around this place like people who are in a different city or on vacation somewhere. And we all sit down to eat at a large table and they bring an enormous pot of stew with pieces of human in it. A stew of people, which rather disgusts me, but only in a general sort of way, so I still try it. During the second course I see a woman's hand with badly painted fingernails in the giant pot and I think several things: that I hope they've washed it well, and that I wouldn't like to eat any recognizable piece. So I take a plate with little squares of meat so I don't know which human part they might match.

In other words, during the day I want to eat Joe alive, and at night, well . . .

Entomologies

In some species of insects the female eats the male after copulation.

As there might be some resistance should the female of the featherless biped species attempt to do the same, in the absolute secrecy of their solitude the human female eats insects—if you don't believe me, read Clarice Lispector's *Passion According to G. H.*, or the chapter on slugs in *El Buzón de la Esquina* (The Corner Mailbox) by my friend Alicia D. O.

Can't be distracted for even a minute. In front of me: the blank page that I was about to imprint with—an idea? But I got distracted and the idea went flying through the air.

Everything is anecdote, anecdote. What do we do with an anecdote?
We ver-ba-lize it.
We paint-ify it.
We don't ver-ify it in the least.
(that would be to invalidate it)

Joe has returned to the fold, it's been more than a month since Joe returned to the fold, gentler than ever, loving. That's why I don't write about it; I'm writing my novel with four hands and I don't even have time to put down in black and white what I'm writing in color with my body at night.

I promised David Rieff that I would hand the novel over to him on Thursday. And from what I've just seen, flipping through this notebook, Thursday it will be exactly nine months to the day since I began the book in Mexico. Time flies, and thanks to lavishing so much attention on novel-writing, I'm hardly paying attention to my marginalia.

Joe has taken away two of his own notebooks, and I never photocopied his poems, nor did I steal or secretly photocopy those really unpleasant things he once wrote about the pleasure of killing. The pleasure of killing floated around us like a promise. Or, let's say the desire to kill—or whatever word-shield we can use to defend ourselves. From the pleasure of killing or better yet from its novelistic recognition: *I am a killer.*

The generic ambiguity of English allowed me to appropriate that sentence of Joe's.

To Write

A peaceful Sunday writing on the fire escape you could call a balcony. I thought about the days when I began *The Lizard's Tail* in the López Cámaras' garden in Mexico. These situations that repeat themselves, with or without luxury, as much as possible with good weather, who will write them? Who will write me? I think that someone could be writing me too. It wouldn't be a bad idea.

May first already. Day of the lily of the valley that arrived without my realizing it but with the early morning call from Robert F. in Paris, and the question, Why does love always come to me from where it's least useful? And then the response: Who says that love is ever useful? *Au contraire*: the beauty of love resides precisely in its gratuitousness, maybe even in its impossibility.

What a wonderful month. I feel the same way I do when September begins in my country. I'm full of creative energy; flowering along with the plants. I would like to *be* a flower; listen to what Alan Watts says: the beginning of pleasure, localized in the genitals according to Freud, and the reality principle, located in the mind according to Freud, are always in conflict because they are separated from each other. Something that doesn't happen in flowers, which have their genitals in their head. Like many women, I note, at least according to the old joke.

Freud, Freud, Freud, what big eyes you have! (The Viennese witch doctor, as Nabokov called him.)

Classes on dream literature. Good thing I still remember a few things, and suddenly I remembered the dream from the other night where we talked about learning to read the silences of texts like in music. And I was saying, of course, that's what I was working on in *Pedro Páramo* and they said, yes, D'Annunzio wrote an essay about that. Did he really write it, I wonder, or will it appear between the lines?

I'm putting together the series of stories that I call *Other Weapons* (years after having written the eponymous piece) and I feel that although the three are so different, they go really well together. They have a lot in common: they're siblings. Of course, since I'm the mother. But they have different fathers. And from one of the fathers who was more metaphorical than anything—terrifying. I believed it was my idea of the military, but now I wonder—is it my vision of men?

The second piece today is called "Fourth Version." The Ambassador and Bella reduced to a digest; I discovered that all the initial chapters that were put together through months and months of work were superfluous (I'll have to convince myself sometime that things start when they start, and there's nothing you can do about it). And anyway, these pieces are just a way of cleaning out the underbrush. Hacking away with my machete, so that from the long novel there are only seventy pages left (and there were more than three hundred), a fourth version that sums up something that will never again be said.

How brilliant, the dialectic of life, the inversion of desire. Human chess. Writing about the Coyote, I note that in the south, man is white and the phone black. Here in the north, in New York, things are reversed: white phone, black man. This as a way of confessing that I'm waiting for the self-described Wolf to call me again. Once again. After a really interesting afternoon spent in bed but that left me rather frustrated because he wasn't all here. Or maybe because I couldn't accomplish everything with this character who won't give me more. Although he did give me a lot, and very moved he told me on the last of his repeated returns: I don't want to sound corny, but it's been such a long time, such a long time, thank you. And then a little kiss on the palm of my hand, as he does on the rare occasions that he wants to show how touched he is.

And here I am, wanting more, and more, without end, because this is desire and the other stuff is just a substitute. Or am I wrong?

Tuesday, no, Wednesday!

What a day! What accumulated from before. What came up today. I was told that I got the Guggenheim and I dance on one foot, metaphorically, and I dance all through the house with joy. I was thinking of moving, but I don't like the apartment I was offered so I'm not going to take it (not taking what comes along because you're afraid of losing something). Later, the party at Strauss's place, and me being me there with Susan and all the other people that I feel are almost like family now. I was happy too to see Mark Strand again, even if it was just in passing.

And the other stuff and the latest (because several days have gone by), especially yesterday's. The consciousness of love. However it is. Accepting what it is, like a secret life, recoveries and returns of my dark desire. I'm writing this to the rhythm of drums.

Another game of identities and truths that get transformed—where is the lie? *Is* there a lie?

A bag of cats: these notebooks I'm slowly burying my past in. My present: a month ahead of me to relaunch the darkness. I tried trips, mysticisms, appetites. What I want now is to go up in the black freight elevator and get lost among Gylles's and Eric's theater monsters.

Gylles and Eric show me photos of Ed, dying in some, acting the part of a dying man in others. And the photos always there, between death and death.

To appreciate everything that shrinks when the lights are turned on in that kingdom of shadows, Gylles's theater-house. The jewels and the jewelry box shrink—and the jewels entirely of paste—the rugs shrink, and the rocks are of Styrofoam when the lights go on, but they're almost never on. Only candlelight on the perpetual night in the theater-house.

As the stories are told, light focuses on the various angles of recurring obsessions.

One day Inga says that they told her about Ed's toenails, in the hospital, painted with little white spots. Another day she says she saw his toenails, and the feet in a V underneath the sheets.

While we watch the videos about Ed, the old Russian choreographer for whom the boys were putting together this theater, Gylles insists that we should write a book together, he and I. About our loves. Yes. Brave comparison. He asks me how many men I've had in a single night—one, I answer him. Fifty, he says indifferently, fifty when he goes to the public restrooms.

I feel like venturing into the dark side of life, the heaviside layer, as T. S. Eliot put it. But the spreading of AIDS and the journalistic campaign about this new, terrifying disease stops me short.

She got out of the car *and the three guys thought: I should get out with her. Each one on his own, and for his own reasons—the third one out of cowardice, in order to escape from the redhead who had him trapped.*

Men and beautiful women.

The woman who got out was less beautiful and not as young as the redhead, but she had more substance: a challenge that none of the guys was ready to accept, even though there wasn't any risk: you could tell that she was going to reject them.

The car disappeared into the night, taking with it three dreamers and a redhead with her feet on the ground.

The other woman remained alone on the corner with her feet who knows where and waving her hand good-bye, almost smelling the regret in the air.

This is my cave and for lack of anything else, I adorn it with phalluses. They impose themselves on you, I grab them, and today I hang them up in wreaths, trying to revive them one by one. I accuse others of reifying me, and here I am doing the same thing— and maybe I've always done it.

I am the appropriator of phalluses, but I am also their great admirer. Worshipper. Devourer? No, although I would like to be, I haven't been able to.

Hairy, chubby like *saucisse platte*, or enormous cocks that make their own owners jealous, and now this last one like a big coat hanger or like a raised fist with pink trim. Beautiful, anatomical.

And the phalluses of dreams, like my friend's on Tenth Street or the one that grew on me in a dream giving me a sensation of power, a phallus that proved interesting but useless.

False/Phallus: here we have a rather disturbing landslide of a game; the dichotomy of metonymy, if you'll pardon the expression: they put something that doesn't exist inside you, and nevertheless it bursts into bubbling sperm, leaving you feeling like a tree wet with sap, and your blood galloping.

A life a love a trip an apprenticeship a horror a love a world.
Let's turn the page over:
A horror a love a world a trip a life an apprenticeship,
Or vice versa.

The delicate line that separates the mythical hero from the fool, upon which many of us, men and women, usually balance, falling alternately to one side or the other.

The Theater

Amnesty International conference in a Canadian city. Many passions, politics, demands abound. And other passions as well. With regard to the latter, she feels as though she's on a stage. The other characters are backstage, and there are a lot of characters present and absent in this work that, as it should, respects the three unities of theme, space, and time:

Conference in a modern hotel, four days.

The first day, nothing happens; we scent each other from afar and there are casual glances.

First Act

On the second day, the male poet from Barbados enters from the stage left, very young, all decked out, dark skin, pretty tasty. She herself is just the open stage, the beginning of a scene that doesn't always get swallowed down, and which, to her later regret, she often spits up.

They converse and converse, he talks about himself, she talks about him, and he can't help but feel dazzled. He falls in love with her. He tells her so in French.

She frames her space (it really isn't any more than a stage).

She says: This is my vital space and these are my measurements and you don't fit. At least tonight you don't fit. I have to concentrate on my big performance that will take place tomorrow morning. It won't be a performance about love; it will be about pure power. Today, love doesn't fit.

He says: It will fit afterward. At five o'clock, I'll kidnap you and we'll forget about power and other banalities, because I'm going to remind you of other, deeper things. You are the most extraordinary woman I've ever met.

She says: I'm only a stage.

1st Intermission

Another actress arrives who puts me in bed. A vast bed, part of the set. I let the other woman have some room but draw a dividing line, a border. Not one more inch, and surely not with your boobs showing.

I say: Don't be too hard on me, don't turn on too many spotlights. I'm the boards. I'm the floor of the stage; don't crush my head.

The prompter is gone. Luckily. The second act is already written, but after that the I prefer to improvise.

Second Act
The actress who burst in during the intermission, changed now, observes the me from the first row of the orchestra and takes notes. The dark poet of the first act is nowhere to be seen; their date is at five o'clock and it's barely nine in the morning. From the height of the dais—from my own height—I, the stage/woman, recite my text with the necessary conviction, having written it myself and having thoroughly rehearsed it, in any case, through many presentations of the same themes: human rights, censorship. Among other things, this text contradicts the great Joseph Brodsky's declaration on the same subject, and he is present on the same dais. I don't share his opinion that censorship is bad for the writer but beneficial for literature.

There are motions for support and voices of protest. She who is the stage itself has fulfilled her role and has transformed into an entire, secret theater, all straight lines, under scrutiny.

A Viennese critic comes on stage late and sits down at the back hurriedly with his raincoat still on and his legs open. From afar, she imagines herself passing her tongue very slowly over his balls and the skin of his member which she suspects is erect under his raincoat. He looks at her. With her face resting on her right hand, and her mouth open, she looks at him and licks him. All the way up. She has nothing better to do. From where his cock begins, a curve for each ball and again up in a straight line, very, very slowly. He gets the message. She no longer feels like a stage, she feels like the protagonist, the stage manager, the director, the author all at once. Is he a *metteur en scène*? Only because she thinks that at some moment in the future he might allow her to undertake in reality the healthy activity she's imagining . . . only because of that.

The actor playing the Viennese critic is also young, not as young as the other actor though, and he seems older because of his straight gray hair. Green eyes. His beauty is rather solemn, distant, very slightly feminine.

During the intermission following the second act, the scene moves because she moves. I am the scene, don't forget. In self-defense or through neglect, all feelings were left out of this work. There are more peremptory problems, questions of state terrorism in many countries. Denunciations. Reflections and the proposal of means to incite change. Sexual urges placate the horrors.

In the dinner scene everyone is seated at a big table; certain characters are superfluous. Five o'clock has come and gone and she spent that time outside of love. Certain characters at the table are superfluous; others are catalysts who provoke lightning-quick reactions.

(Threads that were being tied backstage have become knots now. The Viennese critic, we discover, is the lover of the wife of the man she so loved in other times and who loved her in return. The Viennese critic is therefore like family and has let her know that he wants to become part of her scene and she has tacitly accepted, but now other vibes are in the air and she's not so sure.) During the second course, the Viennese critic seems to be attracted to a French journalist. She likes him too because he's more cheerful, and the licked balls of this morning are forgotten. She believes, and she whispers this to the Viennese critic, that in a hand-to-hand fight, she would win the Frenchman.

Viennese Critic: Maybe so, in these things one has to move very slowly; for a man like him with no experience, the other man has to conquer him slowly, through friendship, with a lot of patience.

End of the third act.

Backstage the supporting actress comes in to measure the height of the French journalist and swiftly directs him to her bed, liberating the other woman. For her part, she who knew how to be a stage moves on to other scenery and discovers that the Antilles are always sunny, even at night.

Curtain.

Literaturesses

Enrique Lihn says that in prose language is a means of transportation. ("Take Route 60 and put the poem together," I translate, or more locally, "take IRT Uptown and finish your novel.")

The photographer's theory: flashes. Capture what's happening, with the necessary speed.

The anecdotal present versus thought's present.

Poe talks about music in relation to poetry and mathematics in relation to prose. The joke is that today mathematicians talk about music in relation to mathematics, not to mention quantum physicists, whose language already verges on poetry.

Does the unconscious work differently when one is writing prose as opposed to when one is writing poetry? More likely it would seem that one is simply taking different roads to access the same enigma.

Substitutions

His name wasn't Germán de Laferrere,[5] it was something else, and this by way of trying to understand how pseudonyms are born. Why someone needs to hide behind an invented name in order to protect their own name or to be someone else.

With Germán de Laferrere, it wasn't a case of a pseudonym being used for protection, a name like a mask, always making clear that behind or around the invented name there's your very own name, which is your own skin.

Germán de Laferrere. The name was born after a thousand stories were heard, and then one irrepressible temptation: to write these stories down. What's usually a justification for a writer was for him a denunciation. The urgent need to write something that will finish you. Depicting with words the shape of your own life sentence.

Germán de Laferrere—or the man who then occupied his shoes— couldn't resist such a temptation. He wrote word after word, the first one first, and then all the rest, flowing like a waterfall. The story was

---

5   Translator's Note: A journalist, writer, and diplomat who wrote under the psyeudonym Germán Dras.

printed on paper, and it was true. The story that was at the same time a life sentence.

It's necessary to read between the lines, they always recommend: you have to see beyond the anecdote.

The real writer of this story whose name we won't divulge didn't have a hard time understanding these wise literary precepts. Even before rereading what this person had written, perhaps even before putting down the final period, he already knew what would be left out, but was clearly implicit. And it was terrifying, the most terrifying anecdote of all: one's own death.

This story was a death sentence, and nevertheless he was going to publish it along with some others, and the only defense he chose was donning this mask of a pseudonym.

A year later, the book published, the man who was no longer Germán de Laferrere (or who would be Germán de Laferrere forever) confronted his nemesis—in other words, his character—as he left the corner store in the town of Eldorado in Misiones. This thug faced him and said I am Pereira and you wrote that I'm a murderer, using my full name, and now I'm going to pay you back. His hand went to his thigh and when the terrified writer thought he would soon no longer be Germán de Laferrere or anybody else for that matter, the other man took out not a pistol but a wad of folded papers and handed it to him.

The poem had a simple rhyme scheme, the writer's whole life was painted in crude strokes, but there in Eldorado, Misiones, in the '20s, a lesson was learned: words are paid with words.

I don't know why I decided to tell this story I was told years ago now. Maybe because, in accord with this anecdote about Germán de Laferrere, I am harboring the hopeful terror, or the terrifying hope, whichever, that while I write about them, some of my subjects are in turn writing about me. "Your *tipos*," John says, and I don't know how he knows the Spanish word.

The only thing that consoles me—well, let's not exaggerate, a lot of things console me, although unfortunately few are of flesh and blood—the only thing that consoles me is when I open Gide's diary haphazardly and find that I don't have to write anymore about whatever is keeping me awake at night because he already described it a thousand years ago and much better: the headaches, the drowsiness, the screen that comes between you and your ideas, the feelings of guilt for not writing. Everything. And over and over again.

I want to be a woman of action: decisive, energetic, merciless at times; not this sorry wretch with a headache.

Gide says in his diary (I don't feel so alone anymore), in 1912: "Rien encore. Je vis dans l'attente de moi."

What I want to do with these notes is cure myself. Not cure myself of myself: find myself.

There are situations that distract me from this stress. There was for example the starting-up again of the lunches at the Institute, yesterday, with new sparkling blue eyes observing me. And they belong to an interesting Englishman, ex-director of the Index on Censorship, with whom I will share an office—where I already know I'll never go, since I hate offices.

Wonderful. What I'm most interested in are coincidences, points of intersection. I go out with Martha G. thinking that I'm going to buy some clothes, but I land in a paperback bookstore. I look for the unfindable: Pasternak's *Safe Conduct,* which Susan recommended for my continually postponed autobiographical project, or *The Hanged Man* by Sheldon Kopp, which is nowhere to be seen. So I buy Gertrude Stein's *Ida* and some ghost stories by Sheridan Le Fanu. *Ida* for the woman who raised me, and the ghost stories with the secret hope of finding the story of the soon-to-be decapitated victims that my sister read to me to make me eat. I opened my mouth terrified, she put in the soup spoon; I listened to the story about the woman with her brains hanging out who was looking, axe in hand, for someone upon whom to take her revenge; I waited for the ending along with the kids on the ground floor of the abandoned house, but then my mother interrupted, asking if these stories were appropriate for a five-year-old girl. This *cuentus interruptus* made me hallucinate that very night and gave me an eternal thirst to know the end of the story. So today I dedicate myself to reading: *Ida* bores me (the novel). S. le Fanu bores me. So I start reading *If on a winter's night . . .* by Calvino, and love it. It happens to be the story of the constant search for the endings of various interrupted stories. He masterfully tells me what I already know I don't know.

There are days—like tonight—when I feel that I've grown. Not morally but physically. The table is lower, the bathroom sink really low. They aren't the happiest days. They are the sad days that elevate me beyond reach of myself.

Written Down after a Not-So-Culinary Recipe

There are and there always will be deserters.
There is always a cigarette hanging like that so that whoever passes by gets burned.
There will—always?—be applause that wakes you back up.

Enough of going around the world; I know that New York is my world, it's *the* world. No more sitting on the doorstep to watch the corpses of our enemies go by—but instead to watch all these passersby, alive and kicking, and become, from such a distance— though living so far away—so intimate. *The Lizard's Tale* is translated, and will be out in English before it's published in Spanish, for obvious reasons, though I do want to publish it in Argentina, when things have changed. And I am so grateful to David Rieff for his arduous dedication to putting the finishing touches on the English version (though he didn't come right out and tell me this; he let me know with a lot more than just a nose for Spanish, and he was right and together we found the appropriate word).

Tepotztlán

The Guggenheim grant that I've always dreamed of and have now pocketed is burning a hole in my pocket. And so: Mexico and the need to be isolated during this winter vacation in order to submerge myself in a new novel and complete the project I had in mind. In Mexico, in the most inspiring place: Tepotzlán, a sacred, vibrant town. And in Tepotzlán, waiting for me: the house of my dreams, the same charming little house at the entrance to the town that was lent to Nenuca when we went to give ourselves the ritual bath in a sweat lodge, and which is now for sale and of course costs exactly the amount from the Guggenheim, and I don't hesitate an instant. If the purpose of the grant is for the happy recipient to write in peace, there's nothing better than to buy the *place* to write instead of buying time, which is supposed to be what one does and always turns out to be an illusion. So I buy my place in the world, the here-place that I've dreamed about forever, and naturally it's a magic place to which I will return as many times as the job in New York lets me, and where I will live—I know that already. All kinds of emotions, from the unexpected and constant jolts that I've suffered to the simple joy of flowers, new to me, unknown, opening up in my little terraced garden; from the many rites and holidays of the town, the praying for rain, the fireworks, to the fears, the intense fears in the dark under that mountain eroded by the centuries, ancestral and surprising.

My house in Tepoztlán awakens so much love in me! It's named Tlatlapechco—it's already been baptized and I have a lizard painted on the entrance gate. Standing higher than the neighbors' roof, which from this altitude only comes up to my knees, I can see the enormous convent and I see behind it the wall of wrinkled rock that is Tepozteco and which has at its summit a tiny white pyramid. It is said that this is a place of energy, one of the few places in the world where there are negative ions and it makes you feel as if something is passing through you, and sometimes it makes you afraid, especially on moonless nights when in some house they're "watching over the tallow," in other words, celebrating the vigil for the candles that on the following day will adorn the enormous, austere convent.

So much love, this house made of stone and adobe and old beams, love that I have to put away for now, keeping it between my breasts so that it nourishes and warms me when I return to the New York snow.

Epiphany. Donations. The piled-up crosses spell out a secret, although intelligible, message. And the new novel? Nothing. Of course now that things are happening outside: a lizard making little lizards, for example, in the terraced garden of my little house in Tepotzlán, in the San Miguel neighborhood, those worlds are catapulting me to another time.

The pets I have for now are the spiders. There's Aracné the round one, and Pepita the big-footed one. They don't worry me, but they aren't much company either. I should talk about the house, the big old trees, the joy of sitting on the porch at night and seeing distant lights. Better not to talk about the leaks. Sometimes I feel as though I've bought a pricked balloon, but it's not true. The house won't deflate, it keeps its solid structure, its country atmosphere, intact. And besides, I'm in the San Miguel neighborhood, the archangel with his scale; and the neighborhood's symbol or totemic animal, the *nahual*, for whom the locals are named, is the lizard. I'm just one more lizard, from the San Miguel neighborhood, and during the Chinelos carnival I will jump around behind the banner that confirms it for me. I take all this into account, and one more pertinent detail: the god Tepozteco, the one who lives up there where I see the little white pyramid—as a child, he was left on an anthill so that the ants would eat him, but instead of eating him, they fed him with honey. Pure serendipity, in Tepoztlán—and the San Miguel neighborhood, no less—but I didn't choose them because of these legends . . . I didn't know about them, but I couldn't have ended up in a better place, with *The Lizard's Tail* under my belt. And now, how can I write a new and different novel?

If they fall like flies, why bother flapping your wings?

What a brusque arrival from New York. My internal brakes are still squeaking—I can't help feeling anxious. I want everything to be done *now* and not at some later time, which in these latitudes means never. "Okay," the plumber says to me when I tell him what I need, and he just leaves, and never comes back, after having taken all the plumbing apart. "Oh, why don't you go to hell," I think, whenever I hear them agree to something and not do it.

Unexpected gifts that come from people and places I least expect to hear from. Ida Vitale and Enrique Fierro come to visit me. An afternoon of poets. And she, who always seemed so distant, here is perfectly charming and full of stories. She gives me a photograph of Felisberto Hernández that I don't like as much as his stories, except for one detail: Felisberto and Paulina Medeiros are in it, together. Felisberto put together a scrapbook of the two of them. Half articles on him, half on her. Pages with columns, like the Bible. The other stuff, no, I don't like it—Felisberto and the women who venerate him, he ignoring them; like the one who fell into the basement while he was writing and he didn't even move. He writes, she breaks her back (three ribs). He leaves the house and abandons her. Like he does with others. Felisberto playing the piano in shoddy movie houses or in concert halls while his wife gives birth. The first time. The second and third will come later. Who stands up to him, who demands anything? The death of his granddaughter, Felisberto catatonic in the morgue. What happened to her? the man burying her asks. I was writing a story, Felisberto answers, while he perhaps was eating those water biscuits he liked so much. Later he will die, enormous, all wrapped up in himself, and at his house in Montevideo they'll have to tear down part of the window frame to be able to take out the coffin made to his size because it won't fit through the door.

I accept favors, that is to say I listen to stories and then I have to pay them back somehow and I want to lock myself up and write. Not talk, not crumble, not be torn to pieces.

The source was left exhausted after *The Lizard's Tail*. I can no longer write, all I do is jot down landmarks on a route that others won't be able to piece back together again. Because I don't feel like telling stories, I feel like remembering, telling myself, pointing out the road. It's the road of my own consciousness as a woman. A woman writer, what luck. "Every woman who writes is a survivor," Tillie Olsen said. I've never read her. What to read? How to point out the road? *Nel mezzo del camin di nostra vita . . .* the jungle of my own cunt. The mixed-up one, like that guy said. The confused one.

I was crying for so many things but now I've made myself a little nest.

Guilt. Cancel guilt or at least put it in parentheses while this work lasts (while I write this writing, while I'm still in the saddle, whatever).

The story about the notebooks is good. The one that Anne Sexton gave Erica Jong with the following warning: "Life can only be understood backwards, but it must be lived forwards."

And later she wrote: "'How do I save my own life?' the poet asked. 'By being a fool,' God said."

The fool would become *le fol* of the Tarot deck, the first, the one without a number, the zero, the one who walks around with a little bundle on his back. When Fernando Arbeláez would do Tarot readings for us, back in Iowa, he would say that *le fol* was the mystery of love, young love about to step into the abyss. In the solitude of this mountain town, I consult the I Ching, which talks to me in its usual elliptic language. Everyone here seems to speak an elliptic language, made of water when they resort to speaking in Nahuatl. Sometimes in the distance the teponaztli, the sacred drum, sounds—and I heed that call. Sometimes a procession praying for rain passes in front of the house. The men throw little flying reeds to prick the clouds and the women carry enormous bouquets of flowers in their arms. I follow them to the convent and I too sometimes leave a floral offering. The women pray silently, the men outside set off fireworks.

Warding off fear. Maybe I write, in part, to try to ward off the fear that half the human race has of the other half. Something more and more evident as masculine security, that clay-footed idol, weakens.

I would like to stop here. Go backward. Follow Anne Sexton's advice, if it is indeed advice, if it is indeed Anne Sexton's. Backward so that the forward part is improvised, not analyzed.

All these changes that I'm going through. These changes of context. Of focus. Another new lens.

Life has marvels that the marvel denies.

The second firecracker goes off. A sigh escapes me almost soundlessly, asking for forgiveness. What loneliness, my own, and what loneliness, his. If I didn't know he was alone then I would really feel like an ass. But he is really, truly alone, and a lot more than I am, because he won't admit it. And he is a lot of *he*s, I can mention three just for starters, and there would be more than three if I started to think methodically, which I don't want to do. I don't want anything to do with methods, or to have to think about loneliness. Loneliness scattered all over the place, how horrible. Communication is difficult when you try to hold out your hand to reach someone and discover that we are all unable to touch, and blind too, like characters in a play by Beckett, wandering through an eternal night.

Literary advice for stopping a train: *Life is a one-way ticket, and if you're afraid of taking the ride, then get off in a hurry. Still, who's to say you won't be one of the lucky ones? In case of emergency, pull lever.*

The memory struck me like a train going full speed ahead down the tracks. What I don't understand too well is why the tracks are empty and not crowded with images: a dense and thick barrier, through which unexpected and subtle memories shouldn't be able to insinuate themselves at all. But no, this memory came from far away, from its own deep unknown depths, and advanced at full speed, as if nothing could stop it. It advanced, even though it was a static memory, tiny, almost sublime in its tininess, a memory to keep separate in some out of the way corner and only bring out during moments of unease. A useless memory, a memory of peace, something round and small and sweet and that lasts a long time, like those candies of my childhood called *media-hora* (half an hour).

But it advanced swiftly and galloped by; just the vision of a corner store in some lost town in Formosa. There's also a yellow church, a few radiant flowers, an incredibly blue sky. The store has eaves made of straw, and underneath this roof and under his own white hat, an old man rests or sleeps and it's as if he's meditating, exuding peace.

Where did this little memory come from, falling like that from the sky?

Or rather, where does it want to take me?

The memory leads to all the provinces in Argentina, to all the many trips I never wrote about and will never write about, though not because they don't deserve it—oh no, *au contraire*. I didn't take notes but I wrote down a lot of facts, largely devoid of any poetry, since I was writing for a newspaper at the time.

I am not a journalist, nor do I want to be. Nor do I want to be? But I will be one again whenever someone proposes it to me, along with the possibility of a trip—but each time it will be harder for me to accept a commission to write something.

From the other side of the story, I *narrate* the story. If I narrated the way I live, if the voice were the same, if the perfect autobiography existed, the story would have only one side, or else it wouldn't be real—as a story—or we wouldn't have lived it at all. (Möbius strip of an indispensable option.)

If once and for all I could get the hang of the picaresque style, I'd have some nice stories to tell. And they'd be my very own private property, not thefts, even if only thefts of the imagination. Moments of rearranging the fauna of one's memory. And also write stories about love and the lack of love as much as possible. Take advantage of the bucolic atmosphere.

Love is something we practice daily without even realizing it, without taking responsibility for it. Destruction is another thing entirely: the militancy of a forced encounter, all one's ruminations about renouncing and forgetting. It happens when you least expect it, perhaps precisely because you don't expect it anymore. Though you've made attempts.

The Difficult Apprenticeship of Turning the Page

I run a finger along your smooth skin; two fingers would be too much in this particular embrace. Because this one finger that I keep running up and down your skin drawing in some of your lines is the best I have (I am my best when I'm at your side).

Your feral odor isn't in you; it's in me—that tame certitude with which you confront life, looking at my window. Later, I'm going to cross the street, heeding your mute call, and you will know how to give me back to myself, cradling me in your arms.

It would be good to have some round, fleshy fruits in my mouth to replace the juicy void left by your lips. A fruit of pure pulp, a ripe reward shot through with insatiable veins.

And after the act of love, how can you not become self-absorbed, inside yourself, burning up? How can you walk, live, and live in company with others after so much death?

We sing to make the sun come up. On the beach, we look for the best hidden spot to make love. Knowing that with or without us, the sun will keep rising but that our love would end in just a few days. Perhaps that cruel inevitability was approaching in any case. And to know that from the moment of our meeting we won't be the same; we will emerge cleansed, purified, as usually happens after these encounters (however brief they are, or perhaps precisely because of their brevity).

Corollary
The general attitude is one of searching, peppered with such volatile encounters and once in a while a real spark of recognition. Our missing half is spread throughout the world and we have to go searching for it piece by piece and—like in a bewildering jigsaw puzzle—the pieces don't always fit into only one person. They are antagonistic, loose pieces of a counter-figure that is perhaps also loose, dispersed, in each one of us. Therefore, it's useless to sit too long in front of ourselves trying to complete the puzzle.

Defense of the Polished Style

This hard, dry style that has formed on me like a shell. More like a barrier, to help me be able to get a little closer to the domain of the ineffable. Because it's a barrier not of separation, but showing the way, like a guide. I walk along the barrier as if on a tightrope and many times I defy my vertigo and peer into the abyss.

From the austere and almost ascetic corner of a polished style, the abyss doesn't seem at all threatening.

The liberating text and the imprisoning text. I have these notebooks and notes spread all around me on the tiles: links in the chain of the imprisoning text. That's why I want to stay here, in my little house, writing on the porch or under the trees, and not run away from this solitude that wears me out, simply because I need to liberate myself from the imprisoning text. But when I do liberate myself, it won't be by fleeing, submerging myself in a completely different text or even image. No. With this same material, I will make myself a liberating text like someone making a poncho to wear outside, into the cold. Internally speaking, of course. Now, even if I wanted to, I know that (oops, I got up for a second and now I'm already thinking about something else. That's running away for you!) I *bought* this place to stay here—at least for a while, as long as I can—although sometimes I think that I really bought it to have somewhere to put all these objects, all this junk and rustic furniture I love. The house as a box, and an excuse for me to buy up half the market.

How to write novels if you don't have all the necessary information in your hands and at the same time feel the merciless certainty that at any moment you're going to make a fist and tear all this information to pieces?

Ornithology

The grand flight with open wings, with the feathers separated like fingers. The predatory flight. Claws ready. Sometimes you see them

*coming like that, hovering over you and all you can do is sit there
with a docile air while you see them coming, threatening.*

*The glory resides in the blue-plumed birds' quick sparkle. In the
middle of the forest, the blue woodpeckers open their wings and,
against the nocturnal green of the pine trees, their color is so intense,
it's almost happiness.*

*Indigo blue, cobalt blue, methyl alcohol blue. None of these blues
and all of them at the same time, a fleeting revelation before they
unfold their wings and show us only their dark hood with a crest
that sketches in their heads. It's like the flash of green from the quet-
zal hidden in the jungle. Not at all like the other hoods, the terrifying ones that they usually put on for the hunt.*

*The hooded hawk waiting for its prey. The other prey, the human
one, wearing a hood and waiting for the executioner. The executioner also hooded.*

*And the flight interrupted. No more blue wings, just broken wings
with the feathers open like fingers that then draw close and clench.*

Another instant, something more positive: to write with the fire
crackling. To crackle with the writing of the fire.

Back in Tep after an incursion into the city. Squeezing *mate* to ex-
tract a novel and not the coarse confessions and more confessions
and notes about so-called reality that could constitute a novel if
I let it, because the novel exists somewhere in me and I exist too
and so we're bound to coincide if I squeeze hard enough. I got a
grant to produce it but the miracle isn't happening and the Christ-
mas vacation is going to end soon. I preferred going with Nenuca,
Javier, and company to visit friends and take part in the Mexican
tradition of *posadas*, or taking a two day drive to El Llanito to celebrate the New Year with the Huehuenches. These are rituals that

I'd love to write about and I don't. Maybe I'm saving them for the future novel, maybe I'm saving them for me, to dream about.

Julio Marzán has sent me a poem:
> When he came in this morning,
> Hungrier than ever,
> I told him I was unhappy.
>
> I miss my legs after all,
> Tongueless, I gnarled,
> I miss my wholeness
>
> Moving by itself. I feel
> Heat in the space
> Where my fingers were
> (. . .)

I like the poem a lot. It's the very cruel story of a man who lets himself be slowly eaten by another man and loses his vital organs. Something that can happen in the domination game and which really has nothing to do with hunger. I'm trying to understand the themes of power (understand what power exercised to its limit is), and how we women are so often accused of being devourers, and in a few days I answer Julio wanting to explore the other side of the coin. I do it with a lot less poetic talent, but what can you do.
> A woman slowly
> Ate
> A man.
> First she told him, Open your mouth, and he opened as if to swallow,
> But he was swallowed

(the ambiguous condition of the glove that contains the
hand and loses its identity as a glove: it is the hand)
The man obeyed and opened his mouth, wide,
The woman slid down his throat and began gnawing
Bit by bit,
Starting with the sleeves of his intestines until she reached
His heart.
The hunger of the swallower was less urgent than the
hunger of the swallowed
A very voracious man swallowed a woman and was very
calmly eaten.
El hambre *es el lobo del* hombre. (Hunger is man's wolf.)

Anthropophagy is not out of place in my beloved Tepotzlán. Sacred place of the Aztec princes, where still today the purest Nahuatl of all Mexico is spoken, where people come from far away like I once did, to participate in the sweat-baths, that scorching ritual in a mud oven. This is a center of power, and there are those who come looking for this negative ion power, Karin tells me, and then she tells me about the blind man who sees auras. This is a town of sorcerers. I've met a few. Here. And over there too, but that's a different story.

I would like to write a story that I'd like to read, not the one that's beating inside me. On the other hand, I'd like the story to work as a recovery of memory. Contradictions within the system, as they say.

My love life (if you could call it that), along with the life of the fascinating slugs (in New York: the beautiful, incredible Inga's puppets, not to mention Gylles and his theater, and *uy uy!* Ava), keep getting in the way. Instead of driving them away, I would like to incorporate them. It's not easy. I'm looking now for something radiant—I envy Alicia Dujovne, but she doesn't see the other stuff.

New York as the place where all my fantasies simmer, and now Tepotzlán, the place of my dreams, which at times turn into nightmares of loneliness and leaks, but then again become green dreams of plants and flowers, all mine, and even the kitten they gave me today on the street because I looked like I wanted one (or a dog, why deny it). Any animal that walks . . .

All this as a way of saying that I finally took off with what I might call *Crónica de los Demonios* (Demon Chronicle—the story of the Ark). That is, I finally took off with it here and now, because I've been working on this story for years. But along the way I found this old dream and that's what's being realized now, the house in the mountains, the house isolated amid such beauty.

Only, not that isolated, luckily, but at times I feel as alone as if it was and I try to take hold of something incapable of being held (the mountain), and I have my dreams of abandonment like last night's: my fortune was told (by reading the tablecloth, and on the underside, to top it off) and my destiny was to remain alone all my life, something like crucified by my work. And I was very upset and said: but it's already happened, I'm a real writer, I've published ten books; yes, they told me, fine, but you're still going to be alone, although what does that matter? And it did matter to me, it upset me and that's why they called in the nurse to give me an injection presumably against loneliness. I prefer the anguish! I shouted. Now, now, they tried to calm me down, but then the guy stuck the needle in my thigh and my leg was totally tense and the liquid didn't penetrate. At least let me relax my leg!

I woke up then, luckily, and in my next dream I was able to relax my leg, being duly stroked by a very attractive stranger's bare foot, under a table.

Return to New York Dream

Now I'm in the other person's place—the person who is kicking's place.

I'm with someone who could be Amalia on a beach looking for shells. We don't find any; she walks away and when I'm about to leave the beach, I kick a bunch of sea wrack and underneath the debris there appear the most beautiful and varied shells imaginable. There are some strange ones too, white and transparent rectangular shapes. I take them over to Amalia and we are amazed and dazzled by them, and discover that the triangular shapes are alive—they're mollusks with a flat animal nose that are moving forward with triangular rectangles erect. One of them gets near another one. We think they're male and female and yes, the two mollusks mate and they're like two hands stuck together and I don't think of prayer, but rather of my lectures: that's how I should stand in front of the public, with my two hands clasped together.

How to live where you don't disturb others while they sleep? How to let yourself get caught up in new currents if you haven't yet left any mark on the old?

Corrientes is the name of my father's province. Corrientes is the liveliest street in my city. But the ideas that with any luck we manage to sketch out don't flow at all easily; we are dragged down a bit of course by the currents.

She crossed Avenida Corrientes and went into a bookstore to buy a book, and there she read everything that was happening to her. She didn't want to know any more and tore out the pages. This is the book, that's why it's incomplete.

I think I'm writing useful literature when I write. I think—oh, innocent me—that there *is* useful literature.

Final message. Final message. Heaven to hell. Urgent communication. Heaven to hell, Final message. Urgent communication. Over. Final message. Heaven to hell, heaven to hell. Or vice versa. Over and out.

Today Minetta Street was being cleaned. Not today, yesterday. Same difference, for all I care about their hygiene. With great gushes of water, grand sweeping gestures that almost knock me over. But I did manage to take photos—the eternal spectator.

Being with the other is being *in* the other. Become a part of him, lose yourself. Do I really want that? I don't mean the man; I mean do I want to lose myself?

I dreamed about the dove: a round, dark little dove wearing a doll's embroidered jacket. It's perched on a tree facing a very busy street. It tries to fly, but can't. I catch it after a short chase and try to take off the little jacket that's covering its wings. Poor thing, underneath it has a little harness on that I also take off. I let it go but it still can't fly—it's very numb. I think that it's dangerous to leave it there among so many cars and decide to take it to my building's garden and let it loose there. On the way I look at it and think that it's very tender, very delicious—I want it for myself, but it would make me sad to put it in a cage.

The phone wakes me up. It's very early. Joe is calling to say he regrets not having spent the night with me. Now I wonder if the "tender, delicious" that I just wrote—with all their gustatory connotations—and which in the dream seemed to be just a harmless, affectionate observation, aren't indeed making reference to something else . . .

Who can escape the cannibalism in every act of love?

Who takes the first bite?

Subways

Back in the Bronx.

The black man who's traveling while suspended between two subway cars, swinging his head. Then he puts his feet on my car and his shoulders against the other one's door. Tired of his acrobatics, he gets into my almost empty car and as he passes by me he shows me the index finger on his right hand, pointing upward, near my eyes. Up yours, it means. I follow him with my eyes and my best indifferent, almost understanding, air. I should have bitten his finger. Eat to eat . . .

Everything in life is a demand: the comings and goings, the turns and returns, the humiliations, the encounters, the mute deceptions, the waiting. Everything. Demands about something called love and to which we never know how to completely give ourselves.

Now I stay at home a lot, intending to write, but all I manage is to stay at home a lot.

Wanting to hit the nail on the head, I stop to think of a certain intense encounter that I never mentioned, perhaps because it was a frustrated encounter, a rapturous contact to which neither of us could offer the possibility of concretion . . .

The River

1) Birth

A man and a woman feed a river. The river separates them. They don't feed it as if feeding hope, no. They give it food and nourish it with their fears. The river is the opposite of other rivers and during freezes it becomes uncrossable and in certain thaws it's barely a trickle of water.

He never crosses the river. She thinks he's the one who should cross, and that's why she stands on the bank and every once in a while makes an almost imperceptible signal. She waits, uncertain whether she wants him to cross the river or not. He says he's afraid. She is too but she doesn't say so, why should she? The shared fear could serve as a bridge over the river. But neither one of them wants to reach the other on a bridge made of fear. As if there was any other way.

She thinks that he should take the first step, and at times only one step separates them. At other times, the distance separating them could be measured in leagues, and the waters becomes stormy and dialogue impossible.

They should forget the bridge and try jumping.

She believes she's already jumped. She believes she's on the correct bank, the far one. On his part of the river, he thinks he's where he should be, and he's accumulating dead weight now that makes jumping impossible.

She observes, she talks, she listens to him, and sometimes takes a tiny step backward, complicating things. Then he takes a step back, getting ready to jump, but then he falls asleep on the way. This river seems to be rather soporific, although at times they give it their dreams, which sail by like beautiful galleons, dazzling them both.

2) Riverbed

And here we come to what is unthinkable about this river: on certain days it achieves what is desired by so many and overflows its banks. So many of us would like to overflow our banks, and cut the cord or the ropes and drift away. Sometimes this river manages to do that and that's when he and she peer into its waters because they're not flowing through the riverbed and given the circumstances it's not a good idea to even mention the riverbed.

Neither one of them is the kind of person who allows metaphors to pass them by, and that's why they create fear for themselves. They give each other fear; they offer it to each other with arms outstretched. Fear as river, riverbed as bed, riverbed as inscrutable depth. On the banks, the river; on the river, the galleon; on the galleon, the masts; and the two of them refusing to come down from the mizzenmast, escaping the mainmast as if it were the plague. Even though they've sailed other waters and know the terminology by heart. They know about the masting and the sails; they recognize the main topsail, the pawl, the mainsail, and even the spinnaker. They know how to arrange the braces and the lanyards, they understand about floor timbers and rigging; hauling in the canvas is an everyday thing for them. There's nothing she doesn't know about a boltrope.

But this galleon of dreams is sailing of its own accord, barely pushed by secret sighs. It's a phantom boat on a phantom river over an unspeakable riverbed.

3) The Estuary

Then there comes the time when all by himself he starts playing war games and sinks the galleons. With letters and numbers—especially with letters—he keeps score and ends up sinking the dream. A new bubble that's punctured. And all of this to avoid sex. They both forget that static detail and drift away.

She too inflates bubbles and then her head hurts or she has small secret malaises. She doesn't confess it but she knows that these indispositions are a barrier, like the river.

She writes about the river, distorting it; he blows new bubbles and the river fills with festive foam. When the foam dissipates, all that's floating in the river are the cadavers of little fish that used to be colorful. The galleons are evaporating, the river is a thousand leagues away. There is no more happiness or dreaming or jumping possible. Neither a river nor a barrier to articulate encounters—nor is there even separation.

That's why all that's left is to swim, dive into the high seas and disperse.

Back from all these—whew!—lectures with the sensation of having reached my limit. Not of my strength, or my talent, or my creative capacities, but of my internal permission to do things. I have to break this barrier, now!

Another turn of the screw and of the symposium, and the sensation of inappropriately falling in love again. Southern California and more specifically a certain hot tub under the moon. I've changed once again my object of desire: not proletariat, not hard, but I overcompensated and fell on the other side of things. A beautiful, neat, and tidy man, with plenty of bitterness and anxieties that are entirely alien to my—let's say, ironically—daring and adventurous character.

Although in the hot tub I got him to join in my adventure—or rather, he stepped in, and then I didn't let him get away, something which he thanked me for by growing . . . repeatedly. In the hot tub and over the next week. Of course I managed to blurt out one of my famous dissuasive sentences . . . Astronomical in this case, because I had just read the inconceivable news about the discovery of a star very far away that seemed to be shooting off in two opposite directions. I feel like that star, I told the heedless one who must still be wondering what I meant by that. Interesting question, doctor. I too have to wonder.

There are Fragments

The wine that I'm drinking, I'm drinking alone. The love that I felt I felt so very much shared. In this house where someone who didn't know better might count two inhabitants, or sometimes one (a four-legged animal), there is also another—the other of my memory, and who knows how many more on his side of things— he who penetrates.

I didn't feel good with him in that bed: I felt confused. And now I don't know (who knows, who ever knows?) if that confusion, which we could qualify quite well as a supreme sort of invasion, wasn't unilateral and defensive.

I mean, there I was, *infraganti*, defending myself against everything that I always liked to accuse him of, accusing him of everything under the sun, but never actually saying the word that can't be mentioned (you see, the ineffable becomes obvious when we most feel like talking and communicating).

You were somewhere else, I was somewhere else, and what a shame to un-meet like that just when we were so close—on top of each other, in fact.

Dark tentacles tempting us when the lights go out. If everything went dark (it can happen), if everything went dark forever, some day we would grow eyes on the ends of our fingers to be able to see by touching.

Waiting for the black ink I always use, I didn't write about certain subjects. As if there wasn't plenty of blue ink and blue dreams and blue desires like feathers. Dreamed of blue feathers, half-glimpsed birds. Back to my bird theme, why not?

Like when I claimed to be writing my long text on the defense of the phallus, poor thing, more commonly known as the penis, so untrustworthy, so temperamental and sometimes pitiful. My intention was to present the other side of feminism. But laziness won out and then of course people started talking too much about "the new masculine impotence" and other such gabble, and the thing lost substance (the thing itself no, fortunately: the project). So many book projects that end up going down the drain. And me, drained, drained of all enthusiasm when I don't write, or when I don't travel, or when I don't fuck (it would be more beautiful to say, when I don't love, but I'm afraid that's rather hard to say).

What are we playing at? What are we talking about if all that's in play here is getting to the essence of things? This turns out to be the most arduous, the most incomprehensible thing for others.

If there's already a man who fits the form of my desire, why try to hammer my desire onto someone else, like a wedge? With all its limitations, this is my very own desire, I can hold it in my hand.

Today I'm dying to see you. Tomorrow who knows, and yesterday not so much. And I'm frozen in time because really, it's better to die from wanting, and from wanting to see you, than to die from nothing.

Now I really am going to have to force myself to write (just write!) in this blank book I've been given and that's so beautiful. The writing is going to be very private. Not deprived of meaning or feeling, just private.

I would like this to be my ship's log, all told, my notebook of being adrift, and today I feel more adrift than ever. I think. I know that I'm on a tightrope (mostly by my own choice, I have to admit), and I think my headaches and other illnesses are due to the unreliability of my navigation.

Stormy seas, life.

Today I tell myself, I repeat to myself and I forget, enough already of this stuff about the tightrope.

Uncertainty is the mother of all creation.

The Great Doubts I

A rock of salt
Stop it from getting worn
Don't lick it
Leave love to one side
Invest in stocks
Avoid wear
      And tear
      And dreams

      Or

Go further every time
Reconcile with love
Collect all its juices
Drink it down to the last drop
Don't leave one drop
Get wildly drunk
Get beautifully drunk.
And the salt rock becomes diluted
Dripping like tears.

The Great Doubts II

Return and remain
Comforting yourself
Leaning on the solid and known
The moist warm familiar warmth

Or

Leave dryly
Not having support
Recognize fear, sharpen fear
Take every step blindly
Foment mystery

Or

Neither return nor leave nor
The opposite
Poke one's nose into the secret:
Dilute.

What I want is to withdraw. Close the store for a while. Because I scare myself. I have a sort of exhaustion of the brain and I forget things, important or not. Things that later turn up in other places. Like writing about fear (and the smell of fear that I smelled more than once) as excrement, and feeling like the great discoverer, presenting it in a conference on the subject and then completely forgetting that Kristeva had already written about it, her concept of abjection. Stupid me for not recognizing it.

Second turn of the screw: Okay, it's a form of appropriation. Forgetting things gives time for digesting them and then using the repressed material in literary form. Capturing it, I would say. But appropriation isn't always comfortable. It looks too much like dishonest theft. Am I a kleptomaniac of thought?

The law of compensation and involuntary equilibrium. I participate in a group that considers fear, fear as an element of political discourse; the exploitation and appropriation of fear and the resistance to it through the arts. And on the other hand, S's seminar drifted toward the subject of laughter and jokes as a social process. There we talk about liberation, thanks to laughter, thanks to plays on words that operate as a physical stimulus, like tickling.

Then I think of humor's capacity to produce relaxation in the middle of the enormous tension of fear. And I also think of the direct relationship between language and the body.

And speaking of that, do I miss my beloved Argentina? No sir, I hurt, but I don't miss it. Because my beloved Argentina is in my soul, I always carry it with me, and in the place where the conventional mapmaker puts it, there's only an enormous wound we hope will heal with time. There are already signs of this.

Salomón Resnik, I remember again, said that you have to take your roots with you wherever you go, and I'm a carnation of the air—I have aerial roots. I feed off ambient—and other—dampness.

Anyway, the Buenos Aires that I loved so much doesn't exist anymore, it would be impossible to return to the same place because the same place is different now.

And thus the charm of returning or not returning to New York, which is *always* different. The energy changes place constantly; it moves, bifurcates, and gets more complex every day.

Pastoralisms

In the beautiful Massachusetts house, at the edge of the forest, uncle and nephew compete to see who can prepare the most succulent and refined dishes. The most succulent and delicious, I should say. I lick my fingers. But I don't lick any single finger. I know that when these two compete—as usually happens with men, however much they're my friends—they aren't doing it for me, they're competing with each other. In everything, even from their long walks through the woods they usually bring back tasty scenes to present to me, just this side of fantastical, like the story about the camouflaged guy, with his face painted and everything, who instead of talking about the pheasants or the wild ducks he's out hunting tells them about mushrooms. A mushroom hunter, let's say, and there isn't a single mushroom in the woods because it hasn't rained lately. And I'm not talking about the sort of mushrooms school kids like to pick. No, I'm in a pastoral frame of mind, and I think of John Cage and his mesostic letters like mushrooms in the forest, and of the music he composes, hidden and remote.

And that's what we talk about, Uncle Julio and she who is writing this, and we hear the story of the little blond boy with clear eyes that the nephew found on the banks of the lake. The angelic little boy was petting a cat very tenderly, until suddenly he threw the cat into the air and gave it a huge kick, as if it were a soccer ball.

What can we do? Wherever you look, the road to heaven is paved with malicious intentions.

And that's how it goes. Some set the table, others will sit at it.

I want to take things from each place and I look on the floor, I look in the trees or in the sand or on the side of the road. I would like to take the place or the moment. I don't want memories at all, I hate memories—they're a form of stagnation. I don't realize that each place usually has its own stories—like wool in different colors, with which to weave the texture of a text that won't be at all static like a tapestry or like an eye looking back at a landscape. It will be a constant flow (damn it!).

I always expect something from the other person, like from the sun I expect warmth. The sun—when it appears—does warm; it doesn't let us down.

I lie on the ground with my arms open in a cross and my body parallel to the brook. May the earth absorb my troubles, may the water flowing beside me cleanse me. With open arms, yes, but my right hand clutching a feather I found on the way. To not surrender completely. Or to be able to fly a bit.
   (And that night, who would have thought, the little red insects devour me, they write all over my body, leaving tiny welts—they don't let me sleep.)

In the city, another Saturday with a headache even though I'm doing everything I can to remove this hood of pain that separates me from the world. This pain today could be to do with the death of María Luisa Pacheco, who I met a few times and who never once recognized me (and maybe the pain of *that*, too). The possibility of dying far away with a bilingual eulogy. Inga said it well: Where is our home? When my mother died, she said, I knew I no longer had a motherland.

Border

Who said that the only
Place is the border?

Who suggested
Borderly
That living in two worlds
Is the truest form of truth?

If we opted for one side
Or the other
We might receive a pardon
And who wants a pardon?

The border almost reaches the forbidden
It's only a few steps away
To access the forbidden is unthinkable
To be on the border is dangerous
Uncomfortable
Nonetheless, whoever said
That the only place to be

Is the border
Knows.

Now I know an internal freedom in which there are no more tuggings. I hope it lasts. This must come along with my chiropractic adjustment and resettling of my vertebrae. With a good spine, you can stand a lot of shocks.

Any port in a storm, say the old sea wolves—referring of course to a more sexual subject than simple shelter. But I only find ports with strong waves. Joe keeps playing his nice game of visiting me every two weeks, now that he's working deep in the pit of New Jersey. Joe just comes to be serviced now, and I'm afraid I've gotten tired of writing about it.

It's too easy to keep acting out sexual fantasies. Too easy in this city and at this time. But meanwhile, here I am trapped in the act of desire. Or at least its intention.

I think I'm old enough to begin giving love without demanding reciprocity, tooth and nail. Something I've been experiencing through different religions: with Claudine and the Sufis, with the Dominican Santeros last night. The joy of offering. I usually offer a lot but I often feel pulled, forced, and that's why I give and take right back and feel tense. Is it because I want retribution?

Trip

All this time gone by. All this space. Now in the very beautiful house in Geneva that was lent to Nestor—I was on the verge of writing other things, something about how beautiful and recuperated I feel, and bam! The flow was cut off. I should really give some thought to these flows of mine that start and then, just as quickly, get cut off. The heavy burdens that others foist on me.

It's logical: who doesn't think of spouts in Geneva, with its Jet d'eau, like the flow from a giant, living Manneken Pis? A spout of 140 meters high so that it drizzles a little, or a lot, depending on your taste for drizzling. The most beautiful part is the natural change of colors, its integration into the sky. I feel so very elegant, sitting on the balcony watching the sky turn the color of a Mexican rose, writing . . .

Tidy little notebook, now I'm writing in you in front of the beautiful bay in Korčula. I could write that Marco Polo was born here but it sounds so accidental, so little related to this calm of cicadas and gentle seas, *plaf, plaf,* like hands clapping. Like the way the streets plop in Venice, but the other way around. That was the setting for an old recurring nightmare: I'm walking through a Venice I'm not familiar with but I know it's Venice and the streets are tiny, with arches, little bridges, and I almost go into the houses and it's as if I were crossing living rooms, the lights are red and gold, Visconti-like. I'm lost in that oppressive labyrinth, and when I finally think I've arrived somewhere, the alley ends level with the water. Abruptly.

Only that now, in reality, I've discovered, along with the fear of being lost (and this time the fear is more concrete in solitary streets populated with occasional drunks), the fascination and charm of being lost. And the surprise. All that's missing is the novel; though novelty abounds.

The fact is that I always claim to be producing, or at least doing something substantial and practical. I can't even give myself the joy of a more or less deserved vacation. Look at what I got myself into when I went to Buenos Aires—instead of prowling around there enjoying friends and beautiful things. Will I never let myself return to the womb? Did I have such a bad time there?

At least I had an idea: dynamic myths can sometimes be explosive, and they're called *dynamyth*.

I write inspired (?) letters with my right hand. With my left ear, the deaf one, I listen to the silence of a phone call that doesn't come.

Everything is finally a very intense internal voyage, and wanting to hold on to someone else is a way of stopping the internal voyage and feeling like you have a companion. But one can only wander alone, like someone I don't remember said, maybe in relation to Baudelaire. Wanderer, yes, and also wonderer, absolutely. I wander alone as a form of marveling—a way like any other to try to get off this rollercoaster we call life.

The so-little-recognized attempt to be where you shouldn't be at the least opportune moment (the wrong place at the wrong time). The utterly dislocated correspondence—referring to letters that will never be sent—working from here to there, with the there being, as it should, a solemn and imperfect place.

One day the saint enters you, as they say in the Macumba religion. One day, or rather, one night, a pure erotic strength is yours. It's yours. Later you'll have to see who wants to play your game, who can hold your gaze. Because there's always someone—

don't listen to the saint who wants you to stay alone up there in limbo, poor little sad animal of the weekdays. A day off comes—and one not necessarily on the calendar—and you start dancing on the tables and laughing wholeheartedly. Even more: you drag others along, you incite others who for a few instants shake off their drowsiness and let themselves be infected by your enthusiasm. Excessive, no doubt. You don't have good light nor can you see what you're writing but it's also true that you're not writing; you're jumping up and shaking yourself, you're saving yourself to the rhythm of the world.

And later you say that your head hurts. You feel like the color of earth, huffing and puffing along roads that are always uphill. But tonight you're the queen of the wild frontier that you've created around you, and there was a look that seemed to understand what you wanted, and if later you gave up on it, if you chose to return to your corner of the ring and forget the call, it doesn't matter. The moment of contact seemed to go on and on, was really long, your eyes and the others lit up like flashlights; they read each other's depths.

A new move—this city is so mobile, and on those few occasions it stays the same (pretty much impossible), it makes *me* change. NYU has accepted me completely and they are offering me lodgings. I'm going to miss the decrepit building on Carmine Street that provided me with such great moments, but now I no longer depend on the absence of Jeanet, the real tenant of that highly sublime bed . . . and the lease contract of this new studio is in my name. The place is big and I have a dressing room and a garden balcony, really a luxury in this part of the Village. I have sun, and a smile on my face because a promise just called up. A cousin insisted that we meet her cousin, that we were made for each other. Since English is genderless, I never know who's made for whom, which is rather worrisome, but the cousin assured me that her cousin is very good-looking, and I'm ready to believe her. Partly. The man calls me, and so as not to get stuck with a dud (he has too many degrees), I suggest that we meet at the cocktail party they're giving for Vargas Llosa on the other side of Manhattan. All my friends will be there, and if my blind date proves to be boring, I'll say I have a previous engagement and bye-bye, see you one of these years.

I'm going to wear a red hat so that you'll recognize me, I told him, and he assured me that he would be able to find me in the crowd, no need of any signals. I avoided telling him where the red hat came from and that it brings me luck . . .

So here I am in the middle of the reception for Varguitas, and since I arrived early I'm spending time with my friends, who aren't necessarily Mexican, but they are dear friends, some of them, plus some others I always get together with on occasions like these. I keep an eye on the door, a corner of my eye on the door, and in a while I notice a tall stranger, a bit ungainly, dark-haired and nice-looking. He stops in the entrance and looks around with an inquisitive expression and I say gulp! and I turn around. The stranger tries to surprise me taking me by the shoulders but I already know who it is when he says, It's me, and I introduce him casually to my circle of friends. Where did you find this little potato? Edith asks me clandestinely, in her bad Spanish. And I look at him and ask him, whispering, *Screw* or *Saturday Review of Books*? I'm alluding of course to two mutually exclusive publications, no misunderstandings there. *Review*, he answers, and I tell whoever wants to hear: I met him through an ad in the paper. And he, showing off his good reflexes adds and elaborates: Yes, I placed an ad saying that I wanted to meet a Latin American writer . . .

And I, upon reading the ad—I keep going in the local language, so that he'll pick up all the irony—picked up the phone right away and invited him to meet Vargas Llosa!

Right then we liked each other. I didn't have to say I had a previous engagement, *au contraire*, and the two of us made a quick exit while the night was still in diapers.

This has a strength that has to be ridden. If I don't ride it I'll feel completely devastated.

Ride the strength. That's the secret. I can't always do it. And when I can't, I hope to be reasonable and/or I get desperate. Especially the latter. What shit. But how many times and until when will I be able to ride it? And where is this strength? It doesn't always appear.

Fucking is the easiest way to ride this strength, when it goes smoothly. After all—and I don't know why I didn't realize it before—the only moments of true security, of feeling truly in my own skin, are while I'm fucking, because I'm generally lying down. That keeps me from wandering around wondering where the hell I am.

In periods of forgetfulness, weakness emerges. Forgetfulness of the internal impulse that summarizes and devours everything. I think that in the long run, love affairs weaken me. Because it's easier, and so I forget.

Nothing. No doubts. Of course, it's also a question of self-defense, to appear strong because I can't always—oh, so few times am I able to—ride my true strength.

Wanting to have everything under control. Or those that claim to have everything already under control. They perturb us. It so happens that control and creation are opposed terms.

Lose in order to find.

A Walk Through Fire

I've resorted on more than one occasion to seeing Elaine de Beauport so that she can help me calm my anxieties. She works with energy and knows how to tell me the exact word I need—my balm, my chamomile tea, my Valium. And it seems that she wants to change approaches because she's left me a message on my answering machine saying, Your specialty travel agent is offering you a walk through fire on Saturday night. And to top it off, I accept, though I know—because I know her and she's told me a little about it—she means a walk over burning coals. The walk won't take place in Fiji, no; they cater to any taste here in the belly button of the world, and this particular firewalk has been organized in a public school in the middle of Manhattan, Saturday at seven in the evening—when the pesky students will all be at home. I hand over the stipulated two hundred dollars, Elaine is also along for the ride; one young man will guide us for seven hours through all our emotions and a few other bits of gringo nonsense as a bonus, shoeless . . .

I'm there because Tim has gone to Los Angeles and I have to calm my new anxieties somehow, and also and especially because on Monday, when at the University they ask me what I did this weekend, I'll say indifferently: Oh, I walked through fire. I have to surprise them with something, sometime, these cool New Yorkers who are always on top of everything. But when I sign the release form that says I won't sue the organizers of the Firewalk Experience for any physical or psychic harm, I start to worry. Okay, so I burn my feet a bit—but go crazy? Just because of trying something new? Okay. I'll have time to regret it later tonight, and indeed I'm about to regret it several times, especially when we go out on the patio to "be friendly" (as the organizer says) with the coals and then the enormous bonfires, as though waiting for Joan of Arc. I won't write down everything that was said and done as in preparation for the walk, but given what the organizer told us, maybe so much chatter was unnecessary. No one knows how or why human beings can—once reason has been left behind, and only the body alone is left to act—walk on burning coals that can reach more than three hundred degrees centigrade. Maybe anyone can do it at any moment. Better not to try. But there are more than three hundred of us who firewalk as if it's nothing, at the order Go!, repeating *cold moss* and looking above and to the left so that the right hemisphere of our brain takes the initiative. Nobody should burn themselves and nobody does.

If this isn't writing with the body, then I'm Joyce (James, I mean, not Carol Oates!).

Nothing that happens here tonight is important, the organizer tells us, crossing that brief, burning red rug isn't important. The main thing comes afterward. You all, who have overcome fear, will face life differently.

And there it is. You do what you can.

Monday

At NYU they're celebrating the annual dinner with the trustees, the millionaires who put up their money so that the University can function in all its splendor. I'm to preside over a table with two really loaded millionaire couples. Of course they ask the inevitable question, because we're in the US and we are artists of small talk.

"How was your weekend?"

"Oh, fine," I answer nonchalantly. "I walked through fire."

There and then I lose the tiny bit of clout I had managed to obtain. My friendly conversation partners very elegantly change the subject and I will no longer be the center of attention. I get the drift: one more Latin American writer, one more practitioner of magical realism; we're not here to listen to your fantastic exaggerations. I hear this perfectly across their distant smiles.

EPILOGUE

A long text that opened with a Foreword closes now with an Epilogue. Everything very tidy—in appearance only, because there really isn't any ending. As long as we're alive, life keeps writing *in* us, through us, in spite of us. We are the blank paper of the one who, in the inescapable stenography of the Secret, we call God.

And then every last period that we type is a fraud. The period that will appear much sooner than many others, because there were too many notebooks superimposed on others, because time became sticky from my not having written down the corresponding dates, because there are so many things crossed out and omitted: acts, facts, and words that persist in memory but didn't find their moment in the body of writing.

Everything outlined here that seems brusquely interrupted followed its logical and biological course of entry and exit, the goodbyes and losses of new relationships. Re-beginnings. What was really interrupted were the sporadic notes and disordered reflections. If writing confers existence onto events beyond the facts, I accept that the story with Joe—linked to the story of the one I called Tim— culminates in the last novel that I signed. I can't say "my last novel," simply because nothing about these novels (and the others with whom I shared the road) belongs to me. The disguises I had to invent to narrate lived material aren't mine either. In this book, on the other hand, I don't use any disguises, only a loincloth made from writing's death rattle. These are diaries. Born through spontaneous generation and silenced by progressive degradation or overuse. Scribbled pages floating adrift. I didn't intend to write *something*, and now, at the end of all these copied pages, I do have something. I didn't know beforehand what would become of recovering these notes I made between 1979 and 1982—an arbitrary date, this last one, because I kept living in New York for seven more years, passing through Buenos Aires to celebrate the return of democracy—where there were so many more emotions and commotions.

Now all that's left is a mirror turned around. New York is no longer the paradigmatic city I so loved, nor are we in the same millennium. And I, impossible to avoid it, am another. Always like everyone I am being another. But this is also the product, the product, the product, the product of what?

Today, September 30, 2002, for the thousandth time, I again take up wandering.

LUISA VALENZUELA was born in Buenos Aires, Argentina in 1938. In 1958, she moved to France and wrote her first novel while living in Paris. In 1979, she moved to the United States and lived in New York for ten years, working as a writer in residence at the Center for Inter-American Relations at NYU and Columbia. She was awarded a Guggenheim Fellowship in 1983.

SUSAN E. CLARK is the translator of Esther Tusquets's *Stranded*. She lives in New Mexico, where she resides with her Costa Rican husband and six dogs and cats.

SELECTED DALKEY ARCHIVE PAPERBACKS

PETROS ABATZOGLOU, *What Does Mrs. Freeman Want?*
MICHAL AJVAZ, *The Golden Age.*
The Other City.
PIERRE ALBERT-BIROT, *Grabinoulor.*
YUZ ALESHKOVSKY, *Kangaroo.*
FELIPE ALFAU, *Chromos.*
Locos.
IVAN ÂNGELO, *The Celebration.*
The Tower of Glass.
DAVID ANTIN, *Talking.*
ANTÓNIO LOBO ANTUNES, *Knowledge of Hell.*
ALAIN ARIAS-MISSON, *Theatre of Incest.*
IFTIKHAR ARIF AND WAQAS KHWAJA, EDS., *Modern Poetry of Pakistan.*
JOHN ASHBERY AND JAMES SCHUYLER, *A Nest of Ninnies.*
GABRIELA AVIGUR-ROTEM, *Heatwave and Crazy Birds.*
HEIMRAD BÄCKER, *transcript.*
DJUNA BARNES, *Ladies Almanack.*
Ryder.
JOHN BARTH, *LETTERS.*
Sabbatical.
DONALD BARTHELME, *The King.*
Paradise.
SVETISLAV BASARA, *Chinese Letter.*
RENÉ BELLETTO, *Dying.*
MARK BINELLI, *Sacco and Vanzetti Must Die!*
ANDREI BITOV, *Pushkin House.*
ANDREJ BLATNIK, *You Do Understand.*
LOUIS PAUL BOON, *Chapel Road.*
My Little War.
Summer in Termuren.
ROGER BOYLAN, *Killoyle.*
IGNÁCIO DE LOYOLA BRANDÃO, *Anonymous Celebrity.*
The Good-Bye Angel.
Teeth under the Sun.
Zero.
BONNIE BREMSER, *Troia: Mexican Memoirs.*
CHRISTINE BROOKE-ROSE, *Amalgamemnon.*
BRIGID BROPHY, *In Transit.*
MEREDITH BROSNAN, *Mr. Dynamite.*
GERALD L. BRUNS, *Modern Poetry and the Idea of Language.*
EVGENY BUNIMOVICH AND J. KATES, EDS., *Contemporary Russian Poetry: An Anthology.*
GABRIELLE BURTON, *Heartbreak Hotel.*
MICHEL BUTOR, *Degrees.*
Mobile.
Portrait of the Artist as a Young Ape.
G. CABRERA INFANTE, *Infante's Inferno.*
Three Trapped Tigers.
JULIETA CAMPOS, *The Fear of Losing Eurydice.*
ANNE CARSON, *Eros the Bittersweet.*
ORLY CASTEL-BLOOM, *Dolly City.*
CAMILO JOSÉ CELA, *Christ versus Arizona.*
The Family of Pascual Duarte.
The Hive.
LOUIS-FERDINAND CÉLINE, *Castle to Castle.*
Conversations with Professor Y.
London Bridge.
Normance.
North.
Rigadoon.
HUGO CHARTERIS, *The Tide Is Right.*
JEROME CHARYN, *The Tar Baby.*
ERIC CHEVILLARD, *Demolishing Nisard.*
MARC CHOLODENKO, *Mordechai Schamz.*
JOSHUA COHEN, *Witz.*
EMILY HOLMES COLEMAN, *The Shutter of Snow.*
ROBERT COOVER, *A Night at the Movies.*
STANLEY CRAWFORD, *Log of the S.S. The Mrs Unguentine.*
Some Instructions to My Wife.
ROBERT CREELEY, *Collected Prose.*
RENÉ CREVEL, *Putting My Foot in It.*
RALPH CUSACK, *Cadenza.*
SUSAN DAITCH, *L.C.*
Storytown.
NICHOLAS DELBANCO, *The Count of Concord.*
Sherbrookes.
NIGEL DENNIS, *Cards of Identity.*
PETER DIMOCK, *A Short Rhetoric for Leaving the Family.*
ARIEL DORFMAN, *Konfidenz.*
COLEMAN DOWELL, *The Houses of Children.*
Island People.
Too Much Flesh and Jabez.
ARKADII DRAGOMOSHCHENKO, *Dust.*
RIKKI DUCORNET, *The Complete Butcher's Tales.*
The Fountains of Neptune.
The Jade Cabinet.
The One Marvelous Thing.
Phosphor in Dreamland.
The Stain.
The Word "Desire."
WILLIAM EASTLAKE, *The Bamboo Bed.*
Castle Keep.
Lyric of the Circle Heart.
JEAN ECHENOZ, *Chopin's Move.*
STANLEY ELKIN, *A Bad Man.*
Boswell: A Modern Comedy.
Criers and Kibitzers, Kibitzers and Criers.
The Dick Gibson Show.
The Franchiser.
George Mills.
The Living End.
The MacGuffin.
The Magic Kingdom.
Mrs. Ted Bliss.
The Rabbi of Lud.
Van Gogh's Room at Arles.
ANNIE ERNAUX, *Cleaned Out.*
LAUREN FAIRBANKS, *Muzzle Thyself.*
Sister Carrie.
LESLIE A. FIEDLER, *Love and Death in the American Novel.*
JUAN FILLOY, *Op Oloop.*
GUSTAVE FLAUBERT, *Bouvard and Pécuchet.*
KASS FLEISHER, *Talking out of School.*
FORD MADOX FORD, *The March of Literature.*
JON FOSSE, *Aliss at the Fire.*
Melancholy.
MAX FRISCH, *I'm Not Stiller.*
Man in the Holocene.

FOR A FULL LIST OF PUBLICATIONS, VISIT:
www.dalkeyarchive.com

CARLOS FUENTES, *Christopher Unborn.*
  Distant Relations.
  Terra Nostra.
  Where the Air Is Clear.
JANICE GALLOWAY, *Foreign Parts.*
  The Trick Is to Keep Breathing.
WILLIAM H. GASS, *Cartesian Sonata*
  and Other Novellas.
  Finding a Form.
  A Temple of Texts.
  The Tunnel.
  Willie Masters' Lonesome Wife.
GÉRARD GAVARRY, *Hoppla! 1 2 3.*
  Making a Novel.
ETIENNE GILSON,
  The Arts of the Beautiful.
  Forms and Substances in the Arts.
C. S. GISCOMBE, *Giscome Road.*
  Here.
  Prairie Style.
DOUGLAS GLOVER, *Bad News of the Heart.*
  The Enamoured Knight.
WITOLD GOMBROWICZ,
  A Kind of Testament.
KAREN ELIZABETH GORDON,
  The Red Shoes.
GEORGI GOSPODINOV, *Natural Novel.*
JUAN GOYTISOLO, *Count Julian.*
  Exiled from Almost Everywhere.
  Juan the Landless.
  Makbara.
  Marks of Identity.
PATRICK GRAINVILLE, *The Cave of Heaven.*
HENRY GREEN, *Back.*
  Blindness.
  Concluding.
  Doting.
  Nothing.
JIŘÍ GRUŠA, *The Questionnaire.*
GABRIEL GUDDING,
  Rhode Island Notebook.
MELA HARTWIG, *Am I a Redundant*
  Human Being?
JOHN HAWKES, *The Passion Artist.*
  Whistlejacket.
ALEKSANDAR HEMON, ED.,
  Best European Fiction.
AIDAN HIGGINS, *A Bestiary.*
  Balcony of Europe.
  Bornholm Night-Ferry.
  Darkling Plain: Texts for the Air.
  Flotsam and Jetsam.
  Langrishe, Go Down.
  Scenes from a Receding Past.
  Windy Arbours.
KEIZO HINO, *Isle of Dreams.*
KAZUSHI HOSAKA, *Plainsong.*
ALDOUS HUXLEY, *Antic Hay.*
  Crome Yellow.
  Point Counter Point.
  Those Barren Leaves.
  Time Must Have a Stop.
NAOYUKI II, *The Shadow of a Blue Cat.*
MIKHAIL IOSSEL AND JEFF PARKER, EDS.,
  Amerika: Russian Writers View the
  United States.
GERT JONKE, *The Distant Sound.*
  Geometric Regional Novel.
  Homage to Czerny.
  The System of Vienna.

JACQUES JOUET, *Mountain R.*
  Savage.
  Upstaged.
CHARLES JULIET, *Conversations with*
  Samuel Beckett and Bram van
  Velde.
MIEKO KANAI, *The Word Book.*
YORAM KANIUK, *Life on Sandpaper.*
HUGH KENNER, *The Counterfeiters.*
  Flaubert, Joyce and Beckett:
  The Stoic Comedians.
  Joyce's Voices.
DANILO KIŠ, *Garden, Ashes.*
  A Tomb for Boris Davidovich.
ANITA KONKKA, *A Fool's Paradise.*
GEORGE KONRÁD, *The City Builder.*
TADEUSZ KONWICKI, *A Minor Apocalypse.*
  The Polish Complex.
MENIS KOUMANDAREAS, *Koula.*
ELAINE KRAF, *The Princess of 72nd Street.*
JIM KRUSOE, *Iceland.*
EWA KURYLUK, *Century 21.*
EMILIO LASCANO TEGUI, *On Elegance*
  While Sleeping.
ERIC LAURRENT, *Do Not Touch.*
HERVÉ LE TELLIER, *The Sextine Chapel.*
  A Thousand Pearls (for a Thousand
  Pennies)
VIOLETTE LEDUC, *La Bâtarde.*
EDOUARD LEVÉ, *Suicide.*
SUZANNE JILL LEVINE, *The Subversive*
  Scribe: Translating Latin
  American Fiction.
DEBORAH LEVY, *Billy and Girl.*
  Pillow Talk in Europe and Other
  Places.
JOSÉ LEZAMA LIMA, *Paradiso.*
ROSA LIKSOM, *Dark Paradise.*
OSMAN LINS, *Avalovara.*
  The Queen of the Prisons of Greece.
ALF MAC LOCHLAINN,
  The Corpus in the Library.
  Out of Focus.
RON LOEWINSOHN, *Magnetic Field(s).*
MINA LOY, *Stories and Essays of Mina Loy.*
BRIAN LYNCH, *The Winner of Sorrow.*
D. KEITH MANO, *Take Five.*
MICHELINE AHARONIAN MARCOM,
  The Mirror in the Well.
BEN MARCUS,
  The Age of Wire and String.
WALLACE MARKFIELD,
  Teitlebaum's Window.
  To an Early Grave.
DAVID MARKSON, *Reader's Block.*
  Springer's Progress.
  Wittgenstein's Mistress.
CAROLE MASO, *AVA.*
LADISLAV MATEJKA AND KRYSTYNA
  POMORSKA, EDS.,
  Readings in Russian Poetics:
  Formalist and Structuralist Views.
HARRY MATHEWS,
  The Case of the Persevering Maltese:
  Collected Essays.
  Cigarettes.
  The Conversions.
  The Human Country: New and
  Collected Stories.
  The Journalist.

ARNO SCHMIDT, *Collected Novellas.*
Collected Stories.
Nobodaddy's Children.
Two Novels.
ASAF SCHURR, *Motti.*
CHRISTINE SCHUTT, *Nightwork.*
GAIL SCOTT, *My Paris.*
DAMION SEARLS, *What We Were Doing and Where We Were Going.*
JUNE AKERS SEESE,
Is This What Other Women Feel Too?
What Waiting Really Means.
BERNARD SHARE, *Inish.*
Transit.
AURELIE SHEEHAN,
Jack Kerouac Is Pregnant.
VIKTOR SHKLOVSKY, *Bowstring.*
Knight's Move.
A Sentimental Journey: Memoirs 1917–1922.
Energy of Delusion: A Book on Plot.
Literature and Cinematography.
Theory of Prose.
Third Factory.
Zoo, or Letters Not about Love.
CLAUDE SIMON, *The Invitation.*
PIERRE SINIAC, *The Collaborators.*
JOSEF ŠKVORECKÝ, *The Engineer of Human Souls.*
GILBERT SORRENTINO,
Aberration of Starlight.
Blue Pastoral.
Crystal Vision.
Imaginative Qualities of Actual Things.
Mulligan Stew.
Pack of Lies.
Red the Fiend.
The Sky Changes.
Something Said.
Splendide-Hôtel.
Steelwork.
Under the Shadow.
W. M. SPACKMAN,
The Complete Fiction.
ANDRZEJ STASIUK, *Fado.*
GERTRUDE STEIN,
Lucy Church Amiably.
The Making of Americans.
A Novel of Thank You.
LARS SVENDSEN, *A Philosophy of Evil.*
PIOTR SZEWC, *Annihilation.*
GONÇALO M. TAVARES, *Jerusalem.*
Learning to Pray in the Age of Technology.
LUCIAN DAN TEODOROVICI,
Our Circus Presents . . .
STEFAN THEMERSON, *Hobson's Island.*
The Mystery of the Sardine.
Tom Harris.
JOHN TOOMEY, *Sleepwalker.*
JEAN-PHILIPPE TOUSSAINT,
The Bathroom.
Camera.
Monsieur.
Running Away.
Self-Portrait Abroad.
Television.
DUMITRU TSEPENEAG,
Hotel Europa.

The Necessary Marriage.
Pigeon Post.
Vain Art of the Fugue.
ESTHER TUSQUETS, *Stranded.*
DUBRAVKA UGRESIC,
Lend Me Your Character.
Thank You for Not Reading.
MATI UNT, *Brecht at Night.*
Diary of a Blood Donor.
Things in the Night.
ÁLVARO URIBE AND OLIVIA SEARS, EDS.,
Best of Contemporary Mexican Fiction.
ELOY URROZ, *Friction.*
The Obstacles.
LUISA VALENZUELA, *Dark Desires and the Others.*
He Who Searches.
MARJA-LIISA VARTIO,
The Parson's Widow.
PAUL VERHAEGHEN, *Omega Minor.*
BORIS VIAN, *Heartsnatcher.*
LLORENÇ VILLALONGA, *The Dolls' Room.*
ORNELA VORPSI, *The Country Where No One Ever Dies.*
AUSTRYN WAINHOUSE, *Hedyphagetica.*
PAUL WEST,
Words for a Deaf Daughter & Gala.
CURTIS WHITE,
America's Magic Mountain.
The Idea of Home.
Memories of My Father Watching TV.
Monstrous Possibility: An Invitation to Literary Politics.
Requiem.
DIANE WILLIAMS, *Excitability: Selected Stories.*
Romancer Erector.
DOUGLAS WOOLF, *Wall to Wall.*
Ya! & John-Juan.
JAY WRIGHT, *Polynomials and Pollen.*
The Presentable Art of Reading Absence.
PHILIP WYLIE, *Generation of Vipers.*
MARGUERITE YOUNG, *Angel in the Forest.*
Miss MacIntosh, My Darling.
REYOUNG, *Unbabbling.*
VLADO ŽABOT, *The Succubus.*
ZORAN ŽIVKOVIĆ, *Hidden Camera.*
LOUIS ZUKOFSKY, *Collected Fiction.*
SCOTT ZWIREN, *God Head.*